# HELME HOUSE

A TROUBLED SPIRITS NOVEL

J.R. ERICKSON

# COPYRIGHT

# DEDICATION

*For my mother. Thank you for always believing in me.*

# AUTHOR'S NOTE

On October twenty-fourth, 1961, a thirty-one-year-old woman vanished mysteriously from her home in Lincoln, Massachusetts.

The woman was a homemaker with two small children and it was the older child, her four-year-old daughter, who alerted a neighbor that her mother wasn't home and the kitchen was covered in red paint.

That paint turned out to be blood.

In the summer before the woman vanished, she had checked out multiple books from the library covering unexplained disappearances. A theory was developed that she might have staged her own death, though many people believe she was abducted from her home. The woman was never seen again.

For forty years, investigators have been searching for the truth of what happened that fateful day in 1961.

*Helme House* was inspired in part by this woman's story; however, the story, that follows as well as the characters and locations are completely fictional.

If you'd like to know the details of the true story, visit www. jrericksonauthor.com.

# 1

"Almost there now," Garrett announced, turning off the paved road onto a winding, densely wooded driveway that led up a steep hill and disappeared around a curve.

Garrett's truck bounced over the uneven driveway. Thick tree roots had ruptured the pavement and left craters in their wake. Rowan rolled down the passenger window and inhaled the warm, fragrant air. It smelled of the dank forest surrounding them, swept through by the breeze rolling up from Lake Michigan.

The house was isolated, which Rowan had expected, but the isolation grew more apparent as the driveway stretched on and on, crooking around enormous oak trees and continuing to climb. "I can't see anything through the forest. Are there other houses nearby? Or—"

"Nope, not for a quarter-mile at least. This place is its own little haven," Garrett said.

"Good thing we're not spending a winter here. My Civic would have never made this driveway."

"Your Civic will be lucky to see another winter as it is. I thought you could do some car-shopping this summer."

Rowan ignored the comment. The Honda Civic had been a gift from her father after she graduated from college. She'd always loved the car. Now that her dad was dead, she cherished it.

Garrett steered his pickup truck from shadowy trees and they emerged at the double garage doors of an impressive brick Tudor home.

The house occupied a dense forest bluff overlooking Lake Michigan, though the water was largely obscured by an expansive lawn and a jumble of trees.

Bushes crowded the home's exterior, pushing up toward the windows. Ivy crawled over the brick façade. A wide rectangle of slightly overgrown yard sloped toward the bluff, which was also packed with trees. Another square of yard stood behind the house, separating the dark structure from the dense woods.

It appeared out of place, this brick monster hulking in the deep woods, but that same strangeness gave it a fairytale quality, as if the house had been erected not by the hands of men, but through some magic. The same magic that now shielded it from the modern world.

"Wow," Rowan breathed.

"My thoughts exactly," Garrett agreed, grinning. He climbed from the truck and opened her door, offering his hand, which she took, though she barely averted her eyes from the house as she stepped from the truck.

It had a presence, this house, a mesmerizing quality that left Rowan slightly off kilter as Garrett led her toward the front door.

"The architecture is out of place, isn't it?" Rowan said, noting the sharp lines, the steep gabled roof. "Most of the houses we passed had that light, beachy look. This place belongs in a rich suburb in Boston."

"That's 1800s for you. Anyone with money went big and brick. They'd sooner go broke than let a neighbor outshine them."

"But there are no neighbors. You can't even see this house."

Garrett tilted his face up to the sky. "Maybe they were showing off for the gods."

Concrete steps bordered by black wrought-iron railings led to a charcoal and glass-paned front door. Garrett slid the key into the lock and turned, pushing the door open.

Cool and dim, the interior held the same aura as the exterior. 'Secret' was the word that arose in Rowan's mind. Though once inside, she realized the furnishings of the previous owner appeared out of place in the dusky rooms. The woman who'd owned the home had had more of a shabby chic style. Distressed bureaus, ornate mirrors with paint peeling at their edges, and a mishmash of furniture from little stiff French-looking sofas to plush velvet chairs. There were no photos of the woman, though much of her artwork remained—paintings of vivid sunsets or framed posters with motivational quotes like, *If your dreams don't scare you, they are too small.*

"I can't believe a single woman lived in this place," Rowan told Garrett, stepping through an arched doorway into the kitchen.

An ebony-patterned tile covered the floor, dizzying in hundreds of tiny whorls embedded within another. The cabinets were stained a dark cherry and the long marble counter was so dark it looked almost black. The kitchen table tucked into a little alcove appeared out of sorts against the somber colors. It was round with turquoise legs. A yellow vase sat in its center.

"Yeah, I love the location, but this house would need a major overhaul for me to want to live here. And alone? Forget it. It's too big."

"Did Alan tell you anything about her? Why would she live here alone?"

Garrett opened kitchen cupboards, revealing rows of glass and plates. "He didn't tell me if he knew. Want me to send him a personality questionnaire so you can find out all about her?"

Rowan scowled at him. "I'm curious. Come on, you're not curious?"

"I'm curious about how old this tile is," he said, leaning down and looking closer at the floor. "I've never seen anything like it."

They maneuvered out of the kitchen and back down the hall, taking the staircase to the second floor. A long dark hallway ended at a blank wall painted a dark green.

"Four bedrooms up here, according to the listing Alan sent me. One bathroom. The master is this first one." He pushed a door open on their right. It did not match the rest of the house. What had once been dark walls were painted white. Shaggy white rugs covered most of the floor. A ceiling fan had been installed on the high ceiling and it whirled lazily.

"Now this is my kind of room. White and bright," Garrett said, striding to the window that faced the lake. "You can even see Lake Michigan from here."

Rowan stood beside him. The grassy yard stretched to the trees, but beyond those lay the sparkling lake. "Wow, what a magnificent view to wake up to every morning."

"And so we will." He kissed her cheek.

Rowan leaned closer to the window. "Is that a deck out there?"

"Yep. It's an overlook. Propped up on huge wooden stilts going into the bluff. Alan said it's sturdy. There's another deck about halfway down the stairs leading to the beach. We'll be getting a workout going up and down those this summer."

They continued out of the room and down the hall, opening doors to find additional bedrooms in dark colors, some bare, others with a scattering of old furniture. At the end of the hall, the last bedroom appeared to have once been a nursery.

"It's freezing in here," Rowan said, rubbing her hands over her arms as they stepped into the room.

It was large and square, occupying a corner of the house that gave it a south-facing window. A large gray rug covered the wood floors. The wallpaper above the wainscoting revealed little bears marching through woods. Some of them carried knapsacks and others picnic baskets.

"I guess we found Quinn's room," Garrett joked.

Rowan studied the space. In appearance it was a pretty room with natural light and soft colors. Something seemed slightly off, though. She stepped to the window that faced the backyard. "You say that like she won't be sharing a room with us for the next two years."

"Two years! Well, I guess that's for the best. I don't want her getting attached to this room right before I tear the wallpaper down."

"Oh, come on, who doesn't love little camping bears?" Rowan asked.

"The billionaires who will hopefully buy this place. Plus, whoever hung this paper did a terrible job."

Garrett was right. Tiny air bubbles ballooned beneath several areas on the wall. In one section, the wallpaper didn't line up properly, leaving the bears chopped in half.

"How much stuff does Alan want you to do in this place?" Rowan asked.

Garrett reached for a corner of the wallpaper and tugged. It started to pull away, but he paused. "This will be a piece of cake. Umm... let's see, rip up carpet in the study and refinish those floors, tear down some drywall in the laundry room. I guess there was a leak in there at some point." He ticked off on his fingers. "Redo the flooring in the downstairs bathroom and put tile in there. And pretty much whatever crops up as the summer goes on."

Rowan opened the closet door, shuddering at the blast of chilly, rancid air that wafted out. She wrinkled her nose. "Stinks in here."

Garrett leaned over and sniffed. "Yeah, it kind of does."

4

"And then what's Alan's plan?" she asked. "He's going to put it back on the market?"

"Yep. He wants to get it listed before the film festival in Traverse City in late August. He thinks his billionaire buyer will be in that group."

Rowan closed the closet door. "It's a pretty amazing house. I'm surprised he got a deal to begin with."

"That's the perk of having half a dozen realtors keeping their eye on everything that comes up for you. Not to mention he rolled the money from his last flip right into this place, so he could pay cash. I think the seller wanted to unload it fast."

"Because the woman who lived here died?" Rowan gazed at the window, where she could see dozens of flies buzzing at the glass.

"Let's go check out that deck," Garrett suggested, grabbing Rowan's hand and dragging her from the room.

"It's like a tree house," Rowan said, standing at the edge of the viewing platform, hands on the rails. The hilly dune dropped out beneath her. The trees rose on either side of the deck, surrounding it in a cocoon of foliage.

"It is. I rather like the jungle feel, but Alan wants to cut it all back. Can't bury the house's best features, he says."

Rowan reached up and tugged at a strand of leafy vine crawling up the rail and clinging to a tall birch tree next to the deck.

"Those need to come down. Invasive species. They'll strangle the trees and then this deck will be a major hazard."

Rowan frowned, taken out of the momentary fantasy of the place— lush and green and perched at the edge of the world. "Why does it seem like the prettiest plants are the invasive ones?"

Garrett chuckled. "At the end of the day, even the invasive ones are just fighting for survival. We call them invasive because they take out the trees we like, but I'm pretty sure Mother Nature is not so discriminating."

Rowan leaned over and looked through the twisted trees to the long stretch of beach far below. Quinn was not quite a year old, but she loved the water. Rowan imagined their summer having picnics on the beach, long swims, trips into town for ice cream.

"It does feel better, right? The change of scenery?" Garrett asked, putting an arm around Rowan's waist and kissing her shoulder.

Rowan stared out at the lake reflecting the golden-tinted clouds above. "Yeah. It does."

～

"I have an idea," Garrett said after they returned to the house and unloaded their boxes from the back of his pick-up truck. He checked his watch. "Let's skip our romantic dinner and christen this house instead. My mom isn't expecting us until nine."

Rowan leaned a hip against the counter. "Is that called flirting, what you just did there?"

Garrett grinned. "Oh, I see. You need a little seduction first, eh?" Garrett started humming as he unbuckled his belt and slid it slowly from the loops. He whipped it and spun at the same time, cracking his elbow on the kitchen table. His face distorted in pain and he cursed under his breath, but continued his awkward dance, adding some come-hither eyes to Rowan.

He struggled out of his slightly damp t-shirt, sweat-marked from hauling boxes.

"You make Casanova look like an amateur." She laughed.

Garrett pulled the rubber band from his ponytail, flinching as it got tangled, and then shook his mane of dark hair out, pouting his lips. "Don't I know it."

He held out his arms and Rowan stepped into him, hugging him and burying her face in the crook of his neck. She inhaled the scent of his sweat mingling with the citrus-scented soap he'd used that morning.

He was still swaying his hips and took one of her hands in his and pressed his other hand into her lower back, singing quietly into the top of her head.

"I love you, Rowan Cortes."

～

They made love on a fluffy burgundy rug in front of the brick fireplace stacked with candles that likely hadn't held a proper fire in many years.

Garrett draped one arm over his face to block the afternoon sun. "Five-minute power nap," he murmured, blowing Rowan a kiss.

6

She stood and pulled on her shorts, walked into the downstairs bathroom and closed the door. Rowan paused in front of the mirror. Her long wavy blonde hair needed a trim. It was nearly to the midpoint in her back, and when she lifted it into the light, a bouquet of split ends met her gaze. She pulled it into a messy bun and washed her hands, dried them on a seashell towel hanging from a metal hook beside the sink.

The color in her face looked good, blue-green eyes clear, the skin beneath pale rather than purple. She'd grown used to thinking of herself as haggard the last few months and she was pleased to see today, for the first time in too long, she looked healthy.

Rowan walked to the kitchen and grabbed one of the bottles of iced tea she'd bought on their drive to the house. She carried it across the lawn, the grass spongy beneath her feet, and took the three steps that led onto the half-moon platform.

Lake Michigan stretched dazzling and infinite toward the horizon. This would be good, a summer in this house, a change. Rowan needed it. Garrett had said as much, doing his best not to push her, dropping hints in the previous months until finally she'd been the one to bring it up.

"Maybe we should all three move to the house in Empire for the summer," she'd said over coffee one morning.

She'd taken her leave of absence from work several weeks earlier. It had started as a week of bereavement after her father had died and snowballed into two weeks of bereavement and then three until finally, she'd filed for a three-month leave, a sabbatical they called it at the *Daily News*—they were writers after all. Sabbaticals were the appropriate way to say, 'I'm having a nervous breakdown and don't want to do it here in the office.'

There was no reason to stay in Gaylord for the summer with Garrett working on the house in Empire. Plus, he'd said it was amazing what a change of scenery could do for the mood. Everyone had agreed. Her mother, sister, Rowan's friends all insisted that yes, Rowan needed a vacation, a break.

And already their half a day in the house felt like a fresh start. She'd thought little of her father and hadn't cried a single time all day, not about him or about Quinn. She hadn't been feeling those niggling doubts about herself as a woman, a mother, a wife—the thoughts that had become like rats in the previous house, scurrying across her vision every time she turned around.

Rowan stepped off the deck and walked the perimeter of the yard, viewing the house from the side angle. Sunlight reflected off the windows, turning the dark panes into mirrors of the woods and sky.

A rectangular, darkly stained porch jutted from the back of the brick house. Wooden benches lined the porch and a jumble of plastic lawn chairs stood stacked in the center. Rowan walked up the steps and started toward the sliding glass doors that opened into the kitchen.

She recoiled at the slick warmth that coated her hand when she grabbed for the door handle. Jerking her fingers back, she searched for whatever coated the plastic. Dark red smeared across her fingers and palm. It could have been paint, but it wasn't. It was darker and more fragrant. It was blood.

"Garrett," she yelled, stepping back from the door.

A moment later, he appeared, long dark hair mussed. He slid the door open, rubbing one eye. "What's up?"

She held her arm out, palm exposed. He looked puzzled.

"What?"

She frowned and tilted her hand to look at it. Bare. No blood smeared across her fingers.

"What the hell?" she muttered, stepping back to the door and leaning toward the handle. She swiped one finger along the inside, but it came back clean.

"What is it, babe?"

She shook her head. "I thought…" She straightened up and gestured at the handle. "I thought there was something on there. Guess I imagined it."

He bent near the handle. "Like what? A bug or something?"

*Blood,* she wanted to say, but she didn't because now the very idea seemed preposterous and too familiar. She was getting better, and she would not say anything that implied otherwise.

"Yeah, a spider maybe."

"Probably fell through the deck." Garrett gestured at the dark cracks between the deck boards. They were narrow, hardly enough space for even a spider to slip through, but Rowan nodded.

"Yeah, probably."

## 2

They spent the following day unpacking. Quinn raced from room to room in her baby walker, a cacophony of jangling bells in her wake as she played with the gizmos attached to the plastic saucer.

"Ouch, shit. I mean shoot," Garrett grumbled.

Rowan peeked around the corner to see him standing on one leg in the hallway, Quinn grinning up at him.

"She's lethal in this thing." He steered her back towards the kitchen where Rowan unpacked their coffee supplies.

"Come on, Quinnie," Rowan said. "Snack?"

"Nak," Quinn said, rushing down the hallway and nearly running into the doorframe before Rowan caught the saucer and maneuvered her into the kitchen.

Rowan opened a can of baby puffs, little stars and clouds that claimed to be apple-cinnamon flavored, but Garrett insisted tasted like Styrofoam. Quinn shoved a handful in her mouth, half of which rained down into her seat and ended up on the floor. She promptly ran them over in her walker and laughed at the sound, looking at Rowan to see if she thought it was funny too.

"Hilarious, Quinnie. I can't wait to clean those crumbs out of the tiny cracks between the tile."

Quinn smiled and smacked her hands on the saucer, crushing more of the puffs beneath her pudgy fists before maneuvering toward the glass doors that opened onto the back porch.

As Rowan added their own coffee mugs to the cupboard beside the sink, she spotted two mugs left by the previous owner. One was navy blue and said 'Coffee Now, Beer Later.' The second mug was large and round with gold piping on the rim and a large gold 'A' in calligraphy. It was a pretty mug. Rowan tilted it back and forth, noticing how the sun caught the gold paint and made it shimmer. She returned the mug to the cupboard and continued unpacking.

That afternoon she found more monogrammed items, clothes tucked in a single cardboard box in the master bedroom—a t-shirt and a pair of sweatpants both monogrammed with the letters ALP.

Garrett had found a pink and yellow gardening set in the garage with ALP engraved on the wooden handles.

"No, you did not," Rowan said, peeling open a box filled with colored cloth.

Garrett looked up. "I need those."

"All twenty-seven of them?"

"How do you know there are twenty-seven?"

"Because I counted them in Gaylord. You have twenty-seven bandanas. Six of them are red and identical."

He cocked an eyebrow. "Was it just my imagination or have I encountered no fewer than five pairs of those cheap plastic reading glasses already sprinkled around this house?"

"Would you rather I go blind?"

"Of course not, my love. Nor would I prefer to spend the summer working with hair in my eyes and mouth. Thus the bandanas. See? Win, win, win."

Rowan smirked and turned back to another box, this one filled with paperback books she'd brought. She slid the box under a chair with her foot before Garrett noticed it.

"It's peaceful out here," Garrett said that evening after they'd spent the day unpacking and gotten Quinn down for an early bedtime.

He carried a bottle of cabernet to the glass resting on the arm of Rowan's Adirondack chair. He filled it to the brim and winked at her.

"If you're Bigfoot," she quipped.

"Oh, come on, really? You don't love it?"

Rowan rested her head against the chair back and closed her eyes.

The dank smells and sounds of a summer twilight enveloped them. Crickets, frogs, the cawing crows she'd imagined watching her when she walked onto the porch. They all released their chorus, vying to be heard above the others, succeeding only in creating a constant throbbing hum.

"No, I do. It's paradise. It's just so isolated. Do you have any idea what happened to the woman who owned it before? I've found like five things engraved with the initials ALP."

Garrett shook his head. "No, like I told you. She died, according to Alan, but I don't know what from. Old age, maybe. Probably had this house in her family for years and just… passed away."

Rowan nodded, but the explanation didn't sit right. The items she'd found didn't make her think of an old woman. They were the possessions of a younger woman. The clothes looked like garments a twenty-year-old would wear, not a ninety-year-old.

"The corn carbonara tonight was to die for, by the way," Garrett told her, smacking his lips. "Gosh, you haven't made that since—"

"I was pregnant," Rowan murmured. She hadn't made much of anything since Quinn's birth the previous June. It had been a tough year and eating, let alone cooking, had taken a backseat in her life.

"Yeah, it's been a stretch, but it's the dawn of a new day." He locked his eyes on her and raised his eyebrows suggestively. "Shall we finish our wine and head upstairs for a little you and me time?"

Rowan lifted her glass to her lips and nodded slowly.

They made love quietly while Quinn slept in the crib across the room.

When they finished, Garrett traced his finger down Rowan's spine, and she shivered. He kissed her shoulder.

"This has been so good for us," he whispered.

Rowan didn't turn, but nodded. In the previous two days they'd made love more, laughed more, and talked more than they had in the prior month.

He wove his fingers through her long silky hair, pulling it over her shoulder. "Quinn's about to be one. We talked about two, maybe even three. I thought—"

"I'm not ready."

"Okay. No pressure, honey. I'm only bringing it up because, well, I had a voicemail on my phone from the woman we were working with at the adoption agency. She wondered if we were still considering adopting."

Rowan's eyelids drifted down. "Garrett—"

He kissed her mouth. "End of discussion. I shouldn't have brought it up. Water?" he asked.

"Yes, please."

She lay back, tears threatening, and listened as he moved around the room, pulling on his brief underwear. Rowan rested a hand on her lower belly where the scar from her C-section rose in a prickly line beneath her fingers. Garrett left the room, his soft footfalls padding down the stairs.

Rowan thought back to nearly two years before when they'd started the process of adopting. They hadn't found a child, but they'd filled out the paperwork, and gotten their background checks. They'd lain in bed at night and wondered if they'd get a boy or girl, if they'd fall in love with an infant or small child or perhaps an older child like Rowan herself had been when Morgan and Emily had adopted her at seven years old.

Garrett returned with a glass of ice water.

Rowan sat up, braced on one elbow, still naked. Her breasts had shrunken since she'd stopped nursing, but they were still larger than they'd been before motherhood.

Garrett gazed at her appreciatively.

"What?" she asked, taking the cup and pressing it first to her cheek before taking a sip.

"Just admiring my beautiful wife."

Rowan's eye caught on the gold chain around his neck, the miniature gold-pressed image of the Virgin of Guadalupe nestled in the dark whorls of his hair. He rarely took it off and though Garrett had never been much of a practicing Catholic, Rowan had watched more than once as Garrett touched the pendant during moments of crisis as if seeking the Virgin's divine guidance.

He took the glass and set it on the bedside table before hovering over Quinn. "She's sleeping with her butt in the air," he told Rowan, smiling.

"Doing her Droopy Dog impression?"

"Yep, nose down, butt up." He returned to the bed, slid beneath the sheet next to Rowan. He pulled her against him and kissed her ear. "How'd I get so lucky?" he asked.

She lay with her head on his chest, listening to the steady thrum of his heartbeat. "I wonder that for myself every day."

Within minutes, Garrett drifted off to sleep, but Rowan lay awake.

A smell of incense wafted through the room and Rowan sat up, searching for the origin of the scent. She hadn't burned any incense the day before. She hadn't even owned incense since college, and yet that was the smell permeating the room.

'Do you smell that?' she wanted to ask Garrett so that he could confirm she was not insane, but he was snoring, deep in sleep, and she wouldn't wake him.

Early in their marriage, Garrett had suffered from insomnia. In those days, Rowan had often found him at two or three in the morning sitting at the kitchen table, flipping through a magazine or working on bids. He'd hold up his cup of manzanilla tea, or chamomile as Rowan knew it, and she'd give him a quick nod on her way to pee.

For the previous twelve months it had been Rowan who'd suffered from insomnia. It had been a tough year beginning with Quinn's birth. Their daughter had gone breech two days before Rowan went into labor. Rowan had felt the shift, like a tidal wave in her stomach, and dropped an entire carton of orange juice on the kitchen floor. She'd gone to see her midwife, Katherine, who had felt Rowan's stomach and agreed that yes, the baby had flipped upside down.

This had been devastating news. Rowan had had a birthing tub already inflated in their sun room. She'd had a vision of a natural birth that did not include a breech baby. Katherine had been adamant. No breech babies born at home for a first birth.

Rowan had gone into labor in the middle of the night and instead of sinking into a birthing jacuzzi beneath the twinkle lights that Garrett had strung up, she'd given birth by C-section under a line of harsh fluorescent lights in a room full of blue-clad strangers. Garrett had sat on a stiff metal chair next to Rowan's head. A sheet had covered her from the waist down.

Garret gazing down at her was the last solid memory Rowan had from those five days in the hospital. Her uterus had ruptured during the c-section. She'd started hemorrhaging blood and the doctors performed an emergency hysterectomy. The worst might have been over, but then an infection developed in her sutures and a fever had ravaged her for days. Rowan had strange, haunted memories of the hospital. The nurses' faces appeared long and ghoulish and filled with menace. Garrett seemed always to be cowering in the corner. Sometimes she would wake in the night hallucinating that Quinn had died and she'd suffered a mental breakdown—they'd kept her drugged to hide the truth. Eventually the fever subsided and she, Garrett and Quinn went home.

Rowan had recovered slowly. Quinn had recovered slowly, too. They both cried a lot. Garrett had worked during the day while Quinn and Rowan napped and held each other.

Mothers understood the divine secrets of a new baby in a way that fathers never would. It was almost like a repayment for the sacrifice of pregnancy and birth, but the truth was that mothers were forever connected to the child who'd lived inside of them.

There was all of that magic and there was an entire closet filled with darkness too. There were the physical pains as her nipples split and bled. The sensations when her breasts grew so full with milk, Rowan screamed herself awake at night from engorgement. There was the slick, sharp haze of sleeplessness. Nights, many of them, without more than a two-hour stretch of actual sleep.

In the waking moments, there was a tiny, fragile, perfect being desperate for Rowan and only Rowan. Garrett could not soothe her at night. Only when Rowan reached her breaking point would she stumble into their bedroom, bleary-eyed, bawling louder than their newborn child, and thrust the baby into his sleepy arms.

"Please," she would mumble before staggering to the spare bedroom to collapse onto the bed. Rowan would fall asleep and awake an hour later, disoriented and sure that the baby had fallen from the bed. Frantically, she would fling the covers aside, search the crevice between mattress and bed frame until gradually the current world would take shape. She would remember that Garrett had the baby, that Rowan had not lost her, that everything was okay.

But still, those moments were not the truly dark moments. Those came later when Rowan's father's routine surgery rapidly turned catastrophic.

Rowan remembered back to one of the worst days, when her dad had been on life support. Quinn had been awake all the previous night, feeding and crying and inconsolable as if she sensed Rowan's grief.

Rowan had gone to see her father at the hospital the next day. She'd stood beside his bed, her fingers clutching his feverish hand, and she'd known that wherever he'd drifted to he could not claw his way back from that place. Nothing could bring him back now, no drug, no surgery–nothing short of a miracle and a miracle would not be coming.

For the second night in a row, as the hours stretched infinitely long and black, Quinn had screamed and cried as if she'd sensed that death was in the air.

And though the memories blurred together now, Rowan thought it had been that night-sleepless, bleary-eyed, almost hysterical-as she'd walked the second-floor balcony in their Gaylord home, bouncing and rocking her frantic baby, that she'd first had the horrifying thought of dropping Quinn over the rail. Not intentionally, but as if some entity would possess her and force her to do this unforgivable thing. Her body would take on a life of its own, and on wooden legs she'd move to the balcony and open her arms.

That night, as if Garrett had sensed his wife's disturbing thoughts, he'd appeared behind her, groggy from sleep, and hugged her and Quinn both before detaching Quinn from her mother's arms and telling Rowan to go back to bed. That had been the beginning of the unbidden visions that culminated in Quinn's death and the constant terror that Rowan would be at fault.

Now Rowan shook away those horrific memories and sat up, continuing to sniff at the air, at the undeniable smoky herbal scent.

Rowan stood and stepped into the dark hallway. As she gazed toward the end of the hall, something creaked. Rowan stiffened, focusing on the doors, fearing some creature would emerge from the darkness, but nothing did.

Lightly, she moved down the hall to the room they'd dubbed the nursery. She pushed the door in with her foot and flipped on the light. The room illuminated, the bears leering at her from the cheerless wallpaper. Rowan entered the room, paused in front of the closed closet door. She touched the knob, reluctant to open it, as she'd already spooked herself and now envisioned someone crouched inside waiting for the handle to turn so he could pounce.

With a quick jerk, she turned the handle and opened the door, stepping aside. No beast darted out. Rowan looked inside. Empty except for a few pieces of clothing hanging from wire hangers. Rowan picked through them. One was a purple and blue tie-dye sweatshirt, so soft that Rowan pulled it from the hanger without a thought and slid it over her head. When she looked down at the front of the shirt, she saw initials in silvery lettering.

ALP.

Rowan flipped off the light and returned to their bedroom. She crawled back into bed beside Garrett and drifted into sleep.

# 3

Rowan woke to light filtering through the half-open curtains. She looked down at her shirt and remembered the night before, the smell of incense that had pulled her from the bed.

"Is it terrible to wear a dead woman's clothes?" Rowan whispered, running her fingers over the silvery initials.

Rowan had been imagining names for the woman since she'd started finding her monogrammed belongings. Amelia Lillian Post. Amanda Lynn Pruitt. Antoinette Lindsey Plum. She was a woman who liked tie-dye sweatshirts and hand-painted mugs, colorful gardening tools.

"Pancakes?" Garrett asked, startling her. He stood in the doorway, his black hair loose on his shoulders, already dressed in work jeans and a craft beer t-shirt.

Rowan yawned and stretched, looking toward the tall windows that revealed blue skies.

Quinn slept, wearing only a diaper, on the bed in the space Garrett had occupied. He must have put her in bed with Rowan when he woke. Like Garrett, Quinn's skin and hair were dark, but her eyes beneath their fluttering lids were a blue-green that matched Rowan's.

Rowan touched one of her daughter's soft, warm cheeks. Her skin felt like smooth dough just rubbed in flour. Rowan leaned down and inhaled her.

Garrett said nothing, just grinned and watched Rowan marvel at their beautiful daughter. He'd grown used to it.

Quinn had become more known to Garrett in the previous months. The first several had been hard for him. Hard for them both. She was so fragile and shifted between feeding and sleeping. His experience of her was relegated to dirty diapers and those especially exhausting nights when Rowan handed her off, unable to rock her, soothe her or feed her for another second, her exhaustion so overwhelming Rowan sobbed more loudly than their infant daughter.

"Pancakes sound good," Rowan told him, scooting from the bed. She turned on the monitor and directed it toward the bed, closed the door behind her, and followed Garrett to the kitchen.

Garrett usually woke by six am. He'd already had his coffee, sent half a dozen emails and made a list of his plans for the day. Rowan could see the list written in red pen on a sheet of scrap paper he kept next to his laptop. At the top of the list, she saw 'pancakes.'

Quinn wouldn't wake for another hour and Rowan could savor her bit of morning quiet time. When Garrett had first showed her the house, she'd imagined taking a cup of steaming coffee to one of the Adirondack chairs that sat on the half-moon platform overlooking Lake Michigan.

"Let's go out there," Rowan told Garrett, gesturing to the deck, "and start a fire."

"It's supposed to be seventy degrees today."

"So? It's not yet."

"Of course," he told her, winking. "Pancakes and a fire for my hot mama."

Rowan dug through one of the boxes in the doorway and found a battered copy of *Eat, Pray, Love* by Elizabeth Gilbert. She'd read the book three times already, but had started again just after her father died, hoping that some of Gilbert's inspiring story might help pull Rowan from the funk she'd descended into.

Rowan set the video monitor on the counter and boiled water for her French press. She inhaled the coffee beans, black and oily, before dumping them into the grinder. It was a ritual, a simple moment of pleasure she indulged in every morning.

Those had been her lifelines in the months after Quinn's birth. No one had told her how shocking it would be, becoming a mother. How everything would change, everything—her body, her sleep cycle, her brain, her heart. She was no longer a singular person. Now she was two people. It was as if she'd given birth to her own soulmate, but her soulmate was tiny and fragile and depended on Rowan for survival. The thing Rowan now loved most in the world, more than her own father, more than Garrett, was also the most vulnerable being she'd ever encountered.

Rowan glanced at the monitor as Quinn shifted and flopped an arm up over her head. Rowan could see half the room on the grainy screen.

The teakettle whistled, and Rowan pulled it off the burner before it started shrieking. She poured the boiling water over the coffee grounds.

Garrett had gone to the platform to start the fire before making pancakes. Rowan watched him through the kitchen window arranging sticks in the copper firepit.

Something knocked in the monitor. Rowan grabbed it, thinking Quinn had awoken, but she lay unmoving in the bed. Another movement caught her eye. She heard a tap and then the tip of something shifted into view. It slipped back out again. Another knock and a scraping sound. As Rowan stared at the screen, the small wooden rocking horse Garrett's parents had given Quinn for Christmas rocked into view. No one touched it, but still it rocked back and forth, inching across the floor toward the bed.

Rowan gripped the monitor so hard it hurt, and after several seconds of holding her breath and watching the toy moving of its own volition, she raced through the house and up the stairs. She burst into the bedroom, the door banging hard against the wall.

Quinn's eyes flew open, and she let out a little cry.

Rowan skidded into the room to the bed, her eyes going to the rocking horse that stood halfway between the wall and the bed. It remained still, as if it had not moved at all.

"Mmma," Quinn said sleepily, crawling across the bed before flopping down again.

Breathless, Rowan sat on the edge of the bed. She brushed her fingers through Quinn's wispy black curls and stared at the rocking horse, her heart slamming out an angry rhythm, her hands shaking as they touched her daughter.

Had she imagined it?

No, no way. For starters, the rocking horse was clear across the room and it hadn't been there when she'd stepped from bed ten minutes before.

"She woke up?" Garrett's voice startled Rowan, and she jumped, which startled Quinn. Her eyes burst open a second time.

"Hey, polliwog," Garrett said, smiling at his daughter. He walked in and sat on the bed.

Rowan nodded, still watching the rocking horse. "I woke her up. Something weird just happened."

"What?" He twiddled his fingers in front of Quinn and she grabbed his hand and stuck his thumb in her mouth. He pulled his hand back. "Better not," he said, holding both palms up. "Daddy's been outside playing with wood."

"I saw... I saw that horse rocking across the room all by itself." Rowan pointed at the rocking horse.

Garrett frowned, gave her a look to see if she was joking. She clearly was not. He got up and went to the toy, kneeling beside it. He rocked it back and forth. Then he stood and went to the doorway, turning his head sideways as he gazed at the room. He got down on hands and knees and put his cheek against the wood floor.

He stood up, satisfied. "Looks like there's a slant in the floor. That would explain it."

"Really?" Rowan studied the floor, trying to see the slant he described. She couldn't see it. "Wouldn't we all be pooling at the headboard if that were true?"

"This house was built over a century ago. On sand, no less. Consider erosion, shifts in the water table. A slant is realistic but what you're describing is more like tilt."

"Seriously, we're debating a tilt versus a slant?"

He laughed, kissed Rowan's head and swung Quinn up on his hip. "Pancakes?" he asked her.

"Pmcaaa!" she exclaimed, yawning.

"Baby morning breath. Thank you, Quinn."

He left the room, but Rowan stayed for another moment, watching the horse and trying to identify this so-called slant. She wanted it to be true. A logical explanation was far better than accepting that the rocking horse had somehow moved of its own free will, or worse, someone had moved it.

Just to be sure, Rowan pulled open the closet door—empty. She got down on hands and knees and peeked beneath the bed. That too was empty.

Unnerved, she slipped from the room and headed for the kitchen.

～

They ate pancakes and then took the long wooden staircase down to the beach.

"Fifty-two stairs," Garrett exclaimed when they were halfway down. "I counted them our first day."

"Feels more like one hundred and fifty-two," Rowan said, thighs burning.

The tide sighed against the shore, steady and unhurried. The water and sky were a mirror of blue. As above, so below. The temperature had begun its ascent, which would top out somewhere near eighty degrees according to the morning radio, which Rowan had turned on while Garrett made pancakes.

Quinn waddled along the beach, turned toward the water and squealed in delight when the cold surf licked her bare toes.

"Not in the water, Quinnie," Rowan said as Garrett headed her off and steered her back toward the dune.

Quinn bent down to grab at a dark stone and then sat on her butt. The water rushed up around her and she laughed and slapped the ground. Her diaper expanded.

"Well, that's done for." Rowan laughed, squatting down and unhooking the sides of the diaper. Rowan held up the soggy mass.

"Now I don't feel guilty about the couple of times I've not changed her right away," Garrett said, poking the diaper with an index finger. "Those things can hold five gallons of pee."

"Very funny," Rowan said, heaving the diaper in his direction.

He caught it and then grimaced. "It's so... mushy!"

"Now imagine sitting in it."

A thoughtful look came over his face as he squeezed it. "Might not be so bad."

Rowan helped Quinn stand and wiped the wet sand off her butt. Quinn barely let her before starting back off down the beach.

"I need to run into Traverse City in a few hours," Garrett said, bending over to pick up a stone. "Want to go?"

"Sure," Rowan told him, hiding her continued disquiet over the damn rocking horse. She had a paranoid streak and an inability to let a mysterious something go. The horse had moved. Either someone had pushed it or it had rocked itself across the floor. Neither left her wanting an afternoon alone in the house.

"Did you smell incense last night?" she asked, watching Quinn meander toward a hunk of driftwood that had washed onto the shore.

"Incense? No. Were you burning some?"

Rowan shook her head. "I woke up and smelled it."

"Probably just the laundry detergent on the sheets. You know how the mind warps things at night."

"Yeah," she agreed, though like with the rocking horse, Garrett's explanation did little to put her at ease.

As Rowan loaded their breakfast dishes into the dishwasher, her cell phone rang and Mona's name appeared on the screen.

"Hey," Rowan said, wedging the phone between her shoulder and ear as she rinsed the last of the syrup from their sticky utensils.

"Hey, yourself. How come you haven't called to tell me all about the pleasure palace you're on sabbatical in?"

Rowan laughed. When she'd told Mona about her intention to take the summer off of work to live in the house on Lake Michigan, her best friend had insisted on calling it the 'pleasure palace,' to which Garrett said it sounded like they were planning a summer at Hugh Hefner's mansion.

"Well, the pool boys have yet to arrive, or the pool for that matter, so I'd hardly call it a pleasure palace."

"Okay, fine, your lakefront villa, how is it?"

Rowan closed the dishwasher with her foot and slipped back into the living room, where Quinn sat on the floor drooling on a set of plastic baby keys. "It's good, interesting."

"Details, please."

Rowan perched on the arm of a couch and considered the room. "It's... different. Which is good. I needed the change and outside is just beautiful and lush and the lake has all these faces, sparkling or turbulent, so that's been fun."

"I sense a 'but.'"

"Well, it's funny, really. A game I've started to play, maybe not a game. I smelled incense last night." Rowan laughed and wondered why on earth she was even mentioning this to Mona. "I've started thinking maybe it's the woman who lived here before haunting the house."

"I did not think that's where you were going with the incense. I had this momentary vision of you sneaking out of bed to find Garrett burning incense, smoking a joint, and listening to his old *Grateful Dead* CDs."

"Nothing that drastic has happened."

Mona laughed. "Really, though? You think it's haunted?"

Rowan stood and walked to the back sliding doors, where Garrett had hauled several tool boxes and now sat rifling through them. "No, not really. I just haven't been sleeping well. Like I said, it's become my stupid little head game."

"Oh, sure, nothing sends you into a peaceful slumber like the thought that a dead woman is haunting your house."

"Yeah, not the best train of thought in the middle of the night."

"No, but if it keeps you distracted… How are you, honey? Doing better?"

"Yeah. I am. I think Garrett was right, change of scenery and all that."

"Well, don't tell him that or it will go straight to his head."

Rowan smiled. "How are Caleb and the kids?"

"Oh, Caleb's his usual chipper self. His guys from work have started a kayaking club, so he's off doing that today. The kids are at summer camp until Sunday. Sweet Jesus, thank you. I was rather hoping you'd swing by if you're coming back to Gaylord for anything."

"I'd love to. Maybe in a couple of days? I left a bag behind and never picked up my laptop charger from the newspaper. I've been sharing Garrett's, which drives him bonkers even though he's barely opened his laptop since we got here."

"Want a job?" Garrett asked, poking his head into the kitchen.

"So long as it's not a blowjob," Mona squawked through the phone, laughing.

Rowan grinned.

"Mona, quit dirtying the mind of my innocent wife," Garrett called back.

Rowan put her cell on speaker.

"Between the two of us, Row's mind is far dirtier than my own," Mona exclaimed.

"That'll be the day," he retorted.

"Okay, Mona. I better let you go," Rowan said. "My boss thinks I'm slacking on the job."

"No better way to solve an unhappy boss than seven minutes in the supply closet."

"Goodbye, Mona." Rowan laughed. "I'm hanging up now."

"Bye, doll," Garrett called.

"You two lovebirds don't have too much fun," Mona boomed before ending the call.

"Good thing she never suckered you into that erotic book club." Garrett smirked.

"It was not an erotic book club. It was just a book club. I think their first book was *Water for Elephants*."

"Sounds kinky," he said, wrapping an arm around her waist. "Hmmm…?" He kissed her neck.

"Bbbaddda," Quinn shrieked, toddling in and grabbing first Garrett's legs and then Rowan's before turning and heading for the glass doors where she pressed both palms and her mouth against the glass.

"Eeew, Quinnie. I haven't cleaned those," Rowan told her.

"Better she consume dirt than Windex," Garrett said.

Rowan picked Quinn up and balanced her on a hip. "Tell me about this job."

He pointed to the ceiling. "The nursery, the one with all the creepy bears. Could you peel the wallpaper? Not all of it. I just want to get a sense of what's underneath, so I can get the right supplies when we drive into town."

"What do you think, Quinn? Want to peel some wallpaper?"

Quinn grinned and released a mouthful of drool onto Rowan's shoulder. Garrett laughed and gave her a thumbs up.

Rowan set up the playpen in the nursery and plopped Quinn inside with a jumble of toys.

At the wall, she found the corner of wallpaper Garrett had peeled their first day. She tugged it and it pulled easily before catching and tearing on a jagged angle. She moved along the wall, picking at corners with her fingernails, peeling away full strips.

The plastered wall, once painted yellow, revealed itself in front of her. Halfway down one wall she discovered words and pictures scribbled on the yellow plaster. The writing was that of children, most of the words misspelled, the drawings stick figures, rainbows and hearts. Someone had allowed a child or children to color all over the wall.

It surprised Rowan. It didn't seem like a place where children would have been permitted to do such things.

As she revealed more of the wall beneath the paper, she unveiled a disturbing image drawn in marker. It crudely depicted the head of a woman or girl. Yawning red holes represented the figure's eyes and mouth. Brown squiggles had been drawn as the girl's hair and black spikes poked from the girl's neck. The artist had not drawn a body beneath the picture, just the head and neck.

"Sick," Rowan muttered, letting the flap of wallpaper she'd pulled free drift to the floor.

She started on another sheet of the wallpaper, but this one stuck. She needed a scraper to get under the edge.

"I'll be right back, Quinnie," Rowan told her daughter, who sat munching on a rubbery turquoise necklace that Rowan had often worn when she nursed.

Rowan skipped down the stairs and rifled in Garrett's toolbox, pulling out a metal scraper with a red handle. She stopped in the upstairs bathroom and peed, opening the door before she rinsed her hands under the faucet. She heard Quinn chattering and figured Garrett must have gone in to see her.

When Rowan returned, she saw Quinn standing in the playpen at the corner, talking and reaching her arms out as if to be picked up. Garrett did not stand beyond her. Instead, she reached her little hands toward the dark crevice in the closet. The door stood cracked.

"Is Daddy hiding in there playing peek-a-boo?" Rowan asked, grinning and stepping toward the door.

As she lifted her arm, gooseflesh prickled along her wrist, up her bicep and across her neck. She stared uneasily at the dark slit in the door.

"Garrett?" she asked, still smiling, though the mirth had slipped away.

Garrett didn't respond, and Rowan sensed her husband did not stand in the closet. He wasn't the kind of person to hide and jump out to scare her—not with the way things had been in the previous months.

The closet door had been closed, hadn't it? Rowan tried to remember if it had been ajar, and she felt almost positive that it had not.

Rowan bent and snatched Quinn from the playpen with such force the little girl cried out in surprise and started to cry. Rowan stepped back, wide eyes fixed on the black crack. She spun and ran from the room.

# 4

---

As she hurtled down the hallway, Garrett came up the stairs. His grin faded when he saw Rowan and Quinn. "What?" he asked, looking beyond her down the hall.

Rowan opened her mouth, registered her daughter's cries and patted her head. "I... the closet. I think there's something in the closet," Rowan stammered, turning to look back at the open doorway to the room at the end of the hall.

"What kind of something? Someone?"

"I think so."

Garrett frowned. "Take Quinn outside to the car."

Rowan didn't want to. If someone hid in that closet, Garrett would face him alone. "Maybe we should just... both go or..."

"It's okay. Take your cell phone. If I don't come out in two minutes, call the police."

Rowan slipped quickly down the stairs, grabbed her cell phone off the counter and walked to the car. Quinn had stopped crying, shifting instead to playing with the buttons on Rowan's shirt.

Rowan climbed behind the wheel, settling Quinn on the passenger seat before reaching into the backseat to fish a toy from the floor. Rowan grabbed two rubber blocks. She handed them to Quinn, who started banging the two blocks together.

Moments later, Garrett emerged from the house.

Rowan unlocked the door and swung it open. "Anything?" she

asked, though she knew from the look on his face there had been nothing inside.

"Nope. Empty except for a few hangers and some dust bunnies. What made you think someone was in there?"

Rowan stepped out as Garrett opened the passenger door and retrieved Quinn. "Quinn was talking to someone. I left the room for a couple of minutes and when I came back, she was talking and reaching her arms toward the door like she wanted someone in there to pick her up."

Garrett looked at Quinn. "Polliwog, you know better than to ask invisible strangers to pick you up." He chuckled and started back toward the house, but Rowan stood by the car for another minute before following him inside.

"Did you see the pictures drawn on the walls?" Rowan asked, glancing up the staircase. She didn't want to go back in that room.

"Yeah, previous owners must have let their kids run wild. I'm surprised the rest of the house is in such good shape."

"Yeah, but did you see the picture of the girl?"

"With the big red eyes?" He nodded, and then something seemed to come to him. "I bet that creeped you out. That's probably what made you think something was in the closet."

"Maybe," Rowan agreed. "I think I'll take Quinn out in the yard to play."

"Had your fill of wallpaper peeling?" He handed her Quinn.

"In that room, anyway."

He grinned. "Okay, give me like a half hour and we'll head into town."

They loaded into Garrett's truck. Rowan grabbed extra diapers, snacks and toys, the usual necessities that in a year had already become ingrained in her mind. Never leave without the necessities. The once or twice she'd made the error, Quinn had ended up with a blow-out diaper, and Rowan had wrapped her daughter's backside in towels or spare t-shirts until she could get home.

They drove into Traverse City. Rowan gazed at the rolling hill-side and then the sparkling bay when they crested the hill on M-72 that led them downtown. The sidewalks were a steady stream of tourists and locals meandering in and out of pubs and souvenir shops.

Garrett parked on the street in front of the hardware store. Two doors down, Rowan spotted a bookstore.

"Quinn and I will be in there," she told him.

"Okay, see you in fifteen?" he asked.

"Yep."

Garrett kissed Rowan on the mouth, then planted a kiss on Quinn's head. "Have fun, polliwog," he told her.

Rowan carried Quinn into the store, diaper bag slung over her shoulder, and scanned the aisle signs until she found the nonfiction section: *Supernatural, Paranormal and Mythology*.

She set Quinn on the carpeted floor and handed her a plastic block with a rubber bear trapped inside. Quinn stuck her fingers into the plastic holes and tried to pry the bear loose.

Rowan browsed the shelves and pulled out a book titled *Ghosts of the Great Lakes*.

"Oh, Lordy, that child is beautiful. What's her name?" a woman gushed as she stepped into the aisle.

The woman looked to be in her sixties, maybe early seventies, and wore a pink jogging suit with clean white tennis shoes. She reminded Rowan of a Florida grandmother, the ladies who went speed-walking, sipping from water bottles and talking gossip as they planned ladies' luncheons and benefit dinners to provide flowers for the local churches.

"Her name's Quinn, or Quinnie, as I like to call her."

The woman squatted and touched one of Quinn's bouncy curls. "Well, she is a beauty queen in the making. My goodness, it almost hurts to look at her! I have three grandbabies myself and don't tell their parents, but they can't hold a candle to this little angel. Course, my daughter-in-law is to blame for that. I think she only brushes their hair about once a month. If you saw them on the street, you'd think they were homeless." She laughed and stood up, eyeing the book in Rowan's hand, which Rowan had meant to set inconspicuously on the shelf.

The woman cocked an eyebrow. "Like ghost stories, do ya? I've heard a few in my day and have a handful of my own, though I'm not one for sharing such tales. Talk about 'em and they come knocking at your door." The woman winked. "You visiting for summer vacation?"

"Not exactly," Rowan admitted. "My husband is doing some renovations on a house in Empire."

"You don't say. I grew up out that way. A big old farmhouse out on Manning Road. Couldn't wait to escape to the big city. Boy, was that a mistake. The minute my hubby and I retired, we hightailed it right back here to northern Michigan.

"Thoreau had it right. A city is just a million people being lonely together—or something like that. And I'll tell you, it is true. We lived in Atlanta, Georgia for thirty years and you know who I talked to every week? My friends from north Michigan. We never made a friend in Atlanta. People'd come into your life for a season and poof, gone with the May flowers."

Rowan smiled. "I've never been a city girl either. I lived in Minneapolis for a year while I did my internship, but that's as big as I can handle."

"Smart girl," the woman said. "So, where in Empire did you say you're staying?"

"A big brick house up in the woods. The property overlooks Lake Michigan. It's near the Empire Bluffs."

The woman's mouth turned down at the same moment her eyebrows shot up. Rowan realized they weren't real eyebrows at all, but penciled on. "Goodness, no. You're living in Helme House?"

Quinn had gotten to the diaper bag and began pulling the contents out. Rowan realized she'd turned her bottle on its side and it was dripping onto the bookstore carpet.

"Quinnie, no, no, baby." Rowan squatted and picked the bottle up, returned the lid and stuffed diapers and wipes back into the bag. She unzipped a separate pocket and pulled out several of Quinn's toys. "Here, Quinnie." Rowan handed Quinn the crinkle paper.

Quinn crunched it noisily in her hands.

Rowan stood back up. "You can't take your eyes off her for a second."

The woman nodded, her face all serious. "Isn't that the truth?" Her easy happiness had dissolved.

"Um... I wasn't aware the place we were staying had a name. You called it Helme House?"

The woman glanced down at Quinn and her face softened. "So innocent, aren't they? They grow up so fast." She returned her gaze to Rowan's face. "I don't want to scare you, dear, but Helme House has a history."

"What kind of history? I mean, I knew the woman who lived there before us died…"

"Oh, no." The woman shook her head. "Amy didn't die. She vanished, but under very mysterious circumstances. The police found blood in the house and other unusual things, but no sign of the woman has ever surfaced."

Rowan's mouth fell open, and she took an automatic step back, her heel catching on the diaper bag. She flailed an arm out, but there was nothing to grab. Rowan went down hard, landing on her butt just inches away from her daughter, still happily crushing her paper.

"Oh, Quinn." Rowan grabbed Quinn and pulled her against her chest. She'd nearly landed on her.

"Gosh, there I go again, putting my shoe in my big mouth." The woman extended her hand, and Rowan took it, heaving to her feet with Quinn in her arms.

Quinn dropped the paper and tugged at one of Rowan's silver hoop earrings.

"Ouch. Let go of Mommy's earing, Quinnie."

She did, and Rowan set her back on the floor, handing her a plastic baby mirror. Quinn pressed her mouth against her reflection, leaving a gooey splatter of saliva.

"My husband is always after me for clucking like some kind of angry hen," the woman said.

"Do the police think someone murdered her?"

"Well, I guess it's too late to shut my mouth now, isn't it? That's one theory. She wasn't a Helme, that woman. Her father-in-law bought the house as a wedding gift for her and her husband. He had a lot of money. But the engagement got called off, and she ended up moving into the big house all alone. There were rumors floating around about a bed-and-breakfast, but my friend Renata works at the permit office out there and said nothing ever crossed her desk about a bed-and-breakfast. Anyway, Amy lived there for about a year and then one day there was a great big headline in the paper. 'Woman Missing from Blood-Soaked House.' I heard her parents tried to sue the paper for writing such a gruesome headline, but I doubt anything ever came of it, on behalf of the headline being the God's truth. Blood all over the kitchen was what I heard, and some in the master bedroom too."

Rowan shuddered, envisioning the room they'd slept in every night since arriving. It was the only room in the house with fresh paint.

Rowan realized she hadn't taken a breath and she could feel the 'o' of horror frozen on her mouth. She forced her lips closed and clamped her teeth together.

"Anyhoo, there was a huge investigation, but"—the woman shrugged—"they never found her."

"How long ago was that?"

The woman's eyes tipped up as if she had a calendar on the inside of her forehead. "Must have been three or four years ago."

"And the house has been vacant since then."

"Oh, yes. There was squabbling over ownership of the house. I don't know all those details, but then again, who'd want to buy it and live there?" The woman seemed to remember who she spoke to and let out a little gasp of embarrassment. "Good Lord. This is why I can't go anywhere without Bill. I just don't have a filter on this mouth of mine."

"Her name was Amy?" Rowan asked, thinking again of the monogrammed items they'd found in the house.

The woman nodded. "Amy Prahm. Nice girl from what I heard. If I remember correctly, she'd just celebrated her twenty-fifth birthday. Practically still a child. I was just sick at the news. We were still in Atlanta then. We moved back here about two years after, but every one of my friends and cousins and even my brother, and he's no gossip, called me up to tell me about the disappearance. It killed the tourism season in Empire that year, I'll tell you that. Nobody wanted to be lying on the beach while a murderer stalked through the woods behind them."

"I don't blame them," Rowan muttered, thinking of Garrett's friend Alan and furious that he hadn't told them that the previous owner had vanished from the house.

# 5

"Hey." Rowan found Garrett in the hardware store and yanked his sleeve harder than necessary.

He turned around, eyes wide. "What happened?" He looked at Quinn, scanning her as if searching for an injury.

"It's not Quinn," Rowan hissed, tugging him down an aisle of power drills. "What did Alan tell you about the woman who lived in the house?"

As Rowan had left the bookstore, she'd wondered if Garrett had been told about the disappearance and had kept it secret, knowing she would not have wanted to move into the house.

He wrinkled his forehead. "What? Why?"

"Just tell me!" she snapped.

Quinn reached her arms for Garrett. "Bebebebe," she said.

He took her. "Are you talking gibberish again, polliwog?" He kissed her smooth cheek. "Umm... let's see, he said he got an unbelievable deal because the owner wanted to unload it. A woman had lived there before us and she'd died. That was it. I told you as much already."

"Do you swear?"

He cracked a smile. "What are we, eight? Yeah, sure. Cross my heart. Why? And why do you look like you just bit into a moldy peach?"

"The woman who lived there didn't just die. She disappeared and left behind blood-splattered walls," Rowan said, too loud.

An older couple at the end of the hallway glanced toward them before hurrying away.

"What?" Garrett shook his head. "No way. Alan would have told me—"

"It's true. I just met a woman in the bookstore and she told me all about it."

He sighed. "A woman in the bookstore. Seriously? That's your rock-solid source?"

"Why would she lie?"

"Why would Alan lie? We've been friends since elementary school. He would never have kept that detail out. Believe me."

"Well." Rowan stuck her hands on her hips. "Maybe he didn't know, but… it's true. I really think it's true."

He was halfway through an eye roll when he caught the expression on Rowan's face and stopped. "We can find out, but Row, what do you want me to do about it? I've got the study floor ripped out. I can't exactly back out of the renovations."

Rowan sighed and dropped her hands at her sides. She hadn't thought that far. "I want to go to the library and look at some news-paper archives. You take Quinn and I'll meet you for lunch in an hour?"

He shifted Quinn higher so she could grab at his ball cap. "Okay," he relented. "But this is supposed to be your summer off. Remember? You're not going to get crazy over this."

Rowan hoisted the diaper bag off her shoulder and handed it to him before kissing Quinn on the ear. "I'll see you in an hour," she said and headed for the door.

The Traverse Area District Library had moved their old copies of the *Record Eagle* and the *Leelanau Enterprise* into an online archive. Rowan sat in a computer room surrounded by teenagers punching at the keys, some of them laughing, headphone buds tucked into the whorls of their ears.

The headlines weren't hard to find. A search of Amy Prahm's name resulted in a dozen records, more on the following pages. Rowan clicked the first and saw the very headline the lady from the bookstore had mentioned.

*Woman Missing from Blood-Soaked House.*

Rowan grimaced. She'd been a journalist for over ten years and had never understood the desire for such detestable headlines. It wasn't the writer's work, but the editor picking the most shocking words they could pack into the shortest line.

*Police are baffled by the strange disappearance of twenty-five-year-old Amy Lyla Prahm, who lives at 1258 Forest Hill Drive, formerly known as Helme House, in Empire, Michigan.*

"Lyla," Rowan whispered, garnering a glance from the pre-teen next to her who appeared to be shopping online for a bathing suit.

Investigators had first responded to a call from Omar Vardaro, a local exterminator who'd gone twice to Amy's residence for pest control. Her car was in the garage but repeated knocks on the door and attempts to phone her went unanswered. When Omar approached the glass sliding door at the back of the house, he discovered what appeared to be blood streaked on the glass. He summoned police immediately.

Rowan stopped reading and looked at the photo of the house she now occupied.

The next article included a photograph of Amy. She had muddy brown eyes and smooth flaxen hair that framed her heart-shaped face. She smiled, revealing overlarge front teeth. Amy was pretty in a quirky Pippy Longstocking kind of way. Though the article stated she was twenty-five, she looked like a high school girl. Dangly dragonfly earrings hung from her earlobes and though the picture only revealed the top of Amy's t-shirt, it appeared to advertise a summer camp.

A hollowness expanded in Rowan's chest as she considered the picture in light of the strange occurrences in the house.

"Are you haunting me?" she whispered.

As they drove back to Empire, Rowan filled Garrett in on what she'd discovered.

He looked at her sidelong. "Row, I'm not sure digging into this is good for you. I—"

"Garrett, if you think it will make me less crazy to allow my imagination to fill in the blanks, then you don't know me as well as I thought."

After that, he said nothing and Rowan offered no further details, realizing it would only lead to an argument.

After they'd returned to the house, Rowan called the *Gaylord Daily News*.

"Carmichael," Rowan said the moment the phone picked up, though he hadn't yet said hello.

"It's twenty bucks to me," he called out. "Row's on the phone."

She heard a jostle of laughter and groans behind him.

"You had a bet going?" she demanded.

"Whatever do you mean, Rowan dear? I simply made a small wager you wouldn't make the first month without working a story. Maybe I'm being presumptuous. Are you working a story?"

"No," she insisted. "Not technically, anyway. I'm looking for anything in the AP about a woman named Amy Prahm or anything with the name Helme House."

"I'm all for favors, but I'd be a terrible journalist if I didn't get the dirt first. What's the story on this Amy character, and did you say Helme House or Hell House?"

"Helme," Rowan enunciated irritably. "It's the house we're living in and Amy was the previous owner."

"Oh, great. Well, good thing it's Helme and not Hell then. You hoping to find a skeleton in the closet of the previous owner?" He guffawed.

"Amy, the former owner, disappeared from here and… there may have been foul play."

"What? No. You're staying in a murder house. Angie, Row moved into a murder house."

A moment later Rowan heard the phone get jerked from his hand.

"No way. He's yanking my chain, right?" Angie asked.

"I wish, but, well, it's not a murder house. The woman disappeared; no body was ever found."

"Ugh. And Garrett didn't tell you? That scoundrel."

"He didn't know. Supposedly neither did Alan, the guy who bought it… but anyway. It wasn't solved, so—"

"So, you're going to solve it?"

"Ha." Rowan offered a sarcastic laugh. "I'm afraid that's not in my skill set. I've just, well, I've got to know. Right? I mean, could you stay in a house where something like that happened and not find out every detail?"

"Hell, no. But let me tell you, I wouldn't stay in the house at all. I'd have packed my bags the minute someone mentioned 'missing person.'"

Angie yelped, and Carmichael came back on the line.

"Angie's a sissy, Row. Don't let her paranoia get to you. You might blow the case wide open. Can you say Pulitzer?"

"Doubtful, but can you send me those links today? I'll sleep easier once—"

"Once you fill your head with the gory details of the murder that likely happened under the roof you're currently sleeping? Sure thing."

"Rowan." Garrett didn't say more, and he didn't need to.

She minimized the article she'd been reading and closed her laptop. "Okay, there, I'm done. See?" She turned in her chair and gestured at the closed laptop.

"Come to bed. Otherwise you're going to be fried tomorrow."

Rowan sighed and nodded, standing and rubbing at her shoulders, both firm with knots from leaning in to the screen for too long.

Garrett was barefoot and shirtless, wearing his gray sweatpants torn in one knee.

"You need new pajamas," Rowan told him, leaning in as he wrapped his arms around her back and kissed her shoulder.

"It took me five years to break these in."

"Well, they look ready for the garbage dump."

"Along with that ratty David Bowie t-shirt you still wear half the nights of the week?"

"Never," she murmured, squealing when he reached his hands down the back of her jeans.

"Shh, you'll wake the polliwog."

Rowan kissed him. "Guess we better take this to the couch then."

Hours later, Rowan lay in bed listening to Garrett snore and Quinn coo in her sleep. She thought of the articles that detailed the disappearance of Amy Prahm. There weren't as many as she'd expected, all fizzling out within a year, save for a single small paper that had covered the one-year anniversary.

Amy's sister had been the most outspoken in the case, appearing in multiple articles insisting that Amy wouldn't have abandoned her life. Still, the consensus seemed to be she'd done just that. A detective on the case was quoted as saying there did not appear to be enough blood at the scene to imply a major injury had occurred.

Rowan's bladder signaled a need to pee. She stood and crept from the room, easing the door shut behind her. She would not open her laptop, would not read any more about the woman who'd vanished from the house.

Even as she repeated the thoughts in her mind, she made her way from the bathroom to the kitchen where her laptop sat on the table. She turned it on and sat down, the wood of the chair cool against her bare legs.

Rowan clicked to the email from Carmichael. She'd read most of the articles he'd sent her, but two remained unopened. Rowan selected the one titled *Bloody Woman in the Woods*.

*Are the recent sightings of a bloody woman wandering the forest dunes in Empire a prank by local teens or something more sinister?*

*Twice, Empire police have responded to anonymous callers claiming to see a young woman, her face bloody, walking through the woods along the Sleeping Bear Dunes National Lakeshore.*

*The first caller refused to give his name. The second included three local teens searching the woods for morel mushrooms.*

*Taylor Beckham, a 16-year-old Leland native, said, "She looked really confused. She walked with her arms out in front of her like she couldn't see. My friend Porcia yelled out to her, but she didn't even look at us. We had to walk back out to our car to get Porcia's cell and by the time we walked back in, she was gone.'*

*Residents have speculated that Amy Prahm is alive and well, walking the forests to create a mythology around her disappearance. Other insist the sightings are not of Amy at all, but her ghost. Then there are the true non-believers, such as local resident James Groesbeck, who said, "Those sightings are fiction. Kids making stuff up to frighten each other. If you ask me, that girl took a bus south and never looked back."*

As Rowan read, movement in the glare of her screen caught her eye. Rowan froze, hand lifted to slam the laptop shut before Garrett realized she'd returned to her computer. The movement didn't come again and there was no sound. Garrett was not quiet at night. He slept so soundly that if he woke to pee or get a drink of water, he lumbered through the house like a drunk grizzly bear crashing into doorframes and stubbing his toes on the furniture.

Reassured that she'd imagined the movement, she returned her eyes to the screen and read the last line of the article.

*What do you believe happened to Amy Prahm?*

Rowan sighed and shut down her laptop.

As she started back toward the stairs, a sound arose in the living room. Rowan paused and listened. It happened again and after a moment she understood what it was—the sound of Quinn's crinkle paper that crunched when she squeezed it.

Had they left a window open, a fan on, something that might cause the paper to shift and crunch?

As she listened, heart thumping faster, a voice spoke.

"Will you be my friend?" it asked in a high squeaky voice.

Rowan's body went rigid. It was Quinn's stuffed dog, the Laugh and Learn Puppy that Mona had given to Rowan at her baby shower. The puppy had buttons and when pushed he spoke.

As she strained forward, she heard a whispered response, so quiet it might have been a breeze passing through the hall.

"Yessss…" it hissed.

# 6

Rowan turned and bolted up the stairs, banged into the bedroom and startled Garrett awake.

"Garrett, there's someone in the house," Rowan whispered, flicking on the lamp.

He jumped out of bed, blinking at her and bracing one hand on the wall. "Huh? What? Are you sure?"

"Yes. I just heard them in the living room."

"Stay with Quinn," he mumbled, lumbering around the bed. He bumped into the crib and Quinn released a little groan in her sleep.

"Take something. A weapon or something," Rowan insisted.

He paused in the doorway, scratching the hair on his chest, eyelids still heavy. "A what? No, I'm sure—"

"Here," she hissed, grabbing a screwdriver from the dresser and shoving it into his hand.

He barely glanced at it, but nodded and started out of the room.

Rowan waited at the top of the stairs, watching him descend, hands clutching the door frame. She wanted to yell for him to wake up, pay attention, but she kept her lips pressed together.

After a moment, a light flicked on and spilled into the downstairs foyer. Rowan braced herself for the sounds of Garrett yelling at someone to leave or, worse, the sound of a struggle, but she heard nothing.

She lighted down the steps, peering into the living room where Garrett stood checking behind a sofa.

He straightened up and looked at her. "There's no one in here."

Rowan's eyes flashed around the room, seeking a bulky shape beneath a curtain or a hunched shadow behind a piece of furniture. As her eyes trailed over the floor, she looked at Garrett and pointed.

"Quinn's toys. Look at them. They're all over the floor. That's what I heard, Garrett. Someone was in here touching her toys." The Laugh and Learn Puppy lay on its side.

Garrett sighed, his face drawn. "Row, we probably forgot to pick them up before bed last night. I'm sure—"

"No," she shrilled.

He stared at her, more awake now, and she wished she hadn't said the last word. Except it wasn't the word, it was the tone, the 'losing it' tone. It didn't help that she'd done the same thing eight hours earlier, insisted there was someone hiding in the house only for it to be empty.

She blinked and swallowed, stared dumbly at the pile of toys and tried to fit his logical explanation into her very illogical experience. A breeze could explain away the crinkle paper. Automated toys sometimes just spoke. But the reply...

Rowan rubbed her hands up and down her arms, shivering. "You're probably right," she managed, though her eyes continued to drift around the room searching for a person tucked in some unlikely crevice.

"Row, why were you down here? You weren't reading more stuff about that woman?"

He hadn't lobbed an accusation at her, but it felt like one. His words said, *You scared yourself. End of story.*

"No. I needed a drink of water."

"Okay." He ran a hand through his dark hair, loose and tangled on his shoulders. "Did you get it?"

"Yeah."

"Then let's head back to bed. I was dreaming about my mother's tamales."

Mid-morning the following day, a Saturday, Garrett insisted he was taking the day off so they could enjoy the beach during their time on the lake.

Rowan carried a beach bag with towels, sunscreen, extra diapers and a handful of toys for Quinn slung over one shoulder. In each hand she clutched a large plastic cup clinking with ice, straw poking from its lid.

Garrett carried Quinn, whose drooling approached epic proportions, depositing a spreading ooze on his right shoulder.

"Baby teeth are coming in," Rowan said, glancing back at them on the stairs.

Quinn reached a hand towards Rowan. "Mmma."

"Are you getting some fangs, baby girl?" Garrett asked, kissing the top of her head.

When they reached the beach, Rowan spread a blanket on the sand. Garrett rested Quinn on it, handing her a pink duck. He took the beach umbrella Rowan had carried and stuck it in the ground, shielding Quinn from the sun. Rowan had bought a baby floatie shaped like a chicken with a little plastic seat that Quinn's legs would poke through.

"Look, Quinnie, a floating chicken," Rowan told her, pressing her lips to the rubber valve and pushing out a whoosh of breath.

Quinn grinned at Rowan's puffy cheeks, more drool spilling from her mouth.

Garrett stripped off his t-shirt and ran into the lake, splashing mirrors of water as he dove and disappeared beneath the surface.

The long beach stretched empty. The closest public beach was a quarter-mile away, and though national lakeshore lay on either side of them, it was densely wooded with steep forest dunes descending to the beach.

Garrett came back and grabbed Quinn and the chicken, carried her back into the water and maneuvered her pudgy legs through the holes in the inflatable.

Rowan reached for the folder of notes she'd stuffed into the beach bag and pulled them out. She'd read everything Carmichael had sent over about the case of Amy Prahm. The next steps if she wanted to look further were to contact sources in the article, primarily Amy's family and friends. But those were the steps if she was writing about the case, which she wasn't. She was supposed to be taking the summer off, not chasing the strands of a several-year-old missing person's case where the woman had likely left of her own accord.

The thought brought an immediate memory of lying in bed and smelling incense, as if someone had just lit a burner in the master bedroom. What had started as the strange fancy of the midnight mind had grown into a genuine sense that the woman who lived there before them had died in the house.

"Row?" Garrett's voice cut through her thoughts and she looked up. He gazed at her. "I thought we were doing a family day. Swimming? Picnic on the beach. What are you looking at?"

Rowan sighed and shoved the papers back into the folder and the folder back into the bag. "There, see? I'm done." She stood and stripped off her t-shirt and shorts, walked into the water and made a face. "Brrr… it's freezing."

"It's refreshing," he said, flopping back on the water. "Go under. You'll be used to it in no time."

Rowan dove under, breath exploding from her nose as she reached her arms and arced them wide through the water, swimming like a frog for several strokes and then shooting up for air. "Whew, it is refreshing, but still damn cold."

Garrett splashed Rowan, and Quinn laughed, slapping at the water. "Dan's coming over for steak tonight," Garrett said, swimming on his back.

The water warmed up as Rowan paddled her legs, swimming to Quinn and bracing her arms on the chicken floatie. Quinn stared, mesmerized, at the brightly colored faux feathers painted on the chicken's inflatable wings.

"My cousin Dan?"

"Yep."

"When did you talk to Dan?" Rowan asked. Though Dan and Rowan were close, he had an almost daily texting relationship with her husband. They seemed to be always debating about sports teams. Dan was also renovating a house in Gaylord and had a million and one questions for Garrett who'd often, when they were still in Gaylord, just driven over to show him firsthand.

"This morning. He texted me asking what kind of wood he should get for his back porch. I told him to come check out the summer digs and have some steak. We could talk shop then."

"We don't have any steak."

"True, but there's a meat place in Traverse City—Maxbauer's Meat Market. Best steaks in the state according to Alan."

"That's quite a statement considering Alan fancies himself a steak connoisseur."

"Which is why I invited Alan too," Garrett added.

Rowan cringed, but tried to hide her dissatisfaction. "It's a party then."

Garrett stood and shook his long hair at her.

"No," she bellowed, splashing him. "Stop that, you heathen."

He laughed and dove toward her, grabbed her waist and pulled her under. When they both emerged from the water, she pushed his head back under. Quinn giggled and shouted baby babble.

Garrett burst from the water on the opposite side of Quinn and she shrieked and reached for him. He floated her toward Rowan and then pulled Rowan against him, his hands running along her slippery back. He kissed her. "That's okay, right? Dan and Alan coming for dinner?"

"Sure," Rowan said, ignoring the deeper question within his question. *You're okay, right?*

"What is Garrett doing exactly?" Dan asked that afternoon.

Rowan had given him a quick tour of Helme House before leading him to the platform that sat halfway down the long set of wooden stairs toward the beach.

"What isn't he doing? Refinishing wood floors, repairing all the crown molding, fixing drywall, installing new hardware on all the doors and cabinets. The list gets longer every day. I heard him and Alan on the phone this morning scheming about how the kitchen would be gorgeous with a tile backsplash and new light fixtures."

"And how are you handling it all? And by it all, I mean not working?"

Rowan shrugged. "I haven't taken up Jazzercise if that's what you're implying. It's fine."

"There used to be a cop on the force downstate who said anytime a woman used the word 'fine,' you should substitute 'homicidal.'"

Rowan laughed. "I guess he was married."

"Divorced three times, actually. How about the other stuff? Losing your dad..."

Rowan braided her fingers through her long blonde hair, pulling too hard when her finger caught on a snarl. "I'm getting through it."

"Your mom? Olivia and Alex? How are they?"

"We haven't talked about it much. My mom has tried a few times, but… I'm not ready. Maybe I'll never want to talk about it. How long did it take you after your parents passed?"

Dan sighed. "I'm sure I'll be there any day now."

Rowan wove her hair into a braid and then pulled it loose. "That's part of the reason Garrett wanted us to come here, get away from the memories."

"Is it working?"

"Sometimes."

"I get the feeling you're holding back something, Miss Rowan. Quinn still not sleeping?"

"It's not that. I get a weird vibe in the house sometimes, you know? Like… like we're not alone in there."

"Raccoons in the attic?" Dan grinned.

"I wish it were that simple. More like…" She smoothed her hands along her arms where goosebumps ran from her shoulders to her wrists. "A presence. The woman who lived here before us disappeared. She might have been murdered here. I kind of wonder if she's…"

"Haunting the place?"

Rowan laughed. "That's crazy, right?"

Dan shifted his eyes from Rowan's and she could see he was really giving it some thought. She'd expected him to laugh it off. He wasn't.

"It's not crazy. Not remotely."

"Really? That's not the answer I expected. I remember when we were kids, Bennie and I would never go in the rundown trailer back in the woods by your dad's place because we thought it was haunted and you teased us that whole summer."

Dan sighed. "Time gives you new perspectives on things."

"Are you telling me you've been somewhere haunted?"

Dan scratched at the stubble on his chin. "I don't want to get into it, the details anyway, but yeah. I saw a ghost, and she wanted me to see her and I can tell you, I'll never question that shit again."

She frowned. "You're not going to give me any details?"

He raised both hands overhead and then returned them to rubbing at his chin. "It was the strangest couple of weeks I'd ever had or have had since. But it was real. I can attest to that and not much else."

"Jesus." She sighed. "I was hoping for something more clinical, like 'Rowan, you're clearly suffering a nervous breakdown and need to go to one of those mental spas where they wrap you in seaweed and make you lie in a tub for three hours.'"

Dan laughed. "That sounds like hell."

Rowan chuckled. "Yeah, it kind of does."

Below them on the lake, a sailboat drifted by. She squinted and read the name painted in black on the side of the boat. "*Bleak Horizon*," she read out loud. "That's not a very inspiring name."

Dan shook his head. "Nope. What happened to names like *Liberty* or *Morning Star?*" Dan leaned to the side and fished his wallet from the back seat of his pants. He pulled a pressed napkin from an inner pocket and handed it to Rowan.

She unfolded it and read the name. "Sally Mitchell?"

"She lives up here, a little town called Buckley. I spoke with her a couple of years ago during my... incident, and oddly enough we've stayed in touch. She calls me with tips a couple times a year."

"Tips?"

"She's psychic."

Rowan rubbed her fingertips into the grooves beneath her eyes. "I really must be losing my mind. Daniel Webb is giving me a number for a psychic."

Dan chuckled. "I've been there, cousin. Thought those thoughts. Consider calling her. She might be able to help."

"How?"

"Don't underestimate the power of someone who believes it's happening. Someone who's experienced it firsthand."

"I've got steaks. Who's hungry?" a voice yelled from above them.

Rowan twisted around in her seat to see Garrett standing at the top of wooden stairs, Quinn balanced on his hip.

Dan put up a hand. "I could eat a bear."

"Pretty sure these are cows," Garrett called back.

"We'll be right up," Rowan yelled, standing and shoving the napkin in the pocket of her shorts. "What do you think I should do about the missing woman?"

Dan frowned and watched the boat drift out of sight. "If nothing specific is happening, I'd wait and see."

"Do nothing, then?"

He laughed. "I know how good you are at that. Maybe do a little digging. Get some background on the woman who lived here before you. Perhaps she's lonely—her ghost, I mean." He ran his hands through his hair. "I can't believe I just said that."

"Neither can I. Dan the big bad cop has gone soft on me."

"Ha. Soft is the least of it." He stood and started up the steps, Rowan following.

Alan arrived as Rowan and Dan returned to the house. He parked beside Dan's car and climbed out. He wore a pin-striped shirt and dark sunglasses. His usually sparse head of hair looked fuller, and Rowan wondered if he'd gotten hair plugs.

"Dan, how are you?" he said, reaching out a hand.

Dan shook it. "No complaints."

Almost as an afterthought, Alan glanced at Rowan. "Hey, Rowan."

"Hi," she said, wishing Garrett hadn't invited Alan for dinner. There'd always been tension between them. Rowan attributed it to Alan feeling that Rowan had stolen his best friend back in their college days when Alan lived vicariously through Garrett's many amours. Within six months of meeting Rowan, Garrett had moved out of the apartment he shared with Alan and he and Rowan had gotten a place together.

"Hi, Alan. Did Garrett tell you about the woman who disappeared from this house?" She'd normally have softened the question a bit, but a part of her suspected Alan did know and hadn't mentioned it.

"Yeah, bizarre. I guess that explains why it was such a great deal." He chuckled.

"You may have legal rights," Dan chimed in. "If you can prove the property is stigmatized, that is."

"Honestly, I didn't investigate the property at all. A realtor I work with sent me the link. It was such a good deal, I bought it as-is with cash. I didn't even come over to look at it until after I made the offer. I was afraid someone else would swoop down and grab it."

Dan frowned. "Seems risky."

"For the big money flipping real estate, you have to take risks. The land alone up here is worth what I paid for the house. There could have been a massacre in this place and I would still have bought it."

"That's an appetizing thought," Rowan said, moving past him and toward the front door.

"It will be when I make half a million dollars on the sale," Alan said. "Especially with Garrett doing his handiwork in the places that need fixing. And as a bonus, you and Quinn get a summer in a mansion on Lake Michigan. I'd call that mutually beneficial."

"And Garrett makes steaks," Dan announced, giving Rowan's

shoulder a squeeze and trying to defuse the growing friction. "Wish I'd married him."

"First dibs," Alan said, heading toward the house.

"Ha-ha," Rowan said. "You'll be singing a different tune when you have to clean his facial hair out of the sink."

They walked through the house and into the kitchen where Garrett held a cutting board loaded with steaks.

"There's a folding table in the garage," Garrett told Dan. "You and Alan want to grab it? We can eat on that."

"Aye-aye, Captain," Alan said.

Rowan tried not to roll her eyes at Dan, who stifled a smile when he saw the expression on Rowan's face.

The glass patio doors were open, and Quinn sat in her highchair outside. She had her squishy hippo next to an overturned cup of bananas she was smearing across the plastic surface.

Rowan paused in the doorway, thinking of what she'd read about Amy Prahm's disappearance. There'd been blood on the door handle, blood smeared across the glass, blood on the white kitchen table.

After they ate, Garrett brought out four bottles of beer, twisted the tops off and handed one to each of them. It was Stella Artois, the only beer Rowan consumed on the rare occasions she drank beer at all. She lifted the bottle to her lips, the foam tickling her nose, and sipped it.

"Were any more of Amy's belongings left behind?" she asked Alan.

Alan looked at her, puzzled.

"The woman who disappeared. Her name was Amy."

"Oh. Hell if I know. There's stuff all over this place."

"More than what's in the bedrooms?"

Alan took a long swig of his beer and glanced at Garrett as if expecting him to put an end to the line of questioning, but Garrett had started giving Dan a tutorial on deck stains. "There's an attic full of stuff."

"Amy's stuff?"

Alan frowned. "Maybe. The realtor mentioned a couple of the previous owners may have left things. I peeked in, but I didn't do a deep search."

"Do you mind if I poke around up there?"

Alan glanced at Garrett a second time. *Your crazy wife is at it again,* he'd tell his friend with a look, but Garrett was chattering away, oblivious. Rowan stared at Alan until he nodded.

"Yeah, sure. Go for it. I hope you don't find any corpses up there."

# 7

---

The next day Garrett spent the morning ripping up the carpet in the study. Beneath it, he discovered wood floors in alternating boards of maple and walnut.

Rowan tried to share his enthusiasm, but her mind kept wandering to Amy Prahm. She'd spent the day unpacking, cleaning and reading, but by early afternoon she felt stir-crazy.

Rowan stopped at the door to the study where the muted sounds of *Alice in Chains* blared behind the door. She cracked it open.

Garrett lay across a roller seat, a blue bandana tied at the base of his neck, scraping black adhesive off the floor with a metal putty knife.

"Quinn's down for a nap. I thought I'd take a walk," she called out.

He glanced up and squinted, pointing at his ear. Garrett rolled to the radio and turned it down. "What, babe?"

"Quinn's asleep. I'm taking a walk." She set the baby monitor on a built-in shelf.

"Be careful on the bluff, okay? There's some treacherous spots out there."

"I will." She blew him a kiss and walked back through the double French doors. She slipped on her tennis shoes and laced them.

Rowan hadn't explored the woods much around the new house, but Alan had told them there were miles of Sleeping Bear Dunes National Lakeshore, much of it with hidden panoramic views of the shoreline.

She trekked across the yard, bypassed the staircase that led down to the beach and turned into the forest. A narrow path, a deer trail, had been carved from the side of the steep hill. It left only enough width to place one foot in front of the next and Rowan leaned to her left in case she lost her footing. She didn't want to plunge to the right, which would send her down the wooded bluff. She'd not tumble all the way to the bottom, the trees would stop her eventually, but the injuries sustained by such a fall would not be pretty.

As she walked, the trail widened, and she peered through the trees at the glittering pockets of Lake Michigan.

Beneath her, Rowan heard the crackling of branches and noticed two black squirrels leaping amongst the trees, despite their dizzying height above the sloping ground beneath them.

"Oh, to be a squirrel," she murmured, thinking of her backyard in Gaylord and the array of bird feeders she and Garrett had erected over the years. Two years before they'd had an especially clever squirrel who got into the bird feeders no matter how many gimmicks they set up to deter him. Eventually they'd thrown in the towel, named him Bugs after the cartoon bunny who never failed to get his carrot, and started leaving extra treats outside for him, notably oatmeal cookies, which seemed to be his favorite. At some point, the squirrel had moved on or been gobbled up by a pack of coyotes, but from that time forward Rowan and Garrett referred to the bird food as Bugs's food.

The hill widened, and Rowan stepped into a grassy clearing. She continued forward, reeds tickling her bare calves. Delicate white flowers peeked from the grass and Rowan considered picking some to show Quinn, but remembered the sneeze fest her daughter had had when Garrett had brought home a bouquet of lilacs the month before.

On the opposite side of the clearing, tall white rocks jutted from the tangle of vines on the forest floor. Rowan moved closer and realized they were not rocks at all, but headstones. An ankle-high wooden fence surrounded the tiny graveyard mostly buried in ferns and grass, some of it hidden by fallen trees. The headstones too were in poor shape, mossy and bleached from the sun.

Rowan squatted and brushed at the first headstone, pulling off a curl of vines that fell over the name.

"Piper Rothwell," she read, and then dates. "May sixteen, nineteen sixty-four, to August thirteen, nineteen seventy-five. Almost eleven," she murmured after subtracting the birth year from the death year.

The next headstone revealed the gravestone of a four-year-old. The following was a two-year-old. They were all girls. There were other headstones, some so faded she could barely read the names and dates carved into their stone faces. One looked cleaner than the rest, as if someone had maintained only this headstone, allowing all the others to fall into ruin.

Her phone shrilled in her pocket and she jumped, heart thudding in her ears as she drew the phone out and saw Garrett's name on the screen.

"Hey," she said, steadying her voice.

"Quinn just woke up from her nap. I thought we could drive to that place Alan told us about further up the peninsula—Fishtown."

"Sure. Okay. I'll start heading back now."

As they drove along M-22, curving around the wooded lakeshore and catching sporadic views of a shimmering Lake Michigan, Rowan turned to Garrett. "There's a graveyard in the woods."

Garrett glanced through Rowan's window and then looked out his own.

"Not out there. Back at the house. When I went for a walk, I found a cemetery."

"Huh, odd place for a cemetery way up there. Still in use?"

"I don't think so. It was pretty overgrown, though…" She thought of the headstone that appeared recently brushed off, even cleaned.

"Probably settlers lived up there before they realized how much easier it was to live inland," Garrett said. "Or maybe they just wanted the best view for their families' ultimate resting place."

"Yeah." Rowan sighed and rubbed her hands along her arms before reaching forward and turning down the air conditioner. "A lot of kids were buried there."

Garrett's eyes flicked up to the rearview mirror as if checking that their own kid still sat safely in the back. She did, concentrating on the plastic box with the tiny bear inside. "Children died of all sorts of stuff back in the day—diphtheria, tuberculosis, smallpox, measles, sheer boredom."

"It's not funny," Rowan reminded him, but she smiled at his goofy grin.

"I know it's not, babe. That's why I made the joke."

The hostess at the Cove led them to a table butted against a long window perched above the Leland Dam. Through a window at the opposite end of the restaurant, Lake Michigan stretched towards the infinite, clear blue horizon. The afternoon light cast the wood floors in shades of honey and transformed the bottles of alcohol behind the bar into shimmering jewel tones.

"This place is great," Garrett said, holding Quinn close to the window. "Look at the dam, polliwog. See any fish?"

"Fish ain't jumpin'," their waiter, Vinnie according to his nametag, said, pausing beside Garrett, "but if you watch, you'll see the otters down there."

"Otters!" Garrett exclaimed to Quinn. "Even better."

Garrett situated Quinn in a high chair and took a seat opposite Rowan at the table.

"What can I get you fine folks this afternoon?" Vinnie asked, pulling a notebook from his pocket and flipping the cover over.

"We'd like to try the whitefish dip to start…" Garrett started gazing at the menu.

"Best whitefish dip in town," Vinnie said.

"Want to split the bacon burger?" Garrett asked.

"Yeah, with sweet potato fries," Rowan added. "And can we get some apple sauce for Quinn?"

"You sure can," Vinnie told her.

Rowan pegged Vinnie at about sixty, not the usual age for a tourist town waiter, but he had as much or more energy as the twenty-year-olds buzzing around the restaurant.

"You folks on vacation?"

"Yes and no," Garrett said, wiggling Quinn's hippo in front of her. "I'm doing some work for a friend on a big old house down in Empire. Beautiful place tucked up in the woods on a bluff."

"In Empire, you say? You wouldn't be talking about Helme House?"

Garrett's eyes widened, and he glanced at Rowan. "That's the one."

The man's mouth turned down. "Strange place on account of the young woman who went missing. You guys hear any news on that? I wonder from time to time if they ever found her. Thinking no since it hasn't been in the paper."

"No, they haven't," Rowan cut in before Garrett could answer. "Are you familiar with the story?"

"Oh, sure." Vinnie leaned a hip against the booth beside them. "Whole peninsula knew about it. Hard not to. We're not exactly big city folks. A missing girl is news. But then rumor was she left of her own doing, and that pretty well quieted the chin-waggers. I can tell you though, I didn't know her myself, but my sister-in-law's daughter chummed around with her and she was crying foul play from the get go. Seems that girl had a fiancé maybe looking to get rid of her on account as he was marrying someone else."

Garrett sighed, handing Quinn her hippo. "I'm sorry to interrupt, but should you get that order in? I just saw the hostess seat a big table, and I'd hate for it to go in behind them."

Vinnie glanced at a long table quickly filling with a group of chattering seniors. "Oh, righty-ho, you're spot on there. Don't want you sitting here for two hours, especially with a sweet little gal who's probably already itching to get out of that high chair."

Vinnie walked away, and Rowan glared at Garrett. "Why did you do that?"

"Do what? I'm hungry."

"You could see I wanted to ask him more questions about Amy. You intentionally—"

"Rowan, stop," he snapped. "Just stop."

~

Rowan and Garrett rarely fought. It had happened more in the beginning of their marriage. Never loud screaming arguments. Rowan was the master of silence when she was angry. She could go days without saying a word to Garrett. He, on the contrary, reverted to sarcasm when angry.

"Oh, wow, not talking to me again, how original," he'd say, fuming around their house.

Usually, their battles ended with the frantic sex that arose after days of not touching, and Rowan's spiraling fears she'd return from work one day to find Garrett's half of the closet empty.

Garrett was better at apologies, at taking the high road. Rowan, when hurt, could sulk for days. But during their eleven years together, she'd gotten better. The bumps and grooves had smoothed out, or perhaps they'd driven over them so many times they'd been obliterated.

Rowan could be mercurial, but she rarely showed it. She'd learned to arrange her features so that no one but she knew what lay hidden behind them. Garrett had more passion and fire when frustrated, but he was also quick to laugh at his own anger.

As they drove home from Leland none of them spoke save Quinn, who sat in her car seat in the back chattering and squeezing a rubber giraffe that let out a high-pitched squeak that startled Rowan.

At the house, Rowan let Garrett unload Quinn. She hurried inside and busied herself with unloading the dishwasher and wiping down the already clean counters.

It was Garrett who finally broke the silence between them.

"Hey," he said, coming up behind her and pressing his chest into her back. He inhaled her hair and his touch, his closeness, brought her stifled emotions pouring forth.

"I'm sorry," she whispered. Tears spilled over her cheeks.

"I know. I'm sorry too, honey. I love you, Rowan. I love you so much it's scary." He wrapped his arms around her and squeezed. "I just... I'm afraid if you dig into this story it's going to..."

He didn't say the words, but Rowan filled in the blank: *send you over the edge again.*

She thought of her dad then and cried harder, shoulders curving forward. If Garrett hadn't been holding her up, she would have slid to the kitchen floor. There was no straightforward explanation for the overwhelm of emotion, but she couldn't contain it and she stood there, sobbing as her husband held her.

# 8

Rowan woke the following morning and found Garrett already in the study scraping the floors. Quinn sat in her playpen in a sea of crushed Cheerios.

"Icky mess, Quinnie." Rowan leaned down and kissed Quinn on the head before stepping to Garrett.

He stood and hugged her, kissing her on the mouth. "How'd you sleep, beautiful?"

"Pretty good," she said, though she'd tossed most of the night. "I need coffee."

"Already ground and in the French press," he told her. "Just add water."

Rowan made coffee and sat at the kitchen table. She hadn't opened her laptop since the day she'd learned about Amy Prahm, but thoughts of the woman niggled at her. Part of her restless night had resulted from wondering what happened to the woman who used to sleep in the bedroom that Rowan and Garrett now shared.

She wanted to investigate Amy's case, but Garrett would be upset if she did. He didn't understand that Rowan needed a story, a distraction. No distractions meant more time to worry, more time to stress about the future, to mourn the loss of her dad, to question her own inadequacies as a mother, a wife, a human being.

"I'll take Quinn outside," she told Garrett after she'd finished her second cup of coffee.

"Great. I think she's ready to work those little legs."

Rowan spread a blanket on the grass and sat Quinn in the center before dumping out toys. She settled beside her, opened her notebook and punched a number into her cell phone before she lost her nerve.

"Hello?" a woman answered.

"Hi," Rowan said. "Is this Colleen Prahm?"

"Yes."

"My name is Rowan Cortes. I'm a reporter in northern Michigan and I've been looking into your sister's missing person's case." Rowan watched the door to the house as she spoke, irrationally worried that Garrett would come bursting out and yank the phone from her hand.

For a moment the woman said nothing and Rowan pulled the phone away from her ear, wondering if Colleen had hung up on her, but the seconds of the call ticked by.

"No one has contacted me about Amy's case in more than a year. I used to call the detectives weekly, now it's more like monthly. Never a new lead. Not a single one in years."

"I'm sorry," Rowan murmured, watching as Quinn toddled to her feet and took off across the lawn. Rowan stood and followed her. "I wondered if we could meet? Have an in-person interview."

"Yes," Colleen said with more force than necessary. "I live in Grand Rapids, but I have a meeting tomorrow in Cadillac. Would that area work for you? Coffee in the morning, say nine a.m. at Java Jane's. It's right downtown."

"I'll be there," Rowan promised. "Thank you."

"No, thank you," Colleen said.

Rowan ended the call and continued behind Quinn as she bent down and grabbed a dandelion, stuffing it into her mouth before Rowan could snatch it away.

"Quinnie, no, spit it out." She knelt in front of her daughter, pulling the soggy yellow flower from Quinn's mouth. Quinn coughed, her face wrinkled with disgust. "That's why we don't eat dandelions. Yuck."

She walked Quinn to the blanket and grabbed a sippy cup of water. "Here, swish and spit," she told Quinn, who took the cup and drank a big gulp, swallowing the water along with whatever dandelion residue still coated her teeth and gums.

From the house, Rowan heard the high screech of Steven Tyler singing *Walk This Way*. Rowan imagined Garrett inside, a bandana across his forehead, bobbing as he worked. She'd never lied to him, not about the big stuff anyhow, but now she would have to. It was for the best. It was. If Rowan dove into the story of Amy Prahm, maybe, just maybe, she could keep from falling apart.

∿

The day lazed on. Rowan took Quinn for a walk on the beach and then gave her a bath. Around three p.m., Garrett emerged from the study, face twisted in a grimace as he rubbed at his lower back. "Crap on a cracker. I should have taken a break about three hours ago. My back feels like I've been bucked off a horse."

"Want a rub?" Rowan asked, sitting on the couch, feet tucked beneath her. She'd been flipping through a copy of *Reader's Digest*. She'd discovered a stack of them in a dresser drawer in the master bedroom.

"Rain check? If I sit down now, I'll never get back up. I need to run to Traverse City to rent a sander for the study. I can take Quinn, give you time to catch a catnap?"

Rowan yawned at the suggestion.

Garrett grinned. "I'd say that settles it," he told her. He lifted Quinn from the bassinet and gave Rowan a peck on the forehead. "We'll be back in a couple of hours."

∿

Rowan woke feeling too warm. She opened her eyes and then squinted when a slant of afternoon sun cut sharply across her vision. Rolling toward the back of the couch to block the light, she blinked at the apricot chevron pattern of the fabric.

Based on the angle of the sun, it had to be late afternoon, which meant her twenty-minute power nap had turned into three or four hours. No sounds emerged from the study. Garrett and Quinn had likely not returned from Traverse City.

Rowan sat up, putting a hand up to shield her eyes from the intense brightness pouring through the living room window. As she stood, her hair stuck to her neck. She reached to pull it free and her fingers got tangled in a sticky glob that snaked through her hair.

"What the hell," she grumbled, walking to the hallway mirror and pulling her hair over one shoulder to see what had gotten caught in it.

Pale pink gum coated her blonde hair in streaks.

Rowan's stomach clenched, and she shut her eyes—one... two... three—and reopened them. It was still there. Shimmers of sticky gum wound so thickly through her blonde hair, she could barely discern her own strands.

Dizziness swept over her and she stumbled back to the couch, leaning both hands on the back and drawing in shuddering breaths. It was only hair. Why was she freaking out? But it wasn't only hair. It was *her* hair, her long golden, wavy hair that her father had loved so much he brushed it whenever she visited him, just like he had when she was a girl. *Hair is meaningful,* he'd once told her. *It carries our memories.*

Rowan sat back on the couch then lay down, pulling her knees into her chest and shivering. Her stomach flopped queasily. She hadn't been chewing gum when she lay down. She rarely, if ever, chewed gum and neither did Garrett. And yet somehow as she slept, alone in the house, a wad of bubblegum had found its way into her hair.

As Rowan's fingers trembled across the gooey mess in her once-satiny hair, a memory of that same sensation slithered to the forefront of her mind.

Rowan had been in first grade at a new school, her second first grade after Morgan and Emily had adopted her. She remembered the pinch-faced little girl named Kimberly whom the other kids congregated around like she held the secrets to the universe. Rowan had noticed how Kimberly's eyes had filled with jealousy when one teacher braided Rowan's long golden hair before recess.

As recess had ended and the whistle signaled students back to the building, Rowan had jumped off the swing, but before she could take off for the double doors that led back to class, she'd felt a pull as if someone had yanked her hair. When she'd spun around, Kimberly and her gaggle of snickering friends had streamed around her and toward the door. Rowan had thought the girl had only pulled her hair to be mean until the boy sitting behind Rowan in class raised his hand and told the teacher that Rowan Webb must have snuck gum onto the play-ground because it was all tangled in her hair.

Now, dreamily, though it felt more like a nightmare, Rowan stood and walked to the bathroom. She tilted her head, cringing at the streaks of pink wound through her long hair.

She fumbled through her makeup case and then into the black leather bag that Garrett kept his razor and cologne in. There her fingers found the cool metal of a pair of silver shears.

~

"Babe?"

Rowan turned from the mirror, gaze drifting over the mass of blonde hair mottled with pink in the bathroom sink.

She looked at Garrett who stood in the doorway, a coconut cream pie balanced on one palm and a hopeful smile on his face. His smile faltered as he took in her chopped hair.

Rowan opened her mouth to speak and burst into tears.

"Row, oh, honey, what happened?" He set the pie on the stack of fresh towels Rowan hadn't yet put away and pulled her against him. His hand on her bare neck felt strange, the hair that protected that delicate part of her gone. Another peal of sobs burst from her throat.

"It was gu-gu-gum!" she managed, aware that she sounded like a child, that she'd spoken the exact words nearly thirty years before to Emily, her adoptive mother, when she arrived at school after Rowan had sat in the principal's office inconsolable while the secretary used lotion and soap to free Rowan's hair from the bubblegum surely shoved into it by evil Kimberly.

Garrett didn't respond, but Rowan knew he'd seen her mane of beautiful hair piled in the sink.

"Babe, just breathe, okay. Come on, come with me." He led her out to the living room where Quinn sat on her moose blanket gnawing on her rubber giraffe. Another burst of tears ruptured from Rowan at the sight of Quinn.

Quinn's lower lip quivered as she gazed up at her crying mother, and then she too burst into tears.

"Mmma," she cried, holding out her arms. "Mmmmma!" she wailed.

Garrett squatted down to scoop up Quinn and squeezed Rowan closer before settling all three of them on the couch, Rowan tucked beneath one arm and Quinn balanced on his knees. Rowan reached for Quinn, rubbing the side of her face.

"Shh... It's okay, baby," Rowan promised, chest hitching.

"What happened, honey?" Garrett asked gently.

"I don't know," she mumbled, face aching from her tears. "I woke up and there was gum stuck in my hair, all over in it."

"Were you chewing gum when you lay down?"

"No. Were you before you left? Or could Quinn have gotten it somehow?"

"I wasn't and I haven't had gum in ages," he said. "If she got it, I don't know where it came from, but that seems like the most logical explanation. Then again, I don't know when she could have done it. You lay down and she and I walked out the door. Maybe it was stuck to the couch somewhere already, to a pillow or something."

"Probably," Rowan murmured, though no part of her believed it.

# 9

Garrett had barely batted an eye when Rowan mentioned she wanted to make the two-hour drive back to Gaylord to pick up some things she'd left at their house. He'd also been more than happy to keep Quinn with him. His easy faith in her had caused a churning ball of fire to develop in Rowan's stomach as she drove not east toward Gaylord, but south towards Cadillac to meet Colleen Prahm, the sister of the woman who had vanished from Helme House.

Rowan parked on the street in front of Java Jane's Coffee Shop, shoving her notebook and pen in the side of her jumbo purse that sometimes doubled as a diaper bag. She pulled down her visor and studied her reflection. The night before, Garrett had helped cut her hair into something less wild, but Rowan hardly recognized herself. Her hair fell just below her ears and she'd stuffed a wide headband on when she'd realized that morning she could no longer pull it back in a ponytail.

It was warm outside, hotter in the coffee shop, but the smells of cinnamon and milk soothed her as she stepped up to the counter. Rowan stared at the chalkboard display of coffee drinks. There were a hundred variations. Caramel café au lait. Peppermint mocha iced latte.

"Can I help you?" the girl behind the counter asked. She was short with tawny skin and sparkling black eyes. Her nose was pierced with a tiny blue stone. Around her neck hung a silver chain, and on that a miniature photograph of a smiling boy.

Rowan leaned closer and looked at the boy, not much older than Quinn. "He's beautiful. Is that your brother?" Rowan asked.

The girl smiled and touched the photo encased in a silver pendant. "My son, Jay."

"Your son? You look so young."

"I'm twenty-two. He came a little earlier than expected, but my dad always said life is as unpredictable as Michigan weather."

Rowan's smile faltered. "My dad said something like that too." Her voice cracked as her broken heart swelled against her ribcage. She reached a self-conscious hand to her hair and had a momentary desire to run out of the coffee shop and back to her car.

"Would you like to order something?" the girl asked, a small line of worry etched between her eyebrows.

Rowan opened her eyes, but the menu blurred. "Not just yet," she whispered and pulled away, hurrying to a booth in the corner of the little cafe. She sat down and clutched her hands in her lap, knotting her fingers together and squeezing until all the blood had left them. She wanted to shove her face in her hands, allow the gurgling sobs to break free, but she channeled that need into her hands and gulped back the tears.

In the weeks after her father's death, breakdowns had become standard in Rowan's life. So standard that Garrett had no longer looked terrified when he rushed into the room at the sounds of her wails. He'd accepted them, and that scared her. It scared her that she'd invited this huge, unrelenting grief into their world and now he and Quinn, living in the tiny snow globe that was their family, were subject to her volatile emotions.

The summer in Empire had been the healing salve, the magic remedy for a handful of days, but those days were gone and the brokenness had returned with a fervor that left Rowan reeling.

Rowan had not been an emotional child. She'd stuffed it down, buried it, ignored it. She'd done the thing the teachers and social workers said to do—*turn a brave face, don't let it get to you*. But it had gotten to her. She'd just hidden it. Refused to react, to feel, to allow it. But something had shifted. The lid wouldn't close anymore. The feelings burst free no matter how tightly she tried to hold them in.

Several minutes passed. Rowan massaged some feeling back into her hands.

"Coconut lime iced tea," a voice said.

Rowan looked up to see the girl from the counter, a plastic cup of iced tea in her hand. She set it on Rowan's table. "It's new this summer and my favorite. On the house."

Rowan looked at her, the kind gesture causing another bubble of grief to expand in her chest. "Oh, no, I couldn't." Rowan reached for her purse.

The girl put a hand on Rowan's. "Please. Let me. I'm off shift now, but…" She shrugged. "I get a free drink every day. I wanted you to have it."

Rowan tried to say thank you, but a stream of warm tears rolled over her cheeks. She nodded and smiled.

The girl smiled back, untying her green apron. "Try it. It's like summer in a cup."

Rowan watched the girl disappear into the back of the coffee shop. She pulled the cup closer, closed her eyes and lowered her lips to the straw. It tasted cool and sweet with strong flavors of coconut and lime. It *was* like summer in a cup, and it eased some of the turbulence raging within her.

She opened her eyes and checked her watch, grateful she'd come to the coffee shop early and not had a breakdown in front of Amy's sister.

Rowan recognized Colleen Prahm when she walked in. She looked as she had in newspaper articles from four years earlier, though her dark hair was longer. She wore an olive blouse with a cream-colored pencil skirt and black shiny heels.

Rowan stood, smoothed out her wrinkled blouse, feeling under-dressed in jeans. She waved at the woman, who changed her course from the counter to where Rowan stood.

"Colleen?"

The woman nodded and offered Rowan a slender hand. Rowan smelled the woman's perfume, a delicate floral scent that seemed to soften her.

"Nice to meet you, Rowan. I'm going to grab a coffee. Can I get you anything?"

Rowan shook her head, gesturing at her tea and feeling off-kilter. She was the journalist. She should have been the one in the power heels offering to buy the victim's sister a drink. Their roles had been reversed.

Colleen strode across the room and returned a moment later with a tall cup of black coffee. As she slid into the seat across the table, Rowan noticed a small silver bracelet on one of her narrow wrists. It was engraved with the initials ALP.

Rowan grabbed her notebook and pencil from her shoulder bag. "Thank you so much for coming, Colleen. I'm sure it's difficult to talk about your sister."

Colleen fixed her dark blue eyes on Rowan's and shook her head. "No, it's not difficult. I'm desperate to do it. I want Amy found. She's my baby sister. Her disappearance shattered my family, shattered it. I'm the only one who's held it together and I have to because if I don't, who will keep looking? Keep fighting?"

"That takes a lot of strength."

Colleen took a drink of her coffee, wiped her lips on a napkin and left a smudge of dark lipstick. "I've never been one to give up."

"Well, as I mentioned on the phone, I'm a reporter, but technically I'm not on assignment. I came across an article about Amy's disappearance and I got interested."

"Interesting is not the word I'd use. Disturbing is what Amy's case is. There's been plenty of curiosity regarding what happened to my sister, Rowan, but not a lot of action. I need action here."

"And I will do my best to deliver that."

"Good."

"Can you tell me about Amy? A little about her background? Who she was as a person?"

Colleen rotated the bracelet on her wrist, and Rowan could see more letters engraved there.

"Amy was five years younger than me. I still remember her birth. My mother had been in labor for two days. Amy was sunny side up. They had to turn her. It was a difficult birth and when she finally came out, she wasn't breathing. The doctors resuscitated her. I wasn't there for that, of course, but she was in the NICU for two weeks. I visited the hospital with my dad and we'd look through the window where she slept in that little plastic box. She was so tiny. Even to me at five, she looked fragile, like a doll who'd been made too small. My mother claims that experience turned me into Amy's protector, into her advocate. Maybe she's right." Colleen took another drink, her shoulders relaxing as she leaned back.

"Amy never really grew out of that fragile state. She was always small and skinny. Whimsical is how my father described her. She loved poetry and art, reading, flowers. Girl things. I was the athlete, playing volleyball and soccer. I was always very driven and Amy was always very distracted. That's how I thought of us. After I graduated from high school, I got into U of M and stayed until I finished my MBA. Got a job at a Fortune 500 company in Grand Rapids. By the time Amy graduated from high school, I'd been working for a year. She took a year off to join the Red Cross and got shipped all over the country doing disaster relief-type stuff. When she came back, she continued living with my parents and enrolled at the community college."

"Did she work?"

Colleen nodded. "Odd jobs. She sold paintings and handmade greeting cards at a little shop in town, walked dogs and pet-sat for people. She worked part-time at a nature center. That kind of thing. By the time she turned twenty-three, she'd almost finished her bachelor degree in arts. That's when she met Declan."

"Declan was the man she was engaged to?"

Colleen scowled. "A complete womanizer. He swept her off her feet. Showered her with gifts, took her on trips. The works. Then he proposed and left her at the altar. I mean it. He literally did not show up for the ceremony.

"On the day of the wedding, which my parents paid half for even though they were broke, the scumbag didn't show up. Declan's best friend came crawling in to the church like a beaten dog and told my mom that Declan had gotten on a plane to Texas that morning. Asshole."

Rowan frowned. "That must have been so horrible for Amy."

"It was. It destroyed her. They'd already moved into that house. She had this vision of her future and it was just ripped out from under her."

"Why did she stay in Empire? Why not move back with your parents?"

Colleen looked away. "Pride, maybe. She just couldn't bring herself to give up on the fairytale. She believed he'd come back, return to his senses."

"Did he?"

Colleen shook her head. "I think he strung her along. He did eventually return to Michigan and I'm pretty sure he drove up to Empire and stayed with her a few times. He helped out with the money, paid his half of the mortgage, for a while, anyway. But then he stopped. That's part of the reason the cops came up with that bullshit theory of her staging her death. They claimed she wanted out from under the financial obligation. Complete horseshit. She could have walked away from that house. Amy could have cared less about her credit score.

"She was depressed, sure. Who wouldn't be after something like that? But she wasn't suicidal, and she wasn't insane. She'd never have faked her own death and run away."

Colleen pulled an envelope from her bag and took out several photos. In one, Amy sat on a couch with porcelain dolls propped on either side of her as if they were dear friends. "She loved these dolls. She collected them since she was little. When she moved to Helme House, she took only one. This one." Colleen pointed at the most unique doll in the bunch. The doll wore a deerskin vest over a tie-dye shirt. A beaded headband ran across her forehead, and loose waves of blonde hair flowed over her shoulders. "The hippie doll. I think it reminded Amy of herself. She named it Indigo."

"It's cute."

"It disappeared. I searched that house for this doll." Colleen tapped the picture. "The cops looked at me like I was nuts when I mentioned it. As if a murderer is going to steal a porcelain doll, they said, but hello, how about trophies? Murderers who want a trophy aren't looking for bank cards."

"Were there ever any suspects?"

"I don't know. I mean, the police got sick of me calling, showing up. They tossed out a couple possibilities. A lawn guy who cut the grass, Duncan Grundy. He'd been hired by Declan's dad right after they bought the house. Amy told one of her friends up there he creeped her out. They also mentioned some guy who'd gotten busted in town for peeping in windows. No one that ever made sense."

"Did Amy have any friends in Empire?"

"She had a few friends. Amy was the girl everyone liked. Sweet, generous. She'd started doing some of the same odd jobs too, dog-walking and the like. She also got a job as a receptionist at a dental office. Not the kind of money that's going to pay for a house like that one in Empire, even if it was old and out of style."

"Yeah, I'm trying to make sense of that. How did they buy the house to begin with?"

"Declan's family had beaucoup money, millions. His dad bought it and financed them on a land contract. Frankly, they should have eaten it when Declan took off, but Amy didn't want to let the house go. That was part of the problem. She was attached to it, though I think she was actually attached to the future she still wanted to believe she and Declan would have there."

"Was Declan ever a suspect?"

Colleen nodded. "I sure hope so. The police looked at him. Apparently, he had proof he was downstate at the time of her disappearance. The problem with people like Declan is when you come from that kind of money you can buy an alibi. People will line up down the block to claim they were with you for ten grand."

"Was he ever violent with her? Controlling? Anything that might point to the possibility of his hurting her?"

Colleen shook her head. "No. I doubt Declan ever laid a hand on her, but that doesn't mean he didn't pay someone else."

"Do you know if investigators looked into that? Checked his bank statements for large cash withdrawals?"

"They weren't exactly calling me every night to fill me in on the latest discoveries. They put a wall up. I called and heard a familiar refrain—'we can't release details that might compromise an ongoing investigation.'"

"Let's switch gears a bit. Tell me what you know about the day she disappeared."

Colleen rifled through her purse and pulled out a planner. "This was my calendar from the year she vanished. I'm a meticulous note-taker." She flipped through the pages. "I spoke to Amy on July ninth at two forty-five in the afternoon. That was the day before police assume she went missing. She called me to ask about planning a birthday dinner for our mom, whose birthday was July twenty-fifth.

"I tried calling her again two days later, then again on Monday July fourteenth. No answer. That's when Omar, the exterminator, went to the house and noticed blood on the glass doors leading to the back porch.

"I got the call that evening around six. Declan's dad called me because Amy had listed Declan as her next of kin on some paperwork found in the house. They'd called Declan, who didn't have the balls to tell me himself, so good ole Daddy did it. Douchebag. Anyway, my parents and I met in Empire the next morning. We tried to get into the house, but it was all blocked off with yellow tape. No sign of Amy. No cell phone. Her purse was there. Two hundred dollars of cash in her wallet. She didn't have a lot of valuables but what she had wasn't taken, so clearly robbery wasn't the motive."

"But there was blood?"

"On the sliding glass doors, on the kitchen floor and some in her bedroom upstairs."

"None in between? Like a trail going down the stairs?"

"No, and of course they used that to strengthen their case that she'd staged it. If someone had attacked her in her bedroom and dragged her down the stairs, where was the blood? Instead, they insinuated someone had intentionally smeared the blood in specific locations to make it appear that she'd been attacked in her bedroom and dragged out the glass doors at the back of the house."

Rowan shook her head, dismayed at the injustice of such a thing. A young woman likely attacked and abducted from her own home, and the investigators decided she'd created an elaborate ruse to escape her problems. "What do you think, Colleen? Do you think your sister is still alive?"

Colleen picked at the dark purple polish on her nails, then quickly stopped, pressing both hands into the table as if to prevent her picking. "I'm an optimist. I have to believe it's possible she's still alive because the alternative is too..." She shook her head. "I can handle it. I can, but my parents... My dad has a weak heart. My mother is very fragile. You might notice they faded from the media after the first six months. They latched onto the fake death story."

"They believe she faked her death?"

"No, not really, not in their hearts. But they want to believe it."

# 10
---

Rowan thought about her conversation with Colleen as she drove to Gaylord. Rather than going to her own home to retrieve the items she'd told Garrett she was coming to town to pick up, she headed for her best friend Mona's house.

Her friend greeted at the front door with an enormous hug and sloppy kiss on the cheek. "You're here! I was afraid when Garrett whisked you away to the pleasure palace, I'd be going the whole summer without seeing my best friend."

"You know I couldn't stay away from you for that long," Rowan told her, following Mona inside to the kitchen.

Mona stood just over five feet tall and she had a bushel of dark hair balanced on top of her head. She wore black terrycloth shorts and a hot pink dry-fit t-shirt. Mona lived in workout clothes, though she'd never exercised a day in her life. She was petite despite a penchant for sugar and booze.

"Tell me everything you've been up to. I haven't seen you in a month!"

"I'm sorry. I wanted to stop by before we left, but—"

"Oh, stop." Mona waved a dismissive hand. "You're here now. How are things going?"

Rowan sat heavily on a stool that butted up to the kitchen island. "I'm okay. I was in pretty rough shape after Quinn was born and then my dad... I thought I was doing better. Our first few days in the house were great, but—"

"Did you ever ask your doctor about postpartum depression?" Mona asked, plunking a coffee mug in front of Rowan and filling it with coffee.

"I considered it." Rowan shook her head. "I thought women with postpartum hated their babies. I felt just the opposite. I wouldn't let her out of my sight for the first six months. I was a basket case. Am. I am a basket case."

Mona reached for her hand and squeezed it. "Rowan, you're not a basket case. You're wearing jeans. I'm pretty sure I noticed eyeliner, okay? Have you ever met a basket case with a steady hand?"

Rowan laughed, brushed a hand through her hair only to run out of strands just below her ears. She grimaced and felt the irrational tears bubbling up. "And my hair." Her mouth quivered.

"Looks beautiful." Mona stepped around the counter and hugged her from behind, resting her head on Rowan's shoulder. She was the only person outside of Garrett and her parents who'd ever been affectionate with her like that. Mona touched so easily that even as girls, Rowan had marveled at the gestures. Sometimes when Rowan stayed overnight at Mona's house, Mona's mother would climb into bed with the girls and spoon them. Rowan used to stiffen at the touch, but years had dulled the sense of strangeness.

Rowan leaned her head on Mona's and they stood there for another moment until Mona broke away and walked to the refrigerator, pulled it open. "I could make us a salad?"

"No, thanks. I'm not hungry."

"You look like you could eat."

"Thanks, Mom."

"Ooh, I've got it." She opened the freezer door and drew out a box of chocolate éclairs. "There's no way you're turning down these bad boys."

Rowan eyed the box, and her stomach grumbled. "I love those."

"I know you do. I bought them when you were supposed to join us for book club and bailed at the last minute."

"I'm sorry about that. I was so swamped with Quinn and moving out to Empire—"

"Stop apologizing," Mona insisted, pulling the lid off the éclairs and pushing the box toward her.

Rowan took one out and bit into the end. The custard inside was frozen, but creamy and sweet. She closed her eyes and exhaled. "It's so good."

"Let's take our coffee and éclairs out to the front porch. Billie, next year's new quarterback, is due for his run soon. We can watch him jog by in his clingy athletic pants."

Rowan grinned and followed Mona. The eave overhead shaded the front porch, and Mona had six rocking chairs lining the long deck. They'd been in her family for generations.

Rowan sat in a chair and watched the busy street. In fall and winter, Mona's road was a ghost street, but in summer with tourists and family visitors the entire town of Gaylord came alive. Across the road, three kids bounded down the front steps of the house toward an enormous boat that took up nearly the entire driveway. A man in a ball cap followed them.

"Can we ride in the boat, Dad?" one little boy asked.

"Yeah! Can we? Please? Please?" a girl, wearing a ball cap that matched her dad's, chirped.

"Nope. I don't want the long arm of the law throwing your old dad in a cell for child endangerment." The man looked up and spotted Mona and Rowan. He gave them a wave, opening the back door of his Suburban so all three kids could pile in.

"Motoring to the lake?" Mona called.

"You betcha," he yelled back. "Nothing like a relaxing day on a boat with three children under ten. Throw some ice cream and candy in there and it will be a day of R&R."

"Good luck out there, Marty."

He gave her a thumbs up and climbed behind the wheel.

Rowan had seen Marty over the years. He and his wife and their three children visited the house in the summer. They lived downstate somewhere near Detroit Metro and both worked for banks.

"How do people do that? Three kids." Rowan took another bite of her éclair.

"Trust me. It gets easier after the first one. Stewart was hard. Ginger was easier. Now they entertain each other. At least half the time, anyway."

"And three makes a family?" Rowan asked.

Mona laughed. "Ha. No. Two and done. We've done our duty as citizens of the Earth and replaced ourselves. It's up to somebody else now."

"Garrett brought up adopting a child the other night."

"That was the plan, right? You were so excited about adopting. And what better parent to adopt than you, Row?"

"Because I was adopted?"

"Not only because you were adopted, because you have such compassion and empathy for the kids who are... left behind. You always have. And you're an amazing mother."

The éclair in Rowan's mouth tasted too sweet, and she wanted to spit it out, but swallowed instead.

Mona glanced at her and frowned. "What is it, honey? More than the creaky old house? Are you and Garrett having problems?"

Rowan quelled the tears that crept up at the question. She shook her head. "Garrett's great. He's always so great. Nothing ruffles him. Not Quinn or work. Not even me and whatever this is." She waved a hand at herself.

"This," Mona enunciated, "is not an indicator that something's wrong with you. You're a new mom, your dad died this year, you've taken a leave from work, you've moved a hundred miles away to live in some funky old house where a lady disappeared. The ground has shifted beneath you. If all that change didn't jostle you, then I'd think something was wrong. If I were living in the place, I'd scream every time someone passed gas."

Rowan smiled and pressed her toes into the deck, rocking back in her chair. "It has been unnerving."

"Have you told Garrett about the... other things? Smelling the incense? Feeling like you're not alone?"

"Yes and no. Twice I've flipped out, convinced someone was in the house, only to have him search and not find anyone. Not to mention this." Rowan flicked at her now-short hair.

"Do you actually think someone was in the house? That someone put gum in your hair on purpose?"

Rowan massaged the skin beneath her eyes. "Some*thing*... that's how I've started to think of it."

"The ghost of the woman who lived there before?"

"Maybe. Then again, maybe it's me. Perhaps this last year really did... make me go crazy. For all I know, schizophrenia runs in the family. I once read that schizophrenia develops in women in their late twenties to early thirties. I'm past the window, but not by much."

"Don't even joke about that, Row."

"I wish I were joking."

"Have you thought about asking Emily about your birth family? Now that your dad is gone?"

Rowan squeezed the wooden arm rests on the rocking chair, pushing with her toes to rock faster. Rather than answer the question, she blurted, "I met with the dead woman's sister this morning."

"The dead woman? The missing one, you mean?"

Rowan frowned, surprised by her own statement. No evidence pointed to the woman's death, and yet... something was haunting the house.

"What happened when you met her? Did you interview her?"

"Yes. And I didn't tell Garrett. I set up the whole thing a couple of days ago and I drove to Cadillac this morning."

"Are you going to tell him?"

Rowan bit her cheek. "I don't know."

## 11

Rowan stepped into the news room at the Gaylord Daily News. Her friend Angie leaned over her desk, her dark hair twisted in long sinewy braids.

Angie glanced up, brightening when she spotted Rowan in the doorway.

"Rowan!" Angie whooped, rushing from her desk, cell phone pressed to her ear. "I'll call you back," she said into the phone before ending the call. She threw her arms around Rowan. "I've missed you, girl. What are you doing here?"

Rowan smiled, blushing. It had only been a few weeks since she'd last seen her, but it felt more like a year. "I needed to pick up my laptop charger. And I dropped into town to see Mona."

"And not see me?" Angie demanded.

"And you too," Rowan assured her, squeezing her hands.

They settled into the break room. Angie waited for an intern to leave.

"How are you feeling? I mean, about..." Angie was referring to the depression, the strange feelings Rowan had experienced since giving birth to Quinn. Angie herself had gone into a depression after the birth of her second child, Henry. Though Angie's depression had lasted less than two months, it had been a dark period in the mother's life and she'd confided in Rowan. When Rowan found herself in a similar space, Angie was one of the few people she'd opened up to about it.

"Better. Mostly, anyway. The change in pace has helped."

Angie looked at her, and Rowan feared she could see through the lie. She suddenly didn't want to be sitting in that room inches away from a woman known around the office as a human lie detector. She'd gotten hardened criminals to reveal secrets they'd never told another living person. Though that had been years before during her days as a reporter in Detroit. Gaylord offered few in the way of hardened criminals.

"Tell me about this missing woman. Sounds spooky."

Rowan nodded and swallowed the lump in her throat. "It is. I probably should never have looked into it because now I... well, I'm not sleeping very well."

Angie pursed her lips. "It's a hard line to walk. On the one hand, work can be such a great diversion, but when you're living in the story, that's a whole other dilemma. Why don't you and Quinn just come back to Gaylord?"

Rowan shook her head. "No. Because then Garrett would have to commute all the way to Empire. He turned down all the work around here to do this job for Alan. I can't ask him to divide his time and the house is... well, it's peaceful and lovely. It's just that—"

"A woman was likely massacred there."

Rowan cringed at the words, and Angie's inky eyes widened.

"I'm sorry. That was crass. You know I've always had a terrible sense of humor."

Rowan shook her head. "No, it's me. This year has just been—"

"Shit."

"Yeah."

"Except for Quinn, of course. She's the light at the end of the tunnel."

"Yeah." Rowan sighed. Her guts churned at the thought of her beautiful, precious baby girl left home with her dad.

Garrett never complained, but Rowan knew he'd expected to get more work done, since Rowan would be home with the baby. Instead, he'd found himself doing double duty as he worked on Helme House and looked after Quinn too. *And me*, Rowan thought. *Let's not forget he's babysitting me too.*

"What have you found out about her? The woman who vanished?"

Rowan sighed and pulled out her notebook, flipping through the pages, but not reading the words. She'd thought about them enough to know everything in the lined pages.

"Amy Lyla Prahm, twenty-five when she went missing, single, worked at a dentist's office, walked dogs, painted, gardened. Parents lived in Holland. One sibling, a sister in Grand Rapids. She'd been engaged, but the guy, Declan Stilts, stood her up on the day of their wedding."

Angie cringed. "That's terrible."

"Yeah."

"Any suspects?"

"No one named publicly. Omar Vardaro, an exterminator Amy had called, discovered the scene. He saw blood on the glass sliding door at the back of the house and called the police when no one answered the door or his phone calls."

"Was Vardaro a suspect?"

"No. His son was in his truck playing video games on a Gameboy. He'd missed school that day and been riding around with his dad. There's no chance his dad could have snuck off and done something to Amy. I did get the name Duncan Grundy from Amy's sister. He was the lawn guy hired by Declan Stilts's dad. He'd come once a week or so to cut the grass, trim back the foliage. She told the friend he creeped her out a bit."

"Cops looked into him?"

"It appears they did, but I can't find out whether they cleared him."

"Have you talked to the detectives on it?"

"No. I've been trying to fly under the radar. Garrett doesn't know I'm looking into it."

Angie leaned back in her chair and folded her hands in her lap. "And why is that?"

Rowan shifted her gaze to the coffee-stained table. "Because he doesn't want me to."

"I'm not here to judge or dole out advice, but Garrett's one of the good ones. This is not the time in your life to shut him out."

"I'm not shutting him out," Rowan grumbled. "Anyway, back to Amy. A journalist who wrote a big piece on Amy's disappearance complicated her case. He presented a theory that she set up the whole thing and disappeared."

"Any possibility that it's true?"

"There's always a possibility, but my gut says no." Rowan thought of the sense she had, not only that the woman had died, but that her presence was still in the house.

"It's a mystery, that's for sure," Angie said.

Rowan rubbed her eyes, exhaustion stealing in. When she left the office, she might recline her driver's seat and take a nap in the parking lot. She'd done it a thousand times, during long days when the office was abuzz and she was pushing to get a story finished or she'd been up most of the previous night. Gaylord wasn't a hot news area, but the behaviors were leftovers from her time as a reporter in Minneapolis, when the deadlines really felt like life or death.

"Want me to brew coffee?" Angie asked.

Rowan shook her head. "Better not. I've already drunk half a pot today. I need to sleep tonight."

"Hey, I meant to tell you after I had all the icky emotional stuff post-Henry, my therapist recommended journaling. Seems like we'd be the first to hop on that, being journalists and all, but it helped. You know? Maybe try it."

"Sure. If you told me to stand on my head every morning while reciting my ABCs backwards, I'd give it a shot if I thought it might bring some normalcy into my life."

"Don't do that or Garrett *will* sign commitment papers."

They hugged goodbye, and Rowan walked to her car. She drove to the A-frame house she and Garrett had bought a decade before, a year after they got married. Her father had helped them build the porch, along with Garrett's own father. It had been one of the greatest summers of her life, coming home from the newspaper in the afternoon to see her new husband and father hunched side by side, hammers swinging, laughing and telling stories.

The porch stood bare now. Their lawn chairs were stored in the shed for the summer, the bird feeders hung empty.

Rowan sat behind the wheel in the driveway, struggling to catch her breath as she realized for the thousandth time her father would never walk through the door again, announcing he'd brought a ham or with arms full of presents for Christmas.

Even as she'd gotten older, he'd still insisted on buying her gifts and wrapping them in shiny wrapping paper for every birthday. For her last birthday, he'd given her a mother-daughter bracelet set with an engraving that said *A Mother's Daughter is Her Treasure.* Quinn's bracelet wouldn't fit her for many years, and Rowan had not worn her own bracelet because she'd tucked it away in a drawer and been unable to open the box after her father died.

Gathering her courage, she stepped from the car and unlocked the side door, pushed into the house. Rowan held her breath, not wanting to breathe the familiar scent lest it send her into a crying fit. She raced into the kitchen, snatched the small dark duffel bag she'd forgotten on one of the kitchen chairs, and burst back out into the afternoon light. She hurried to her car, ignoring the wave of her neighbor across the street. She climbed behind the wheel and started for Empire.

That night, as had become their custom, Garrett fell asleep quickly while Rowan lay awake, watching the dancing lights of Quinn's starry sky turtle play across the ceiling. The turtle emitted sounds as well, a lullaby punctuated by hooting owls and chirping frogs.

After a while, Rowan slipped into sleep.

She might have been out for minutes or hours when the smoky herbal fragrance of incense merged with her dreams and lured her out of them like a vaporous hand curling its finger. *Come*, it seemed to say.

Rowan opened her eyes and drew in a long breath, but the fragrance didn't fill her lungs. It was a phantom scent, a smell beneath a smell, slipping away before the shapes in the room slid into focus. Quinn's turtle no longer released light or music.

Garrett slumbered on his side of the bed, breathing low and slow. The breath of deep sleep. Three or four am, Rowan figured, rolling to her side and squinting toward the crib where Quinn too slept in near silence. No murmuring, no rustling, just the thick muted sound of breath.

Rowan stared at the ceiling, gauging the likelihood of drifting back off. Her eyes grew heavy, the lids slipping lower, and then a muffled creak sent them snapping back up to her browline. Breath held, she waited for an accompanying sound, but nothing emerged. Stillness and quiet filled the room.

Rowan willed her eyes closed, imagined she sank into a cloud of feathers and gradually relaxed into the soft bed.

Another creak sounded from the side of the room near the door.

Rowan's eyes shot open. Wide awake, she swiveled her head toward the sound.

She squinted, her body stiffening, as she gazed at the thing that had made the noise.

A figure crouched on the opposite side of the room on all fours with lank dark hair falling on either side of its pale face. Two darkly glittering eyes gazed out from the sallow face.

Rowan's jaw unhinged, and the scream trapped in her diaphragm tried to explode between her teeth. Nothing emerged. A whimper, no louder than Garrett's breath, trickled out.

Rowan watched the face, paralyzed, a sudden weight pressing down on her as if someone had climbed onto her chest and sat there, all their girth bearing down until her ribs might crack and puncture her lungs. Teeth gritted, she forced her eyes closed and tried to breathe, searching her brain for some talisman of light. She'd rarely attended church growing up, but had gone a handful of times with Garrett's family.

Garrett's mother Yolanda spoke the Hail Mary prayer so often that Rowan had it memorized. She latched onto those words now, parting her lips and forming the words silently. 'Hail Mary, full of grace, the Lord is with thee. Blessed art thou among women and blessed is the fruit of thy womb, Jesus. Holy Mary, mother of God, pray for us sinners now and at the hour of our death. Amen.' She repeated the words, eyes clenched shut, again and again until the pressure on her chest seemed to lift, but still she didn't open her eyes.

She gripped the edges of the blanket and pulled it up over her face, still reciting the prayer, sensing the eyes of the thing watching her, imagining it crept closer and closer. The word 'coward' streaked through the prayer. What kind of mother hid beneath a blanket when her daughter slept in the room unprotected, unaware? But Rowan could not bring herself to pull the blanket down. She lay stiff, terrified, praying into the dark.

# 12

Rowan woke drenched in sweat. She tore the blanket from her face and kicked it away, recoiling at the too-bright sun piercing through the open curtains. Overhead, the ceiling fan buzzed at full speed, but did little to cut the stifling heat.

She sat up and the memory of the thing watching her from the night before blasted across her vision. Rowan stiffened, afraid to turn her head and look at the spot where it had stood, but when she looked, nothing was there. The light of the day banished the terror that had stricken her the night before.

She fumbled her phone from the bedside table. It was after eleven a.m.

As Rowan made her way to the kitchen, she listened for sounds of Garrett or Quinn, but heard nothing beyond the drone of ceiling fans whirring in every room. In the kitchen, she gulped iced tea from the glass bottle in the refrigerator, standing in front of the open fridge for an extra minute. It chilled her sweat-slick skin.

She felt grimy and could smell the fear-sweat that had poured out of her the night before. Rowan wanted to wash off, but not in the shower; she wanted to swim in the lake, feel the icy water sluice the pungent odor away.

Rowan half-considered a swimsuit, but the likelihood of encountering anyone on the isolated beach was slim, and if she bothered putting one on, she might lose her nerve.

She left the house and lumbered barefoot across the yard, still groggy, the dream she'd been having trickling away with each passing moment of consciousness.

The stairs to the beach basked in shade and she sighed as she stepped onto them, grateful for a break from the high and hot morning sun.

Halfway down the wooden stairs, something in the lake caught her eye. A bloom of colored fabric floated on the surface of the water. A pale purple color, periwinkle, and as it came to focus Rowan's heart dropped into her feet. The periwinkle of a dress Garrett's mother had bought for Quinn.

"No..." She gurgled more than spoke the word and then screamed it as she fled down the last fifteen stairs. She could see more of Quinn now, her black hair fanning out above the purple dress, her doughy brown arms and legs poking from the fabric in a star-shape.

"No!" Rowan shrieked and plummeted off the stairs, landing awkwardly. Pain shot through her right ankle, but it barely registered as she struggled across the sand and splashed into the water.

Wailing, throat going hoarse, she dove forward and the icy lake snatched her breath. "Quinn!" she shouted, praying Quinn would lift her head and swim to Rowan, but she couldn't swim in her waterlogged dress. She'd only sink if she tried.

Rowan's legs were concrete pillars as she kicked and surged forward in the water. She went under and swallowed a nose- and mouthful of lake, sputtering when she came up, but not slowing, not hesitating.

She reached her and grabbed the dress, yanking it toward her. Rowan flipped it over, her legs trying to tread water as the heaviness of her sodden clothes pulled her down.

Quinn was not in the dress. It was not a dress at all, but the nylon of an umbrella, darker purple than periwinkle and decorated with yellow stars. Rowan gasped and stared at the fabric, dazed, sick, a cramp spasming in her abdomen.

She tried to let the umbrella go, push it away and start her swim back to shore, but her hands clutched it so tight and they wouldn't listen as her brain urged them to open and release.

She groaned and bile rose into her mouth. She spat it in the water and slipped under, catching another mouthful. She came up again hacking, struggling to breathe. The cramp tightened in her lower abdomen, spread fire into her legs.

She paddled her arms harder, finally letting go of the umbrella and trying to will herself back to the shore, but she couldn't. Her legs were numb, two solid stilts sinking. Rowan slipped under, held her breath and then fought back to the surface, gulped more water. This time she barely had time to spit it out before she went under again.

Something slippery and ice-cold brushed against her calf and when she looked bleary-eyed through the water a large pale shape glimmered by. Not a fish, but a corpse. She cried out, her mouth opening and allowing another rush of water. Her legs wouldn't kick, wouldn't move. She flailed her hands up, tried to pull the water down and propel herself up, but she continued to sink.

The thing beneath her slithered by again, fingers wriggling across her ankle. Rowan thrashed and struggled, but it had her now. It was the thing from their room. It had followed her to the lake to drag her down.

∼

Rowan heard Garrett's voice.

"Rowan! Rowan!"

He shouted her name, but she struggled to open her eyes, to feel anything beyond the odd sensation of being pulled in two directions. She had to make a choice, up toward Garrett and her heavy, icy body or down toward warmth and golden shimmering light.

As she allowed herself to descend, Rowan thought of Quinn and jerked upwards. Strong hands gripped her shoulders. A plume of breath filled her mouth and she choked, coughing, her eyes flickering open and shut.

Garrett was above her. In the background, Rowan heard crying. Her daughter, Quinnie, wailing from somewhere nearby.

"Quinn," she croaked, struggling up onto her elbows, her throat raw, eyes burning.

"Hold on, not so fast. Quinn's okay," Garrett assured her, cradling her against his chest.

Through stinging eyes, she spotted Alan holding their red-faced daughter in one arm on the wooden stairs, a cell phone in his other hand.

"Paramedics are on the way," he shouted.

Rowan shook her head and then opened her mouth and spewed

water across her bare legs. Garrett lifted his t-shirt and wiped her mouth.

"There, shh, it's okay."

Eventually the water stopped coming up, but her throat burned as if she'd swallowed sand rather than water.

"I need a drink," she said hoarsely, eyes fixed on Quinn.

She wanted to run to her daughter, snatch her from Alan and clutch her to her chest, but when she tried to stand her legs were rubber.

"Here." Garrett lifted her up, cradling her like a child, and started toward the stairs.

"No, I'm too heavy," she murmured, struggling to be put down.

"Stop. You're making it hard. I can carry you."

She wanted to fight him. Garrett had injured a knee playing soccer in high school. He didn't need another injury trying to heave her post-baby body up the fifty-two stairs to the house above, but the energy to put up a fight drained out of her.

She was no longer hot. Her flesh had turned icy. Goosebumps covered her arms and legs and her teeth chattered as Garrett followed Alan.

At the top of the staircase, he set Rowan down, but kept an arm braced around her waist. Rowan limped across the yard, watching Alan carry Quinn into the house.

Once inside, Garrett guided Rowan to a couch in the living room.

"Please," she croaked. "I need Quinn. Hand me Quinn."

"You're soaking wet, Row. Let's get your clothes off and then I'll bring her to you."

Garrett helped her strip off her sodden t-shirt and shorts. He grabbed her a pair of heather-gray sweatpants and a long-sleeved black t-shirt.

Once dressed, she collapsed onto the couch. Garrett filled a glass of ice water as Alan walked into the living room and handed Rowan a wriggling Quinn.

"Oh, baby, oh, baby, my baby," Rowan murmured, pressing her forehead against Quinn's.

"Paramedics are here," Alan announced as the sound of a siren cut through the muggy quiet.

"Here, honey, let me take her for a minute." Garrett reached for Quinn. Rowan cried out as her daughter left her arms. "I'm sitting right here, Row. We're not going anywhere."

Garrett sat in a chair bouncing Quinn on his knees as Alan let the paramedics into the house. Rowan could see the question in her husband's eyes, but he didn't ask her anything as two white-clad men entered the room, one carrying a red canvas bag.

Rowan lay on the couch, eyes trained on her daughter, as one paramedic checked her heart rate, shined lights into her eyes, and pressed gently on her abdomen and back.

"Does this hurt?" the man asked, lifting her swollen ankle.

"A little, but not bad," she rasped.

"Looks like a sprain. The cold water helped with the swelling. Elevate and ice it." He directed his suggestion at Garrett.

"Okay. We will."

"Everything looks okay," the man continued, "but it wouldn't hurt to come into the hospital and have a more thorough check."

"No," Rowan exploded, wincing at the fireball that roared up her throat. "I'm okay."

Rowan hadn't been to the hospital since her dad died, since he'd walked in for a routine surgery and came out in a body bag.

The paramedic glanced at Garrett and then stood.

"I'll walk you out," Garrett said. He sat Quinn in Rowan's lap before following the man out the door. Alan joined them.

Rowan snuggled Quinn beneath her chin, fatigue pulling at her eyelids.

"Maybe you should lie down, honey," Garrett urged, putting a hand on Rowan's arm and startling her. She hadn't heard him come in and must have dozed off. Quinn slept soundly against her chest.

She didn't want to lie down, but she also didn't want to see the look on Garrett's face for another moment.

"You're right," she said at last, and allowed him to help her up the stairs.

"Quinn can stay with me—" Rowan started, but Garrett interrupted her.

"We'll be right downstairs, babe. I think it's best if you rest on your own for a bit."

"No!"

Garrett winced, but didn't argue. He gave a slight nod and laid Quinn, already asleep, on the bed, pulling the sheet over her legs. Rowan sat beside her, not looking at Garrett as he left the room and returned downstairs.

# 13

Rowan kissed Quinn's cheek and then stood and hobbled to the bathroom. She peed and washed her hands, avoiding the mirror.

In the hallway, she heard faint talking and walked toward the nursery, bracing one hand on the wall to keep pressure off her sore ankle. She stepped into the nursery where one window stood half-open. Garrett must have opened it to disseminate the odd, rancid odor that arose in the bedroom at the back of the house.

"How's she doing?" Alan asked.

Rowan crept to the window, peering out. Alan and Garrett sat on the back porch below. They each had a tall glass balanced on the arm of their chairs, iced tea or beer.

"I don't know. I figured spending the summer here would help, change of scenery and all that, but this today..."

Rowan analyzed Garrett's response, the tone of his voice. It held a lot back. She sensed his reluctance to tell the truth, likely combined with his desire to put it all out there. She grappled with something similar in herself.

"Leah's sister suffered from pretty bad postpartum depression. She told Leah she'd imagined killing their son almost every day for months. I think a doc got her medicated, and that helped," Alan said.

Rowan stiffened at the man's words, enraged, but also ashamed. She would never have hurt Quinn, never. But there had been nights, hadn't there? Long dark nights where she counted the passing minutes and wanted so desperately to fall asleep, to make up for the lost sleep from the night before and the night before that, but the mere thought of the passing hours, the time for sleep slipping away, paralyzed her in a wakeful anticipation. Sometimes, after weeks of those nights, she'd look at Quinn and...

Rowan clenched her eyes shut, but she saw the vision that had repeated itself again and again in her mind so often that it could almost have been a memory. Quinn falling from the second-floor balcony at their A-frame home, falling and falling, landing with a sickening thud on the wood floor below. Rowan would stand paralyzed at the top, staring in horror at her child's broken body, seeing her sightless eyes.

"I've encouraged her to see someone, but..."

"Let me guess, therapy is beneath the high and mighty Rowan," Alan retorted.

"No," Rowan muttered, fluttering her eyes open. She hadn't spoken loudly, but Garrett's head twitched.

"What about brass for the kitchen hardware?" Garrett changed the subject. "I found a store online that sells antique brass knobs and hinges. They'd look great and be in line with the original hardware."

"Brass? Sure. Whatever you think will up the resale value on this place."

Rowan listened for another moment, but it was clear their conversation about her had ended.

Rowan lay for an hour watching her child. She stroked Quinn's forehead. A tiny bubble of spit formed on Quinn's baby lips and popped.

Garrett appeared in the doorway. "Did you get some sleep?"

"A bit," Rowan lied. She hadn't slept. She had lain beside Quinn thinking of that periwinkle dress that was not a dress at all.

Garrett leaned down and kissed Rowan on the temple. He sat on the opposite side of the bed and ran his fingers along Quinn's row of tiny, perfect toes. "She's so beautiful."

"Sometimes I wonder, looking at her, how my mom could have done it," Rowan murmured, sliding a dark curl behind Quinn's ear. It sprang free.

Garrett gazed at her, his eyes soft and filled with the afternoon light. "How she could have left you?"

Rowan swallowed the sticky lump that had formed in her throat and nodded, sure if she tried to utter a word it would come out as a croak.

"Maybe it's time to look into your birth family. Your dad is gone and—"

"No." Rowan cut him off and stood, gritting her teeth against the pain in her ankle. "No. I can't. It would break my mother's heart. Plus, why should I, you know? She left me. She doesn't deserve to know who I am. Or who Quinn is."

Garrett sighed. "It wouldn't be for her, Row. It'd be for you. To close one of those loops in your head that you're always stumbling over. The huge 'why' that's followed you your entire life. And maybe..."

Rowan stiffened. "Maybe what? Maybe I can find out my family history so we know if anyone was completely insane?"

Garrett's eyes widened. "No, God, no. Quinn's about to celebrate her first birthday. There's still time to have a relationship with your birth mother and for her to be a grandmother."

Rowan frowned and reached for her hair. She wanted to run her fingers nervously through the long strands, but her hand found air and she let it fall back to her side. "Are you okay with her? I'm going to take a walk."

"Honey, your ankle—"

"It's just a walk, Garrett. I'll take it easy and I need some fresh air." Rowan ignored his wounded expression and hurried from the room and down the stairs. She slipped on her tennis shoes, cringing at the tender black and blue flesh above her foot. She stood and plodded across the yard to the trail that led along the forest bluff.

It took Rowan over five minutes to reach the cemetery in the woods. She took frequent breaks to rest her ankle and her winded lungs.

As she stepped into the clearing, she froze.

A man stood in the little graveyard, a handful of red flowers in one fist. He hadn't heard her, so Rowan watched him.

The man looked to be older than her, early fifties perhaps, with ashy blond hair cut close to his head and deep-set grey eyes. He wore a long-sleeved black shirt despite the heat and dark jeans. He was tall and lean, handsome.

He stopped at one grave and rested the flowers before it, brushing away dead leaves and staring intently at the stone.

Rowan felt like a terrible intruder spying on this grieving stranger. She took a step back, and a twig cracked under her foot.

The man's head jerked up, and his eyes narrowed on her face. Rowan swallowed, half-considered turning back for the house, then lifted her hand in a limp wave.

"Hi, sorry." She stepped from the cover of trees and into the clearing. "I didn't mean to interrupt. I figured no one came out here."

His face softened, and he moved away from the graves, his stride long. He was taller than she'd realized, well over six feet.

"That's okay. I rarely see anyone here. You startled me." He smiled, and she noticed one of his front teeth turned in slightly. He stuck out his hand. "I'm Eddie."

"Rowan." She shook his hand. "Is this your... property, I guess? Your cemetery?"

He chuckled and shook his head. "No. It's national lakeshore, but I have family buried out here, though the county stopped taking care of this place twenty years ago. We had a big storm come through that took down a bunch of trees. The grounds crew stopped coming after that. Now it's forgotten."

"I'm sorry. That must be hard."

He shrugged and looked toward the lake. It glittered in blue strips through the wave of trees that crowded the hill beneath them. "I don't mind. Sometimes it feels like my secret."

Rowan glanced back at the headstones. She'd had a similar sense of the place, as if finding it out there abandoned had made it her secret.

"Do you mind if I ask who you know who's..." She didn't say the word that jumped into her mind—'dead.'

"My mother."

"Oh." Rowan reached for her hair, found nothing, and tugged on the collar of her t-shirt instead. "I'm sorry. That's terrible."

Eddie smiled and returned to the graves, stepping over the small fence. "She died a long time ago. I don't make it out here as often as I'd like, but a few times a year at least."

"It's a beautiful place to be buried." Rowan grimaced at her own words, but Eddie bobbed his head in agreement.

"I can't imagine a better one. What brings you out here? This isn't a usual stop for hikers."

"My husband and I are staying in the big house down the bluff." She gestured behind her.

He nodded. "Helme House. That's a big place for two people. Do you have kids?"

"One, a girl. Quinnie. She's a year old."

He smiled. "That's a good age, or so I've heard. No kids myself, but the consensus around ages seems to be one is good, two is terrible, and three is a toss-up."

"One is definitely good. She's sleeping through the night now. That alone is a lifesaver."

"I bet."

"Do you live around here?" Rowan asked. "I haven't noticed many houses. The guy who bought Helme House said most of this is state or federal land."

"I live in Maple City. It's here on the peninsula, but more inland. No lake view for me."

Rowan smiled. "Ours will be a temporary view. My husband is doing some work around the place for the summer. He thought it might be fun for us to stay here while he works, change of scenery and all that. We live in Gaylord."

"What kind of work is your husband doing?"

"Refinishing floors, repairing drywall, that kind of thing."

"Nice. I'm sure the place needs it."

"I'm sorry again about showing up during your time. I lost my dad this year. It's been… difficult."

His mouth turned down. "The first year is tough. I don't envy you going through it. I walked around in a daze those initial months after I lost my mom."

"But it gets better?"

He sighed and gazed at the tombstones. "Eventually, yeah, it does. I figure we're all heading there. You can't outrun the reaper."

"How about your dad? Is he still around?"

"No dad to speak of."

"I'm sorry. I'm prying into your life, aren't I?" A blush rose up Rowan's neck.

"No. It's fine. My dad died before I was born. I never knew him. That made losing my mom more difficult. She'd fulfilled both roles. She'd been it all. I have some books, good ones on grief. I probably should have gotten rid of them years ago, but… I always thought they might come in handy. I live in Maple City not far from here. Stop by the next time you're out and about. You can have them." He took his wallet from his back pocket and pulled out a business card, handed it to her.

She looked at the card. *Faces of Leelanau*. Oil and watercolor paintings of Leelanau County. He'd listed a website and email beneath, but no name or phone number. "You're an artist?"

"A novice, more like. I'm an odd-jobs guy. Painting is my hobby or my passion, depending on when you ask me."

"That's great. Maybe I'll borrow the books and buy a painting. I'd love to take something of this place back to Gaylord with us. It's just so beautiful."

"I've painted a few times from this very spot. Might even have one of Helme House."

"That sounds lovely. I'd like to see them sometime."

"Sure. If you drive into Maple City and take Burdickville Road west, you'll find my place about four miles out—big gray pole barn. You can't miss it. I don't have a cell phone otherwise I'd give you the number."

"No cell phone? Wow. That's unusual these days."

"I've never been a fan of phones, period. Cell phones are like a nightmare come true. I have a landline, if you like it, but it's easiest if you just stop by. I'm usually home."

"Thanks, I will."

"Be careful off the back here." Eddie fanned a hand toward the woods behind the tombstones. "There's an old cellar. Pretty hazardous if you're not careful."

"An old cellar?" Rowan peered in the direction he'd gestured.

"Yeah, here. I'll show you."

She followed him from the sunny space into the patch of woods that lay at the space where the hill started another upward climb.

Eddie hunched down, grabbing handfuls of vines and ripping them away. Gradually a dark hole appeared.

"Probably the cellar on an old house. It's made from stone. I've been in it a few times. It's well over ten feet deep. A hazardous fall if someone were just walking along."

Rowan could smell the dank, moss-covered rock. "Creepy."

# 14

When Rowan returned to the house, she found Garrett in the kitchen cooking macaroni and cheese.

"Mac 'n' cheese and milkshakes?" he asked. "I thought you might like some comfort food."

Quinn sat in her high chair eating sliced bananas. "Mmma," she announced, slapping an open palm on to a piece of banana.

"Hi, baby girl," Rowan told her, kissing her head. "Yeah, comfort food would hit the spot. Thanks, honey. I'm just going to wash up."

Rowan slipped into the downstairs bathroom and ran her hands beneath the sink. The man she'd met in the woods drifted across her mind. She hadn't mentioned him to Garrett

They ate their mac 'n' cheese on the couch. Garrett had put a DVD of *The Wedding Singer* in his laptop and propped it on a stack of books on the coffee table.

"Row," Garrett said after a half hour of watching the movie in silence while Quinn zipped around the room in her walker. "What happened today?"

Rowan leaned forward and took her chocolate milkshake off the coffee table, taking a sip. She sat it back down and turned to face him. "I woke up, and I was hot, so I went for a swim. I got a cramp and... My body must not have been ready for the cold. I seized up out there."

Garrett looked troubled as he stared back at her, and she knew a part of him didn't believe the story she was telling.

"When I saw you—" His voice cracked on the last word and he closed his eyes. When he opened them, his lashes were wet. "I thought... I thought you were gone."

Rowan broke his gaze, unable to look him in the eye. She scooted close to him and snuggled her head into his neck. "I'm so sorry, Garrett. I'm so sorry that I've been screwed up lately."

"No. This has been a terrible year. I want to help you, okay? Please don't push me away."

"I'm trying," she mumbled.

❧

The next day, Garrett drove into town for drywall. While Quinn napped, Rowan stared at her blank computer screen, remembering Angie's advice to journal about her feelings.

*I feel...* Rowan typed. Nothing arose. No string of eloquent prose poured forth.

*Afraid,* she typed. *Afraid that we're not alone in this house. Afraid that a woman was murdered here. Maybe she's calling out from beyond the grave for me to help her. I'm afraid that if I don't help her, I will go insane, unraveling further and further until I am a ghost too.*

Rowan frowned at the words and closed the computer.

She didn't feel like writing, not journal-writing anyway. At least article-writing was detached, focused, specific. Who wanted to while away the hours lamenting their own feelings? Not her.

Rowan took out the notes from her meeting with Colleen. Amy's sister had written Declan Stilts's phone number, but told Rowan he'd never agree to an interview about Amy. Rowan needed another way in. According to Colleen, he'd started a brewery with some friends in Mount Pleasant, Michigan, called Stilts's Brewing.

Rowan dialed his number.

"This is Declan," a male voice said.

"Hi, Declan. My name's Rowan Cortes and I'm a reporter. I was hoping to do a piece on the Stilts's Brewing Company."

"Okay, yeah, that'd be great. Let me give you the number to our PR person and she can answer—"

"I'd prefer an interview with you directly. The name behind the company and all that."

"Oh, okay. Sure."

After some back and forth, Declan agreed to an interview the next day.

Rowan dialed her mother. Emily picked up before the phone rang.

"Mom?" Rowan asked, when she heard only silence.

"Franny? Oh, how nice to hear from you."

"The phone didn't even ring," Rowan said.

"Didn't it? Well, I picked it up anyhow. I was just working on the quilt for Quinnie. I'd so hoped to have it done by her first birthday, but…" Her mother trailed off and Rowan knew what thought had accompanied that statement. *But Dad died.* Her mother had always called their father 'Dad' when speaking to her children and 'Lee' when speaking to others about him.

Emily preferred middle names. Rowan's father's first name was Morgan, middle name Lee, thus Emily called him Lee. Rowan was Franny or Frances. Olivia was Joy and Alex was Dean, which her younger brother hated, but never told Emily for fear of hurting her feelings.

"How are you, Mom?"

"Oh, I'm getting along. Aunt Trudy has been by a thousand times with casseroles and sandwich lunches. Dad always loved her corn soufflé, but corn doesn't sit well with me. Something to do with the intestines, according to Dr. Cruz, but I don't have the heart to tell Trudy."

"You can set it aside. Garrett loves Trudy's corn soufflé," Rowan told her.

"Oh, of course, he does. Why didn't I remember that? This brain of mine has been on an extended vacation these last months."

"Me too, Mom," Rowan said, scribbling question marks in her notebook. "I wondered if you'd watch Quinn for a couple of hours tomorrow? Garrett's busy with the house and I have an interview with someone in Mount Pleasant."

"An interview? Aren't you taking a summer leave from work?"

"I am. This is just something I'm helping Angie with." Rowan listened to herself lie and tried to ignore how often she'd been doing it lately.

"Absolutely, Franny. I'd love to see Quinn."

"Great. I'll bring her to your place. I appreciate it."

"Oh, honey, it's me who appreciates it. This house, since… well, suddenly it just seems too big. Anything else going on while I've got you on the phone?"

"Umm… yeah…" Rowan's thoughts flitted to Garrett's words from the day before. *There's still time to have a relationship with your birth mother…*

Rowan tried to imagine the most delicate way she could phrase the question to her adopted mother, but nothing seemed appropriate in the wake of Emily's grief. The woman was just learning how to live without the man she'd spent the previous thirty-five years of her life with. Waking up to make coffee alone, preparing dinners for one, climbing into the queen-sized bed where her husband's indent still occupied the space beside her.

"I wondered if I left Quinn's squishy hippo at your house?" Rowan lifted the hippo from the counter and stared at its bulging brown eyes.

"Oh, dear. Not the hippo. She loves him. Let me look."

Rowan listened as her mom set down the phone and walked away.

Rather than disappointment that she'd bowed out of asking about her birth family, relief coursed through Rowan. It wasn't always better to know where you came from. She considered the stories she'd read about mothers abandoning their children, killing them even.

What if her own mother had suffered such severe postpartum depression that giving Rowan up was tantamount to saving her life? Or maybe the woman had refused to hold her child, to feed and nurture her, to provide the touch and care that was crucial to an infant's development? Denied her the very love that would shape the rest of her life, that would set the groundwork for her own future parenting?

Did Rowan really want to know about the dark secrets her birth origin might reveal? Neglect, abandonment, cruelty…

"No sign of him, honey," her mother said, interrupting her thoughts. "Want me to call some stores and see if I can find one? I could go pick one up today and have it ready for Quinn tomorrow."

"No, that's okay, Mom. It'll turn up. It's probably wedged between the seats in my car."

# 15

Garrett wasn't skeptical about Rowan's story that she intended to visit her mother with Quinn. Instead, he seemed relieved he'd have the house to himself. Rowan knew he'd been feeling the pressure of falling behind on the work he'd thought he'd already have done. She kissed him goodbye, loaded Quinn in the car and made the two-and-a-half-hour drive to her mom's house in Midland.

Seeing her childhood home had a similar effect on Rowan as seeing her own home days before. Her breath stuck in her throat as she pulled into the driveway and parked behind her mother's green Saturn. The garage door was closed, but Rowan could imagine her father's black PT Cruiser parked inside.

"Time to wake up, Quinnie," she told her daughter, who'd snoozed for most of the drive. Rowan unbuckled Quinn, huffing as she pulled her from the car seat. Quinn seemed to weigh twenty pounds more in sleep.

When the fresh air hit Quinn's face, she opened her eyes and blinked groggily at Rowan.

"Time to see Grandma Emily," Rowan told her, kissing her warm cheek.

Rowan paused at the front door, Quinn balanced on her hip, and considered whether she should knock. It was ridiculous. She'd never knocked on the door a day in her life save the one time in high school when she'd stayed out until three a.m. drinking warm beer and contemplating the meaning of life from the tailgate of Randy Kissinger's pickup truck. She'd returned to find the front door locked and her father less than pleased. He'd said in no uncertain terms, "You're too good for Randy Kissinger and if he keeps you out past midnight again, I'll be visiting his parents."

Rowan stared at the door. But it was the memory of that night she saw. How badly she wanted her father to yank open that door, a scowl of disappointment on his face as he watched Randy back down the driveway and disappear into the night.

Before Rowan raised her hand, the door swung in and her tiny mother stood in the threshold.

"Franny," she announced, smiling. "And if it isn't my beautiful granddaughter." Emily reached for Quinn and Rowan handed her over. "My Selena girl," she said, bouncing Quinn and kissing her cheeks and forehead. As she did with Rowan, Emily called Quinn by her middle name, Selena.

Quinn grinned and grabbed at Emily's dark hair, cut in the same style for as long as Rowan could remember—a mushroom cut with the ends curled under. Emily had been fastidious about dyeing her hair since grays had started appearing in her forties, but now inch-thick silver roots protruded from her scalp on both sides of the part. The gray wasn't the only change in Emily. New lines spidered out from the corners of her eyes, and she appeared as if she'd aged since Rowan's last visit weeks earlier.

"My heavens, Franny! You cut your hair." She reached a hand out and smoothed it across Rowan's cheek and into her hair. "It's just lovely, really brings out those gorgeous peepers."

Rowan imagined spewing the entire story to her mother—the gum, the house, the collapsing of her carefully constructed identity—but she bit back the words and forced a tight-lipped smile. "I needed a change."

"Well," Emily exclaimed, "I made apple sauce and colored ice cubes and I found a big box of your and Alex's and Olivia's old toys—"

Rowan stood in the doorway, the smells of the house, of her father, wafting out. Teakwood aftershave and cloves. The scents mixed with her mother's smells, spearmint gum and ocean breeze air fresheners she plugged into the outlets in every room.

For an instant, she was transported back decades, to evenings around the dinner table, arguing with Alex over the after-dinner movie, trying to impress her dad with her latest grades, half-listening as Olivia and Emily discussed which dress patterns they wanted to get from the fabric store.

Rowan took a step back, nearly plunging off the concrete steps and onto the sidewalk. She grabbed hold of the wrought-iron railing before she went down, but the movement sent a shot of pain through her swollen ankle.

"Oh, goodness," Emily said, stepping out onto the stoop.

Rowan straightened up and shook her head. "It's okay, Mom. I'm fine. Just lost my footing. I'm not going to come in because I don't want to be late for this interview. You guys have fun."

She didn't give her mother a hug or kiss Quinn goodbye, though she wanted to do both. Instead, she hurried back to her car and climbed inside, glimpsing her mother disappearing through the doorway as she backed out of the driveway.

Rowan's eyes welled and she blinked away tears. "No," she shouted. "I will not ugly-cry for the next thirty minutes. I am a reporter and I am going to an interview and I will look like a damn professional."

Her shouts did little to stop the tears pouring over her cheeks, but she found herself laughing until she looked through her driver's-side window to see a middle-aged couple staring pointedly forward as if worried about making eye contact with the sobbing, screaming, laughing lady in the car beside them.

Stilts's Brewing Company occupied an industrial glass and aluminum building that looked more like a warehouse than a place to grab a few drinks after work. Pressed concrete floors and a long steel bar with fifteen beer taps behind it did little to reduce the industrial feel when Rowan walked through the glass doors into the chilly interior. Long metal tables surrounded by metal chairs stretched the length of the establishment.

A man swept from behind the counter, flashing her a wide white smile. Beyond the smile, Declan Stilts did not live up to the expectation Rowan had imagined when Colleen described the wealthy playboy who'd stomped Amy Prahm's heart into smithereens. He stood no taller than five feet nine with a rail-thin build and a pasty complexion. Watery green eyes gazed out from his long face as he offered Rowan his bony hand.

"You must be Rowan," he said. She noticed dimples in his cheeks when he smiled.

"Yes. You're Declan?"

"Unfortunately for my father, yes." He released a brittle laugh and gestured she follow him. "We have a girl who does tours of the facility if you'd like to see where we brew the beer. We can sit over here and have a chat beforehand."

Rowan slid into a booth, feeling the cool metal through her slacks. She pulled out her notebook and pen and rested them on the gleaming table. "A lot of metal in here."

Declan's head bobbed up and down. "Urban industrial, my wife calls it. Her uncle designed the place. He's a pretty big architect in Chicago, and we were lucky to get him on board."

"You're married? You look so young."

He smiled, revealed the dimples again, and laced his hands together on the table. Despite his less-than-Hollywood looks, he had the air of someone who thought highly of himself. "I'm twenty-eight, but I get that all the time. I still get carded and I own a bar." He chuckled.

"Is your wife in the beer business too?"

"No. She's an attorney. Not even a beer drinker. She's after me to put some wines on the menu. Now she's got a baby on the way though, so wine is out for a while."

"You're going to be a dad?"

"Yeah." He flushed. "I'm pretty pumped. I figured I can't do any worse than my own dad." He laughed and a brief glower crossed his features.

"Were you ever married prior to your current wife?"

He faltered, glancing toward the bar where one other guy stood staring at his cell phone. "No. Just one wife, Heather."

"And how about Amy Prahm?"

The little color there'd been in his face drained away. Now his eyes darted to every corner of the brewery, as if cataloguing the exits for escape. "My lawyer has advised me—"

"I'm not a cop. I'm living in the house where Amy disappeared and I'm just trying to help her family. Don't you want someone to find out what happened? For the sake of her family, Declan? Imagine if it were Heather or, worse, your future child, all grown up?"

He stared hard at the table, his hands wound into a single bloodless fist. "Okay, fine, but this is off the record. I can give you ten minutes."

"Can we start with why you left Amy to begin with? I know that's personal, but it might shed some light on her state of mind."

Declan scratched his jaw. "Amy was… a mistake. When I met Amy, my girlfriend Heather had just kicked me to the curb. We'd been dating for three years. I'd bought a ring. Girl of my dreams. I went into a total nosedive. Started going to the clubs, drinking all night, sleeping all day. If I'd have been younger, my dad would have tossed me in military school, but I was twenty-five. He couldn't do much. Neither could I.

"I met Amy at the Gladwin County Fair. My buddy had dragged me over there to see monster trucks. Amy was painting faces—little rainbows and whiskers on kids." Misery flitted across his features, but he clenched his jaw and forged on.

"She was so different from Heather. Like I said, Heather's an attorney. At the time, Heather had just graduated from law school and started an internship in Grand Rapids. Heather could melt you with a stare. Amy was the opposite. She was like a kitten. Small and fragile, always daydreaming. I decided the best way to obliterate Heather was to replace her with someone totally different.

"It all happened so fast. Amy and I went on a couple of dates. I took her to Las Vegas to see the Cirque du Soleil, and we flew to Florida and spent a week on the beach. Then one day, I looked in the newspaper and I saw Heather. She'd assisted on a big case. I went into my room, dug the ring out of my sock drawer and asked Amy to marry me."

Rowan gazed at him, barely hiding her disgust. "You asked her to marry you because your ex-girlfriend's name was in the paper."

He didn't look her in the eye, but nodded. "I didn't think she'd say yes," he whispered. "Imagine my surprise when she did. Then things just"—he mimed his hand flying like an airplane—"took off. Marriage announcement, wedding date, invitations, and finally the house in Empire."

"How'd the house in Empire come about?"

"Amy and I took a vacation up there. We were out on a friend's boat. She saw that dark staircase from the lake, all tucked up in the trees. We anchored and swam in, walked up to the house. She loved it. We'd originally talked about going to Costa Rica and spending a year living in an off-grid community she'd found there. I was never sold on the idea. I have terrible allergies and figured in the rainforest I'd be sneezing and covered in a rash twenty-four seven. When she saw the house in Empire, I figured maybe I could make things work with Amy. We'd move up north, and I'd divide my time between Grand Rapids and Traverse City, start a new branch up there or whatever. I was managing one of the branches of my dad's banks."

"And then?"

"And then Heather called me. She wanted me back. She'd never stopped loving me. 'Please don't marry that girl,' she said."

Rowan's stomach churned. She imagined a photograph that Colleen had given her of Amy. Amy had been sitting on a park bench, a baguette sticking from her wide mouth. She'd been making a goofy face, eyes crossed, dark hair framing her cheeks. Colleen said Amy had been twenty in the photo, but she looked more like fifteen, wearing denim overalls and a sunny yellow t-shirt dotted in little black and white panda bears.

"So, you ditched her on the day of your wedding?"

A flush rose into his cheeks, and he still didn't look at her. "Yeah. I got hell from everyone for doing that. As well I should," he added quickly.

"What happened then? You and Heather lived happily ever after?" Rowan couldn't keep the fury from her voice.

"We got married about a year later."

Rowan shook her head. "And Amy moved to a house in the middle of nowhere and probably got murdered by some fucking psychopath." She heard the words—worse, the snarl they emerged as—and knew she was failing as a journalist. Rowan had always been good at the unbiased, indifferent thing. Putting people at ease by keeping judgment out of her questions. She had none of those skills as she spoke to Declan.

"I… if I'd known she was in danger. I would have—"

"What?" Rowan snapped. "You would have what?"

He fanned his shirt out as if hot, though a chill still lingered in the brewery. "Time's up."

He stood and Rowan's hand darted out, grabbing the hem of his t-shirt. Declan looked at her hand as if it were covered in leprous boils. She jumped up as he jerked away.

"When was the last time you spoke with her? Did you know of anyone who wanted to hurt her?" These were the questions she should have started with, the questions that mattered, but they'd come too late and he hurried back toward the counter.

She jogged to catch up and cut him off. "Please, wait. I'm sorry I put you on the spot. I had a baby and my dad died." The words rushed out. "I haven't been myself."

He paused, still looking like he wanted to run. It was the baby comment that had stopped him. She saw the way his eyes darted to her belly. She wondered if he was thinking of his own pregnant wife.

"I hadn't spoken to Amy in two weeks when she disappeared. I called her to let her know Heather and I were getting married."

Rowan's fury tasted acrid in her mouth, but she bit it back. "Did she seem distraught at that news? Upset?"

He shook his head. "Not really. I know everyone thinks I'm the big bad wolf here, but… Amy had her own stuff going on, her own demons she was running away from. That's part of the reason she agreed to marry me. We both wanted to be different, start new lives, run away from who we were."

"Demons? What does that mean?"

He brushed a hand self-consciously through his short pale hair. "I shouldn't say. Colleen gave me hell for telling the police."

"I'm not going to print it."

"Amy… umm… she'd had a problem with prescription drugs. I guess it started in high school after she had her wisdom teeth removed. When I met her, she was six months clean, but…" He shrugged. "Everyone in her hometown thought of her that way, as a hophead."

"A hophead?"

"A user," he explained. "It may have gone beyond painkillers. If it did, she never told me, but she wanted to escape that image, the way people saw her."

"And you told the police?"

Declan chewed his lip. "I regret it now. It strengthened their belief that she…"

"Took off."

He nodded.

"Did the police ever suspect you?"

"I was in Grand Rapids. I had an alibi."

"Do you have any reason to suspect Amy was using again?"

"No, none."

"Did she tell you about anyone strange up there? Enemies? People mad at her?"

He shook his head. "After I called off the wedding, we were pretty over. I only spoke with her a few times. I'd look at the people up there. People she worked with and stuff. I really do have to go now."

Rowan watched him walk away, aware she was no closer to the truth of what happened to Amy, and unlikely to ever get an interview with Declan Stilts again.

# 16

Rowan called her mother on the drive back to Midland, asking if she could meet her with Quinn for lunch at Moonie's. It was her mother's favorite restaurant.

Rowan didn't want to go into her childhood home. The interview with Declan had upset her, and she still hadn't come down from the rushing emotion as she imagined Amy left at the altar and the man she loved skipping through his new life with barely a care for the woman he'd left in his wake.

At the restaurant, Rowan ordered a chicken salad sandwich but took only a single bite. She wasn't hungry. Her mother ate her entire plate of spaghetti, talking about her quilting group and Olivia's new job and how excited she was for Quinn's first birthday.

"Are you ready for the big party?" Emily asked, using a piece of garlic bread to mop the last of the tomato sauce from her plate.

Though her mother had likely never weighed over one hundred and ten pounds, she was always a proud member of the clean plate club. A club Rowan had often joined in her youth to please her mother, but in her teenage years had added an extra fifteen pounds to Rowan's already wide-hipped frame. Eventually she'd learned she couldn't eat like her mother and siblings.

In the previous year, Rowan had dwindled from a size twelve after having Quinn to a size four. Her emotional turmoil had left her rarely hungry.

"Umm... yeah." Rowan nodded and reached for Quinn's apple sauce, spooned some out and lifted it to her daughter's lips. Quinn blew bubbles into her apple sauce and then laughed, swinging her arms. Her hand hit the spoon and sent it flying into Rowan's lap.

Rowan closed her eyes and took a breath before using her linen napkin to wipe away the apple sauce coating her cheek and the front of her shirt.

"Oh, Selena," Emily gushed. "You little gremlin, you. The food goes in your mouth." Emily pointed at her mouth.

"I'm leaving most of the planning to Garrett—well, his family anyway. They do a big one-year celebration in his family and... I just haven't had the energy for it, I guess."

Emily reached over and patted her hand. "And why would you? It takes a long time to recover from giving birth. Longer because you had hysterectomy too. I bought her a b-a-l-l p-i-t," Emily spelled out, winking at Rowan. "It was Joy's idea. Is that good?"

"My sister's ensuring my house will never be clean again," Rowan joked. "It's great, Mom. Quinn will love it."

Emily clapped her hands together. "Oh, goodie. I thought so too. Joy is coming, though not Michael. They're having problems again. I wish she'd find a young man like Garrett. She has always been drawn to those moody boys. The last time I saw Michael I said hello, and he didn't speak a single word to me. Not one word."

"Yeah, Garrett refers to him as Oscar the Grouch," Rowan said. "Olivia will tire of those guys someday, Mom."

"I hope so," Emily sighed.

They finished lunch and Rowan hugged her mother goodbye, wishing again that she could tell her everything that had happened in the previous months. Instead, she plastered on a waxy smile and revealed nothing.

When Rowan turned into the long driveway that led up to Helme House, exhaustion tugged at the corners of her eyes. She wanted to crawl into bed and sleep, but knew she had hours to go before bed. It wasn't even four o'clock.

Garrett came out to greet them. "Alan's coming over with pizzas.

That cool?" he asked, kissing Rowan on the cheek before opening the back door and releasing Quinn from her car seat.

"Sure. We had lunch at an Italian place, so I'm not really hungry, but that's fine."

"Did you guys have fun with your mom today? Get up to anything?"

Rowan nodded, grateful that her daughter couldn't reveal that Mommy had missed most of the day's activities. "Just the usual stuff. My mom talked about her quilting group. We went to lunch. Oh, and she bought a ball pit for Quinn's birthday."

"A ball pit?" Garrett grinned. "Like with all the colored plastic balls?"

"Yep. Quinn will love it, but I can imagine we'll be finding balls beneath our furniture for years to come."

He swung Quinn around. She laughed and waved her arms.

"Get much work done today?" Rowan asked, grabbing her bag and following Garrett into the house.

"I sure did. Completely stripped and sanded the floors in the study. I also pulled up the floor in the downstairs bathroom, so we'll be using the upstairs for a while. I'm going to tile it, but the tile won't get delivered to the store until tomorrow."

Garrett continued listing off the house projects, but Rowan only half-listened, thinking instead of Amy. Had she woken in the night to someone in her bedroom? Or had it been an ordinary afternoon like this one when someone had appeared in the house to take her away?

"Is that okay with you?" Garrett asked.

Rowan looked up to find her husband watching her. "I'm sorry," she said. "Zoned out for a minute there. What did you say?"

"My mom and dad are coming a little early on Saturday for the party. They thought around ten? We told everyone noon, but you know how they love to get an early start on the day."

"Sure, yeah." Rowan maneuvered past Garrett to the cupboard and took out a glass, filled it with water and drank it empty.

"Are you feeling okay, babe? Throat still hurting? Ankle any better?"

Rowan refilled the glass. "I'm tired. I guess that whole thing did a number on me. My ankle is less tender. I've taken ibuprofen a couple times today."

"You almost drowned. It would do a number on anyone."

The front door banged open, and Rowan jumped.

"Pizza, pizza!" Alan yelled, walking into the kitchen with two large pizzas balanced on one palm.

Rowan tore the plastic off a bundle of paper plates. Garrett set Quinn in her high chair on the back porch while Rowan arranged slices of pizza on plates and carried them out, handing one to Alan and another to Garrett. She gave Quinn a bottle of goat's milk formula before filling a glass with wine and sitting in a chair opposite Alan and Garrett.

"Alan, do you have any idea what's up with the cemetery in the woods?"

He paused mid-bite and lifted an eyebrow. "Cemetery?"

"Yeah, it's old from the looks of it and unkempt, along the ridge trail." Rowan pointed toward the bluff trail where she'd discovered the little graveyard.

Alan shook his head. "I've never seen it, but this property only runs to the treeline. The rest is national lakeshore. Probably just an old cemetery created by settlers who lived near the lake."

"There were several children. Mostly children in fact." Rowan tried not to notice the way Alan's eyes flitted toward Garrett before returning to her own.

"I'm guilty of ignorance here," Alan admitted. "I did a pretty cursory look around the property, but that's it. If you drive into Empire, there's a museum and historical center. I've never been there myself, but the ice cream shop across the street is excellent. Best mint chocolate chip I've ever had."

Garrett bobbed his head. "We'll have to try it. Rowan wanted to check out the town there. Maybe this Sunday, if we're not too worn out after the party on Saturday."

"Yeah," Rowan agreed. "I'd like that."

"Leah's ready for the birthday," Alan said. "She bought Quinn a"— he lowered his voice, glancing to where Quinn sat in her highchair —"lawnmower that shoots bubbles." He grinned at Rowan. "Might take her a while to get through the whole yard, so you can catch up on your summer reading. I saw a few of those bodice-rippers in a cardboard box upstairs." He winked at Rowan.

Rowan smiled. "She'll love the lawnmower, Alan. Thank you."

"Oh, don't thank me yet. It also makes a really annoying popping sound when you push it. You'll need earphones to tune it out." Alan stood with his second piece of pizza in hand. "I can't wait any longer. Let's look at the study," he told Garrett.

"The wood floors beneath the carpet are exquisite," Garrett said, standing and following Alan back into the house.

Rowan looked beyond Quinn to the dense woods that sloped from the back of the property down to the road. Miles of woods surrounded the house. If someone had murdered Amy, there were innumerable places to hide her body.

She shivered, a tingling at the back of her neck that made her feel as if eyes peered from the dark forest.

Such woods could conceal anyone, living or dead.

## 17

"I'm staining the floors today," Garrett told Rowan the next morning when she arrived in the kitchen well after nine a.m. She'd slept late thanks to another restless night.

He handed her a cup of coffee, and she sipped it, trying to get her bearings. "Where's Quinnie?"

"In the playpen." He gestured toward the living room where Quinn stood watching her. "Mmmaaa…"

Rowan held up her coffee. "Let me gulp this down and I'll pick you up, honey," she told her daughter.

"You and Quinn can stay here today. I'll close the door to the study and open the windows, but it still might get stinky in the house."

Rowan yawned. "That's okay. We'll go into town. I'll take Quinn to the library in Traverse City. I saw a neat little kids' area when I was there last time."

"Perfect. I'm going to get started." Garrett grinned, tightening his bandana as if preparing for battle. He kissed Rowan's cheek and stopped by Quinn to peck her on the head before disappearing into the study. Two minutes later, AC/DC blasted down the hallway.

∾

As Rowan drove into Traverse City, her cell phone rang, revealing a number unknown to Rowan.

"Hello. This is Rowan Cortes."

"Um… hi. This is Zoe Gibbs. Colleen Prahm gave me your number. I was a good friend of Amy Prahm's."

"Oh, hi, Zoe. Thanks for calling me. I'm on my way into Traverse City if you're available to talk. Do you live in the area?" Rowan searched her fuzzy brain for any mention of Zoe by Colleen, but couldn't place her.

"Yeah. I live on the west side of town. I work this afternoon, but I'm free until two."

"That would be perfect. Though just a disclaimer, I'll have my one-year-old in tow."

"Aww, cool. I love kids. There's a park near me. We could meet there."

"Sure. I'm on M-72. How do I get there?"

Zoe rattled off directions, and they ended the call.

Rowan tilted her rearview mirror down. Her face looked pallid, her hair choppy and askew. She'd intended to make a hair appointment, let a professional clean it up, but it hadn't seemed important. Now it did. She wanted to look like a reporter, not like a deranged mother who cut her own hair and whose clothes hung on her body like rags.

She caught Quinn's eye in the mirror and smiled. "Hi, peanut. How ya doing?"

Quinn continued to slobber on her plastic keys, holding them up for Rowan to admire the glistening drool that made the colors extra-shiny. Quinn's eyes remained locked on Rowan's, green-blue and full of knowledge. Rowan felt sure that Quinn sensed the anguish in her mother. Somehow her daughter knew about all the things Rowan tried to hide from the rest of the world.

Unsettled, Rowan tilted the mirror back to display only traffic through the back window. She reached for the diaper bag and fumbled out Quinn's comb, driving with one hand and yanking the comb through her hair with the other. She didn't have makeup in the bag and half considered smearing a bit of Quinn's jarred strawberries on her face to give her cheeks a spot of color.

"Then I'd really look certifiable," she muttered, abandoning the thought and focusing instead on what she'd ask Amy's friend.

∾

Rowan missed the park the first time, but spotted a young woman on a swing, a book open in her hands.

After pulling the car into a parking lot, Rowan turned around and headed back, parking beside the only other car, a silver coupe.

She climbed out and opened the rear door, unhooked Quinn and lifted her daughter out, cringing when her baby released a mouthful of drool onto her shoulder. "Oh, Quinn. Icky. Those teeth are causing you some trouble."

Quinn babbled a string of baby talk, reaching her arms toward the playground, where inanimate farm animals sat atop large metal springs.

The woman on the swing stood and made her way to Rowan and Quinn. "Hi. Are you Rowan?"

"Yes, thanks for meeting me. I apologize for not shaking your hand. I just got slimed by Quinnie and I need to find a burp cloth." Rowan dug through the diaper bag with one hand while balancing Quinn on her opposite side. Her daughter felt heavier than usual, and Rowan's arm ached.

"Here, let me," the girl said, pulling the bag from Rowan's shoulder. She took out a pink and green polka-dot burp cloth.

"Thank you," Rowan sighed, mopping the drool off her shoulder, though her shirt was already saturated. "You'd think I'd have the hang of this by now."

Zoe smiled. "I used to work in a daycare. I can't imagine how anyone gets the hang of it." She shifted her focus to Quinn. "Hi there. Aren't you sweet? Look at those big eyes and dark curls."

"She's got Mom's eyes and Dad's hair," Rowan said, nuzzling her nose behind Quinn's ear.

"She's beautiful. Want to sit? There's a picnic table over there."

"Let's head for the baby swing. I can strap this munchkin in and have my hands free."

They walked to the swing set that included a plastic baby swing. After several attempts, Rowan got her daughter in. Quinn laughed and talked. Rowan rolled her shoulders and tilted her head from side to side.

"Who knew that one day my greatest challenge would be wrestling my one-year-old into a plastic swing. She's getting heavier. I'm going to have to start lifting her with the other arm to balance things out."

"I bet. Best arms of my life when I worked at that daycare. Who needs the gym when you're hefting sixty-pound toddlers every day?"

"I can't fathom handling more than one at a time," Rowan said. "They should pay daycare workers more."

"Agreed. That's why I quit. I couldn't afford my apartment on ten dollars an hour. I work at an insurance company now. It's not as lively as life with the kids, but at least I'm not getting shut-off notices from the electric company."

Rowan reached for her notebook and pencil in the diaper bag, giving Quinn another push before she flipped open to a blank page. "You work an afternoon shift at an insurance company?"

Zoe nodded. "It's new this year. They're trying to give the staff more flexibility in their hours. I'm a night owl and pushed for a later shift. I guess we'd better get to Amy though, huh? You probably have naps and feeding times and all that fun stuff to work around."

"Yeah," Rowan murmured, though she'd never gotten the hang of scheduling Quinn's feeding and nap times. Other mothers did it. The supermoms with their dry-erase boards covered in daily activities. The mothers who made their own organic baby food, ran three miles a day, and sent newsletters about the latest sex offenders to move into an area. Rowan had never considered she might be one of those mothers, though it hadn't stopped the shame at how far she fell short.

"Before we get started," Zoe said, "I hope you're not taking the same angle as that reporter who wrote a bunch of articles about Amy's case. He printed a month's worth of crap about Amy faking her own death."

"I read a few of those articles. Duncan something or other."

"Leach," Zoe said. "Duncan Leach. Pretty appropriate, if you ask me. His theory was that she set the whole thing up, cut her arm or something and spread blood around at the scene, so she could flee her unhappy life. Do you think he ever talked to me? Or Colleen? Hell, no. But you know who he did talk to? Declan Stilts."

"You think Declan pushed the narrative that Amy faked her death?"

"It had to come from somewhere and he was taking heat after she disappeared. Then the focus shifted to these crime books she'd been reading, like *Gone Girl*, and how the scene looked staged. I was furious about what Leach had written. I mean for starters, who hasn't read *Gone Girl*? I confronted him in the Flapjack Shack in Traverse City. I wanted to throw my coffee in his face."

"I don't blame you. Zoe, can you tell me anything about Amy's life at the time? Was she dating anyone?"

"No, she'd sworn off men after the cockroach. That's what we called Declan."

"How was she spending her time?"

"Doing the usual things, I guess. Painting, gardening. She had this big dream of turning that place into a bed-and-breakfast. She'd looked into the history of the house, wondering if she could get it deemed historical and protected, so Mr. Stilts, the cockroach's father, couldn't sell it out from under her. Obviously, he didn't want his kid tied up in a mortgage with Amy when he was getting married to someone else. It was a cluster, that's for sure."

"Who was she talking to about the history? Or was she just researching online?"

"Oh, no, she was in deep on that stuff. I know she visited the historic place in Empire and she talked to some folks who lived there before."

"Really? The previous family who owned Helme House?"

"No, not the family. Helme House used to be a home for girls. Amy tracked down a couple who used to work there."

"A home for girls?" Rowan's voice hitched on the words and a curtain of gloom swept through her, fast and then gone.

"Yeah, like an orphanage."

"Huh…" Rowan thought of the scribbles on the walls of the nursery. "Do you know the names of the couple Amy spoke to?"

"No, I'm afraid not. Colleen might. But if you go to the museum in Empire, I bet the lady there would know."

"I'll check it out," Rowan said. Quinn bent forward in the swing and got hold of one shoe, yanking it off. Before Quinn could get it to her mouth, she dropped it and squealed in frustration. Rowan bent and retrieved it. "Quinnie, you can't chew on your shoe. It's dirty." Red-faced, Quinn reached for the shoe. Rowan dug her hippo from the bag and offered it to her. Quinn stuck it in her mouth, but continued to stare at the single pink and yellow shoe in Rowan's hand.

"Zoe, who do you think hurt Amy?"

"The cockroach, without a doubt," Zoe said, leaning against the swing set.

Rowan thought of her conversation with Declan from the day before. She hadn't gotten the killer vibe from him, not that she'd interviewed many killers, but he had a meek disposition. She wouldn't have been surprised if people had described him as sickly in childhood.

"Have you ever met Declan?" Rowan asked.

Zoe shook her head. "No. I never wanted to either. I stalked him online a couple times after I met Amy. That's how I found out he was getting married. She didn't know. I wish now I hadn't told her."

"Was she upset?"

"She didn't cry or anything, at least not in front of me, but who wouldn't be upset? The lowlife ditched her on their wedding day. She seemed... surprised. I wondered if they were still involved. That's crazy because more than once she said she never wanted to see him again, but... I'm not sure he hadn't visited the house a few times, maybe even in the days before she disappeared."

"What makes you say that?"

"I saw a text message come in once on her phone, like five days before she vanished. It said, 'Excited to see you tonight.' I had a feeling it came from him."

"Really?" Rowan frowned.

Declan definitely hadn't mentioned that. Rowan had the impression he'd discarded Amy without a look back, not wanting to face the aftermath of his own shitty choices. He presented a meek front, an awkward guy with an important father, but maybe it had all been an act.

"Zoe, did you ever see any evidence that Amy might be using prescription drugs?"

Zoe fixed her shrewd dark eyes on Rowan's, her irritation at the question plain. "No. Absolutely not. And it chafes my ass that those rumors persist. She wasn't a drug user. Maybe she'd scarfed down a few too many Vicodin after high school, but I've met drug addicts and Amy was not one of them. She was humiliated that she'd ever used painkillers at all. When I met her, she wouldn't take a Motrin even if she had period cramps so bad it felt like someone was using her ovaries as a stress ball."

"Okay. I had to ask. Another thing I keep coming back to is the strangeness of Amy living in that house alone," Rowan said, imagining Amy, who looked young and fragile, a waif, a fairy-person who belonged in a little yellow cottage, not an oppressive brick mansion forgotten in the woods.

Zoe nodded. "It was weird. I told her as much the first time she invited me out there. 'Holy shite, who wants to live in this creepy old place?' I asked her, but she'd get that dreamy face and start talking about travelers from all over the world coming up there to stay. Somewhere down the road, it could be a retreat center for painters, writers. If she could get the funding, she could offer an artist residency. She had a lot of big dreams."

"Sounds like it. I can imagine the house serving that purpose. Though I'm not sure how she envisioned making it happen."

"Making it happen wasn't Amy's strong suit. The dreams were aplenty, the means less so. I'll tell you though"—Zoe leaned in—"I wondered if she had plans to blackmail the cockroach. Say he knocked her up and siphon the big dream money out of him."

Rowan frowned. "Did she ever say anything like that?"

Zoe shook her head. "No, but that's what I would have been thinking. I would have sued the pants off that guy. Emotional damages and whatnot."

Rowan parked on the street in front of the Empire Historical Center. She grabbed Quinn's stroller from the back of her car and unfolded it. Quinn smiled and tugged at her curls as Rowan settled her into the seat, buckling her in place and attaching a baby toy to the sunshade.

Rowan pushed the door open with her backside and maneuvered the stroller into the air-conditioned interior. The blonde wood floors gleamed, and the white walls were arranged with large black and white photographs with captions beneath.

"Welcome, welcome," a middle-aged woman in capri chinos and a turquoise polo shirt sang, slipping from behind the counter. She hurried to Rowan and peered into the stroller at Quinn. "And welcome to you," the woman said, reaching for one of Quinn's pudgy hands and shaking it. "She is enchanting."

"Thank you," Rowan said. "Her dad and I are pretty fond of her."

"Could she have a lollipop?" The woman strode back to her counter.

"No lollipops, I'm afraid. She's not quite one, so we're trying to limit the sugar."

"Oh, yes, what a dope." She slapped a hand against her forehead. "I watched a documentary on sugar not too long ago. Apparently most chronic diseases come from people eating too much sugar. I finally kicked my daily ice cream habit after that, though the shop across the street seems intent on ruining me. They're offering two-dollar ice cream sundaes."

"I've heard they have good ice cream. I'm Rowan Cortes." Rowan extended her hand.

"Karen Murphy," she replied, taking Rowan's hand and squeezing.

"A lot of history for such a small town." Rowan gestured at the walls.

"Oh, yes, indeed. This town is rich with history. My daddy was a historian—a hobbyist, he'd say, though everyone in this town and twenty miles around came to him for property lines, lineage questions, who owned what and who was owed what. He could tell you the name of every body buried in Maple Grove Cemetery, even if the name faded decades before. He kept records on everything. Drove my mama mad, to be frank. Notebooks stacked floor to ceiling in his study."

"And you took up the torch?"

"So it seems, though I can't carry the flame he was running with. About ten years back, I hired my nephew to put the contents of those books onto a computer. Not much of a typer myself. I try to keep the history alive as best I can, but..." She gazed around the room decorated with maps and yellowing portraits. "It's a fading interest for many folks. Every year seems fewer tourists come in here. I've barely sold a single map or book all spring. Getting hard to keep the lights on in this place, justify the cost of keeping it up."

Rowan stopped at a table with items for sale, including paperback books with titles like *Remembering Empire* and *The Women of Leelanau County*. There were trail maps and road maps and one map for a self-guided history tour.

"I'll take one of each," Rowan said, gathering up three paperbacks and four maps and then adding a key chain that read 'Those who do not remember the past are condemned to repeat it.' Her eyes lingered on the words and she wished she'd grabbed one of the brightly colored key chains that said things like 'Sleeping Bear Dunes National Lakeshore' or 'Beach More, Worry Less.'

"Can you tell me anything about the house up in the woods? Helme House."

The woman's mouth turned down. "As I said, my daddy was the real historian, but I know a bit about the house. That woman going missing had people talking about it again, but then when it turned out she'd likely run off, the hens stopped clucking. My daddy spoke of the house a time or two, but the woman who owned it and ran the children's home was a private person. The Helmes all were, from what I heard. Doris Helme had a couple who worked there, and they did the grocery runs and whatnot. Doris only came into town once or twice a year."

"When did the girls' home shut down?"

"Sometime in the 70s. Doris Helme had developed some health things. There were rumors too."

"Rumors?"

"Well, rumor had it a girl or two had died up there. The deaths were hard on Doris and she finally just closed the place down."

# 18

"Children died at the house?" Rowan asked, tightening her grip on Quinn's stroller.

"A few in pretty quick succession, but I can't give you any more details than that. As I said, Doris Helme was a private woman and we didn't have the kinds of news responses we get nowadays when a little one passes on."

"Where could I find out more about the children's home and about Doris?"

The woman frowned and walked over to an enormous book. She flipped pages until she found a single page devoted to Helme House.

Rowan looked at the image. A tall, broad woman with a hawk nose and frizzy brown hair stood behind four girls, each wearing dark smocks. Off to one side stood a more diminutive woman with pale hair. She was not looking directly at the picture but down at an angle, as if smiling at one of the girls.

Karen tapped the face of the smaller woman. "This is Wilma Kaminski, part of the Polish community over in Cedar. She worked at Helme House throughout the years. She's in her eighties, husband is too, but they're still around and spry to boot. I couldn't give you a phone number or address, but head over to Cedar and ask around and someone can point you to them."

～

The polyurethane fumes still lingered in the house when Rowan and Quinn returned, despite Garrett opening all the windows on the ground level. They found Garrett on the back porch grilling cheeseburgers.

"Hey there, hot mama!" he exclaimed, dropping his spatula and wrapping both Rowan and Quinn in a bear hug. "How are my two favorite girls?"

"Tired," Rowan admitted. "I've forgotten how exhausting a day out and about is."

"Especially when you're toting this porkchop." He took Quinn from Rowan's arms and Rowan sagged into a chair, pulling up a pant leg to examine her ankle. It throbbed dully. "Aching today?"

"A bit. I might go in and take something for the pain."

"Let me." He set Quinn down. "Follow me, polliwog," he told her. Quinn toddled after Garrett into the kitchen.

He returned a moment later with two ibuprofen and a glass of water. Rowan threw the pills to the back of her mouth and swallowed.

"What did you guys get up to today?" Garrett asked, returning to the burgers as Quinn made her way off the porch steps into the grass.

Rowan followed her, but Garrett held up a hand. "She's okay, babe. If she wanders, I'll get her. She's not moving that fast yet."

Rowan watched Quinn take a few steps into the yard and then plop on her butt, pulling at the grass. "We went to a park and Quinn got to swing." Rowan thought of her story, plucking the bits of the truth from the larger lie. "And we visited the historical museum in Empire. I bought a few books and maps."

"Cool. I'm happy you made it in there."

The following day, the swelling in Rowan's ankle had disappeared, thanks to Garrett the night before elevating her leg on a pillow and arranging it with ice packs.

Garrett sat at the kitchen table, making notes on a sheet of notebook paper. Quinn watched him from her high chair, munching on Cheerios.

"Party time tomorrow, polliwog," Garrett told Quinn, catching her hippo as she flung it off her high chair. She giggled and reached for it.

"Speaking of the party," Rowan said, filling a mug with coffee, "I wanted to run into town and grab a few things, last-minute supplies. Do you mind? I know you said you were working on the bathroom today, but I thought—"

"No, sure, of course. Go. I'm happy you're... excited."

He'd been about to say something else—*taking part, showing some interest in our child's first birthday*—but he'd switched directions and Rowan had no intention of calling him on it. She didn't want to argue. She wanted an excuse to look into the history of Helme House.

"And you don't mind if Quinn stays here?"

"Of course, I don't mind," he said, sticking his tongue out at Quinn, who laughed and crashed her palm into her Cheerios. "Demolition is the name of the day, and Quinn's got that down pat."

Rowan drove into Cedar, a town fifteen miles east of Helme House. As Karen from the historical museum had mentioned, the moment Rowan asked around a Cedar gas station about Wilma Kaminski, two separate people piped in with how to find her home address.

Rowan drove out of town following Bellinger Road until she spotted a purple farmhouse with white trim and shutters. 'The color of wisteria,' the woman working the cash register at the gas station had called it. The man who'd offered a description had said, 'Look out for the rooster mailbox,' and sure enough, at the end of the gravel driveway, stood a large wooden rooster mailbox.

As Rowan turned into the driveway, an elderly man working in the garden at the side of the house glanced up, squinting at her from beneath a wide-brimmed straw hat.

Rowan stepped from her car, inhaling the heady scent of lilacs growing in heaps along the side of the house. She started toward the man in the garden. "Hi. I'm looking for Wilma Kaminski?"

"Basil Kaminski at your service," the man told her, straightening up and wincing as he limped toward Rowan, hand outstretched. "Wilma's my wife."

"I'm Rowan Cortes," she explained. "I hope you don't mind my just dropping in."

"Goodness, no. This here is one big family." He gestured at the rolling farmland around him. "My brother Ernest lives just up the hill there. My daughter and her family yonder down that valley. We've got siblings and children and cousins as far as the eye can see. A day without a drop-in would be a strange day indeed."

Rowan smiled. The man had dark blue eyes that looked young despite his weathered face.

"Wilma's having her morning nap. The arthritis has been blazing like a forest fire in her hands and feet as of late. Doc keeps giving her pills but she'll be darned if she's gonna take them." He chuckled and hobbled toward the pea-green farmhouse behind him. The trim on the house was white, and though the house looked old, the paint looked recent. A covered porch jutted from the front of the home, and Basil waved a hand at Rowan to follow.

"We can find a spot of shade up here," he told her, pausing with his hand on the back of a wicker chair. "Can I get you a drink? Lemonade?"

"No, I'm fine. Thank you."

Basil nodded and settled into a chair, sighing and smiling as he leaned his head back.

"I came here to ask Wilma a few questions about Helme House, if that would be all right."

The man opened his eyes and gazed at her sidelong. "Helme House, eh? That name has come back into fashion these last years."

"Do you know much about the house or about Wilma's time there?"

"Oh, sure I do. I was the groundsman, after all, and the grocery man, and the painter, and the mender of the girls' shoes."

"You worked there as well?"

"I surely did."

"Are you aware that a woman went missing—"

"Amy. Bright as spun gold, that wee girl. Just broke my and Wilma's hearts when we heard the news."

"You knew her?"

"Oh, sure. We had Amy over for dinner three, four times at least."

"Really? Wow, okay. How did that come about?"

Basil smiled and sat forward in his chair. "Seems it came about much like this conversation we're having right now. Amy showed up here one day and wanted to talk to Wilma about Helme House."

"Did she say why?"

"Sure, sure. She wanted to get the history of the place. She had high hopes of turning that old house into an inn of some kind, a B&B, they call 'em, I guess. We told her about the house and then invited her to stay for pieczeń z mięsa mielonego. Wilma's is the best in Cedar, though Cornelia Jankowski would have you believe otherwise."

"What is piezen—"

"Meatloaf," he interrupted her, smiling. "Polish meatloaf." He smacked his lips. "Makes me hungry just thinking of it."

"Were you surprised when Amy disappeared?"

Basil bobbed his head. "We surely were. The girl was making plans. Who runs off when they're making plans? Wilma called her sister up and they spoke a bit, but wasn't much we could do other than get the word out. We organized a fundraiser here in Cedar with a Polish food sampler. That added a bit of money to the reward and brought a few reporters about, but…" He spread out his empty palms. "Not much came of it. How come you're asking about Helme House, Miss Cortes?"

"I'm staying there for the summer. My husband is doing some renovations for the new owner."

Basil nodded. "And is the new owner thinking about a bed-and-breakfast too?"

Rowan shook her head. "Honestly, I think he intends to flip it."

"Come again?"

"Fix it up and sell it for more than he bought it for."

"Ah, yes, okay."

"I'm a reporter, and when I learned about Amy's disappearance, I thought I'd dig deeper. That's when I heard the house was once a children's home. That piqued my interest."

"And you're imagining the girls' house is related to Amy in some way?"

"Not necessarily. I just like to have all the facts."

"Okay, sure. I'll fill in what I can. Let's see. Luther and Cora Helme originally built Helme House in 1910. They intended for many children, hence the grand estate, but Cora lost most of those babies midway through the pregnancy and had a son who was stillborn. It took a toll on her. She gave birth to Doris, their only living child, in 1927. Poor Cora had grown sicklier with each lost child, and by the time Doris arrived, she'd nearly wasted away to bones. She passed a year after Doris was born. Then it was Doris and Luther up in that house for a lot of years.

"Doris was a spinster, as they said in those days, unmarried, in her middle twenties, and I believe Luther Helme was looking for… a way to legitimize her, perhaps. They converted Helme House to a home for girls in 1952. Luther had developed an illness and he moved south. That was the remedy in those days. Warm weather and sun. Turned out to be cancer, and he passed on in 1955. Doris ran the girls' home until 1975 when she closed it down."

"And you and Wilma worked there the entire time it was open?"

"We sure did."

"I found a cemetery. Is that related?"

Basil nodded. "The property all along there was a part of the estate, but in the 70s the state took control, eminent domain and whatnot. Doris didn't fight it except for the girls' home, which they allowed the family to keep."

"Several of the children died quite young."

"Children died young more often in those days, though a few strange occurrences happened in that last year, another reason that Doris closed down, I'm sure."

"Strange, how?"

"The last year, 1975, was a bad one for Helme House. Almost seemed that a curse had befallen that place. Not into superstitions myself, but my wife sure was. Wilma wanted to leave, afraid that black shadow might follow us home, but she stayed on for the sake of the children."

"A curse?"

"We lost three girls in 1975. In the past girls had died. A bad flu, tuberculosis, pneumonia took the children, but usually only the sickly ones. The first girl to die that final year was Winifred Hamilton. Winnie, we called her. You never met a more robust girl, swarthy, big-boned, but a healthy gal. She climbed trees and played sports like the boys. She'd hoof it over three miles to get to Camp Kohana and Leelanau—that was a kids' camp—and she'd be right there with the boys, rough-and-tumble style. Rose-cheeked, bright eyes. There was nothing sickly about that girl."

"What happened to her?"

"Got hung from a tree."

"She was hanged?"

Basil gnawed at his cheek, his eyes troubled. "Not on purpose, we figured. The girls had a treehouse out in the woods, old rickety thing with the pulley bucket for raising and lowering stuff. Somehow, she got tangled in it, the rope got wrapped around her neck. Robin found her. She and Robin weren't close, they butted heads a bit, but… it disturbed her just the same."

"Robin was another girl who lived in the home?"

The screen door creaked open and a woman hobbled out, bracing one gnarled hand on the frame. "I thought I heard voices out here," she said.

Like Basil, the woman appeared to be in her eighties with a shock of white hair loose and frizzy on her shoulders. She wore an overlarge t-shirt that read 'Kaminski Clan Reunion 2008' over the slogan 'Proud to be a leaf on the Kaminski family tree.'

Basil stood and offered his wife an arm. "This here is Rowan Cortes, a journalist interested in Amy Prahm and Helme House." He led Wilma to an empty chair and helped her sit down.

Wilma turned to Rowan. Brown eyes peered out from her rutted face. "Amy was a dear, sweet as pudding."

"Basil mentioned that Amy was curious about the history of Helme House and I have to tell you, after talking to him, I'm pretty curious about it too."

Wilma looked beyond Rowan to where Basil had returned to his seat. Her mouth turned down. "I don't feel real good about sharing those stories with Amy on account of her disappearing just weeks after."

Basil tisked. "Wilma Kaminski, us telling those stories, which are nothing but the truth, is not the reason that girl went missing."

"And how do you know that, Basil Filip Kaminski? Hmmm?"

"Oh, now, Wilma, don't go getting yourself worked into a tizzy. I'm just saying—"

"You're just saying God and the Devil haven't got a hand in the affairs of us common folks. Well, I have a different view, sir, and stories… well, they've got a power all their own."

Basil sighed. "Can I get you a lemonade, dear?" he asked Wilma.

"I would love a cup of decaf coffee, please."

Basil stood and walked past her and disappeared into the house.

"You think telling Amy the stories of Helme House somehow led to her disappearance?"

Wilma massaged her bony knuckles, grimacing as if they were painful to the touch. "Basil thinks it's all nonsense. He reckons Doris and I both got caught up in the paranoia back then. Started believing something supernatural was at work."

# 19

---

"Did you believe that?" Rowan asked.

"Looking back now… yes, I think I did."

"I understand your reluctance to share, Wilma, but I'd like to look into what happened. Maybe I can even find out what happened to Robin or get the police interested."

Wilma gazed uneasily at the long stretch of country road. Across the street rows of ankle-height green leafy plants lazed in the still day.

"Corn," she said, gesturing. "A month from now you won't be able to see the opposite side of that field. Robin loved to run through the cornfields. Basil and I took her a handful of times. We'd bring the girls back to the farm, one or two at a time, teach 'em about planting.

"Robin was a sprite. To Doris she was more like a rascal." Wilma chuckled, and then her smile turned down. "When she vanished… well, that was the beginning of the end."

"Did she run away?"

"That's what the police decided, though they barely batted an eye at the situation. A few of the rich folks with houses in the area had filed complaints about Robin. She was a wanderer, didn't give a second thought to dragging a canoe she found on a beach out into the lake for a row. Nothing menacing, you see, but some of the folks called her a nuisance. They gave Doris a stern talking to a few times. But then one day Robin never came home.

"She was often in the woods and in the lake. Sunup to sundown. In those days, that's just the way it was. Piper was her best friend, but she'd been sick with influenza, locked up in the sick room, shades all drawn. I can still smell the camphor and menthol."

"You saw Robin the morning she went missing?"

"Sure did. Made her a breakfast of oatmeal and honey. We'd had five girls at the start of that year. Winnie and Robin were both twelve, Piper was ten, Delilah was six and then there was a wee little thing, Bonnie, just two.

"We lost Winnie in the spring of 1975. Then Robin went missing in June. The last was Piper in August. She never came home. We thought… well, we thought all sorts of things. That whatever had gotten Robin got a hold of Piper—maybe a wolf or a cougar. There'd be sightings of such creatures in the woods now and then.

"After Robin vanished a rumor started amongst the girls about a monster in the woods. Started by some of the kids at the Leelanau camp, I'm sure. Now if Robin had still been around, I would have put the start of that rumor in her own mouth, but seeing as she was the one who'd gone missing…

"We were just sick over Piper. Basil surmised there might be a kidnapper in the area, but… then we found Piper. Or somebody found her anyhow. She washed up on the beach about five miles down the coast from Helme House."

"She drowned?"

Wilma nodded, eyes welling. Her shoulders sagged forward. "That did it. For Doris, for me and Basil. None of us had the heart to keep on after that. A family adopted Bonnie that September. Only Delilah remained, and we took her with us. Had some friends here in Cedar who'd wanted a child and couldn't conceive. They took in Delilah."

"Where is Delilah now?"

"She lives here in Cedar with her hubby. She has four kids, but two are grown and off to college, two still at home, but they'll be graduating from high school in the next few years."

"And the police never investigated the deaths? Or the disappearance of Robin?"

"Not that I saw. It was another time, simple as that. And these were unwanted girls. I hate to describe them as such, but it's the way it was."

"Did anyone keep tabs on them? Birth families or prior social workers?"

"The best record you'll find on these girls is people. Though you're talking about girls in the system nearly forty years ago. Some of the folks who knew them will be dead. The ones still living might not remember these girls at all."

"Basil mentioned it seemed as if Helme House was cursed."

Wilma shifted in her chair, stood and shuffled toward a wicker hutch. She opened it and took out a cushion. "Would you like one, dear? Those wooden chairs feel like a cement block after too long sitting."

"No, thank you. I'm fine."

Wilma dropped the cushion on the chair and sank slowly back into it. "Cursed. That's how we felt, Doris and I both. Doris was so worried she had an exorcism performed."

"An exorcism?" Rowan's heart thumped faster in her chest.

Wilma nodded. "She was a superstitious woman. After Winnie died and Basil carried her broken body into the house, we were so busy we forgot to cover the mirrors. Doris worried about that for days. And then when Robin disappeared and then Piper died, well… she near lost her mind. She contacted a Catholic church and they sent out a priest to perform an exorcism."

"Why was she concerned about mirrors not being covered after Winnie died?"

"Doris, and many folks in my own family, believed that souls in transition get confused by mirrors. They can become trapped inside and not move on. Doris's father was adamant about this. Most of their life, Doris's father insisted on mirrors staying covered and windows staying open to keep the spirits out. The girls loved mirrors, so Doris had taken to leaving them uncovered all the time."

"Did Doris believe Winnie's spirit had been trapped then? And she was haunting the house?"

"I can't speak to what she thought, but the house was different after Winnie died. It was darker, more glum, quieter. The girls used to laugh and sing. There were always sounds in the house, cheerful sounds, sometimes the girls fighting, but never quiet. After Winnie died, the sounds died too. Robin and Piper would leave at sunup and not come home until sundown. Piper once told me walking into the house seemed like falling into a black hole. I understood her, too. It felt… dark, sad."

"What happened to Doris Helme?"

"She lived on in Helme House for years and years, and then she suffered a stroke and moved into an assisted home. A couple years back they moved her into a new home, Cordia in Traverse City. It's a nice facility, used to be an old mental hospital—the Northern Michigan Asylum. Seemed odd they'd want to turn some of that place into an old folks' home, but I like to see things recycled rather than torn down and replaced by strip malls, so there's that."

It was afternoon when Rowan started back to the house. She turned her blinker on to turn into the long driveway, then realized she'd bought no party supplies.

"Shit," she sputtered, shifting her foot from brake to gas and passing the driveway. She continued up the peninsula until she came to an over-look, pulled in and turned around. She spotted a familiar figure at the edge of the hill that overlooked Lake Michigan.

Rowan left her car running and climbed out, unsure what compelled her to say anything at all. He hadn't looked back at her. She could have easily turned around and driven back toward town.

As she walked across the grass toward him, Eddie turned, expression blank. After a moment of staring at her, he smiled. "Rowan of the forest," he said. "How are you?"

"I'm good. Sorry to interrupt your painting."

He returned his gaze to the view. "Not an interruption. If I wanted solitude, I wouldn't paint at a tourist overlook."

"Makes sense." She looked over his shoulder at the painting. "That's great. I love all the colors of the trees and water. You really captured it."

"Thanks. I could paint these landscapes with my eyes closed. I've been looking at them for so long. I'm not sure why I even come out here anymore."

"Because it's peaceful." Rowan sighed, almost sitting on the wooden bench beside him and then realizing why she'd turned in to begin with.

"That's because it's empty. Introduce people and you introduce chaos."

"Especially if the people include a soon-to-be toddler. Which I need to get back to. Nice to see you, Eddie."

"You too. Listen, why don't you stop by this weekend, pick up those books, check out the paintings? Offer still stands."

"Oh." Rowan lifted a hand to her neck. Warmth climbed into her neck. She wasn't flirting with this man, wasn't setting up some secret rendezvous, and yet she felt criminal just the same. "Maybe. We're celebrating my daughter's first birthday this weekend, so I'll see. Thanks again."

Rowan returned to her car and drove back into Empire and hurried into a gift shop. She filled a plastic basket with beach toys and children's books.

After she'd paid and started toward the door, she paused. A plush kangaroo sat on a beach chair, pink sunglasses propped on his caramel muzzle. Rowan touched his hard plastic nose and a surge of tears raged up through her and spilled onto her cheeks.

"Roo," she murmured. It had been the first toy her father Morgan had ever given to her. He'd been holding it that first day when he and Emily arrived at her foster home to pick her up, to take her to what turned out to be her forever home.

Rowan grasped the kangaroo and returned to the counter. She wanted this kangaroo for Quinn because someday when she had it all together again, she would tell Quinn that story about her father and the kangaroo that Rowan had slept with for more than five years.

As Rowan wound up the long driveway to Helme House, her cell rang. Her cousin Dan's name appeared on the phone.

"Hey, Dan," she said.

"I got in touch with an investigator at the Leelanau Sheriff's Department about the woman who disappeared from the house," Dan told her. "Have a sec to talk?"

"Yeah, definitely. Hold on, let me park." She stopped the car outside the garage, but left the engine running. "Go for it."

"Well, the initial theory was an accident. There was no sign of forced entry, nothing had been stolen. They speculated that the woman, Amy Prahm, fell and hit her head. Maybe she touched the wound with her hand, which led to the smears in the bedroom, stairs and kitchen. The problem was they couldn't find the location of a fall, any obvious smear of blood on the floor or pool of blood."

"Okay, so they ruled out an accident?"

"No, not entirely. It just became less likely when they realized her purse was gone and her cell phone. They wondered if she'd had an accident and called for help. Someone came to get her and then…"

"Never brought her home? Took her? Killed her?"

"Yeah, possibly."

"But then they shied away from that. Why?"

"This is where the case gets strange. A detective found several books in the house. One in particular was of interest to them. It was a true crime story about a woman who'd vanished from her home, but left a trail of blood behind. The theory that she'd staged it emerged in that case as well. The woman was never found."

"A lot of people read true crime. Why would the police lean so heavily on that assumption over a book?"

"Because a reporter printed a piece based on the theory. He did some of his own digging and claimed family history supported the theory."

Rowan sighed. "Duncan Leach?"

"Yeah. And just so we're clear, this is off the record, Row. If the sheriff's office got wind that I was feeding information to a journalist, I'd be shut out by them and likely my own department."

"I'd never betray your confidence, Dan."

"I know, but I still needed to say it."

"What was the detective's sense of the case? His hunch?"

"Nothing solid. He said initially he was sure it was foul play—she let somebody in, a struggle occurred, and he dragged her out. But the blood pattern didn't support the story. They found blood in a nursery upstairs, the master bedroom, on the stairs, in the kitchen and on those back doors. What also struck him as odd is that those doors aren't close to the driveway. Why would a perp take her out that way when it's further from his vehicle?"

"Because it's more concealed," Rowan offered.

"Sure, but that place is already isolated. He could have murdered her in the front yard and there likely wouldn't have been witnesses. The blood smears looked like someone had been injured and started staggering around, leaving traces. The books put the nail in the coffin. They became convinced she staged the whole thing, especially once they got the background on her life. Wronged by her ex-fiancé, no money or prospects and all that.

"There were sightings, too. Two separate people claimed to have seen a woman matching Amy's description the day she disappeared.

One saw her walking along M-22 north, the other claimed she was in the town of Empire sitting near a bus stop. Neither sighting was confirmed."

"Did the detective mention anything else about Helme House? Other unusual things that had happened there?"

"No. Why?"

"Well, I met some people today, people who used to work at the house when it was a home for girls, an orphanage-type place. They claimed the last year they worked there, two children died and one disappeared, all mysteriously. A little girl drowned in the lake, another one hanged herself from a treehouse rope and then a third left one morning to play in the woods and never came back."

"Those are pretty bizarre occurrences all in one year."

"Exactly."

"None of them were ruled homicides?"

"I don't know that autopsies were even done. These were girls without families living in a home for unwanted kids. Not to mention it was 1975."

"You're thinking those deaths are related to Amy's disappearance? That's a stretch."

"I know. But doesn't that seem strange? Two people have disappeared from this house and never been found?" She gazed at the side of the house, the steep roof arching toward the clear blue sky.

"In a sense it does, but when you put it in the context of the house being a children's home, the likelihood of a runaway goes up exponentially. In the time it operated, there might have been multiple children who seemingly vanished when really they hitched a ride out of town."

"Amy was looking into the history of the house. Right before she vanished, she was digging into all that."

Dan said nothing.

"Is there any chance you could ask around about the deaths? See if there's anything from a criminal standpoint associated with those deaths?"

"I can, yeah, but like you said, if there weren't autopsies there may be no information. Your best bet might be to hunt down the funeral director who would have seen the bodies. I'd also look into the girl who disappeared. There's a good chance you'll find out she's alive and well living somewhere else."

"Yeah, okay. I hope so. Thanks again, Dan."

"You're welcome, and hey, I'm sorry I can't make it to Quinn's birthday party. I'm working this weekend. But when you guys come back to Gaylord, I'll take her out for ice cream."

"She'll like that. Bye, Dan."

# 20

Rowan walked into Helme House and found Garrett on the couch watching a movie on the old television in the living room.

"Look at this monster," he said, beaming. "It actually works. There's a VCR connected to it and I found a box with about two hundred VHS tapes."

Rowan looked at the ancient television nestled in its wood console. A scene on the screen depicted Harrison Ford in his signature fedora and brown leather coat playing Indiana Jones.

"*Temple of Doom*," Garrett told her, holding out a hand.

Rowan took it and sat next to him, sitting her bags on the floor at their feet. She looked at her watch. "I'm not sure I've ever seen you watching a movie in the middle of the day."

He grinned. "It's my reward for getting the last of the tile off the bathroom floor with Quinn in tow."

"Where is Quinnie?" she asked.

"Tuckered out. I put her in the crib upstairs." He pointed to the video baby monitor where Rowan could see Quinn sound asleep, butt high in the air.

"Did you have a good morning?" he asked.

"Yeah, I drove into Traverse City and checked out some kid stores, took a walk along the water. It was nice."

"What'd you get?" He leaned over and peered into the bags. Garrett eyed the contents. "Aww, he's cute," he said, running a hand over the tail of the kangaroo.

"I had one like him when I was little. I wanted Quinn to have one too."

"She'll love it," he said, leaning over to kiss Rowan's cheek. He frowned and touched her. "You feel warm. Not coming down with something, I hope."

Rowan touched her own cheek. It felt warm, but her entire body felt warm in part because she'd just lied to her husband for what seemed like the zillionth time. "I am tired. Maybe I'll go lie down."

Garrett kissed her again, this time catching the corner of her mouth as she'd started to turn away. "Hey," he said, pulling her closer and hugging her. "I love you, Rowan."

"I love you too."

Rowan walked to the second floor and stood over Quinn, staring at her sleeping girl. Satisfied all was well, she stripped off her clothes and slid into a worn t-shirt. She crawled into bed, pulled the sheet up over her legs and closed her eyes.

Rowan woke hot and disoriented. The sheet stuck to her naked legs. Her t-shirt had twisted sideways and tugged on her neck. Her panic rose until she'd righted her shirt and ended the sense of being strangled.

Sitting up, the dream shriveling back into her subconscious, Rowan looked toward Quinn's crib expecting to see the form of her sleeping baby. She couldn't see her daughter, and she bolted to her feet and took two long strides to the crib.

Quinn's tangled pink blanket met her eyes. Rowan's hand flew to her throat. She spun around and searched the blankets of her own bed, terrified to find Quinn face down on the mattress or tangled up as she had been in the sheet, face blue, eyes staring sightlessly. No Quinn.

She stepped into the hallway, felt the wood floor cool beneath her feet and almost turned for the stairs, but her eyes caught on the closed door at the end of the hall at the same moment she heard the hushed buzzing.

They rarely closed any of the doors in the upstairs hallway, but that door was shut tight.

Rowan blinked at the door, head swimming as she tried to

remember what she'd been doing before lying down. Had she rested Quinn in the playpen in that room?

Heavily, she moved toward the door. The buzzing grew louder, and she recoiled at the tiny writhing bodies of the flies crowded along the edges of the door, flooding from the crack beneath, but not flying away, not filling the hall. They clung to the wood as if desperate to get out and back in at the same time.

Rowan grimaced and clutched the doorknob. The iron knob was cold and clammy to the touch and she wanted to jerk her hand back, but gripped it harder and turned. The knob didn't twist. Someone had locked it from the inside.

"Quinn?" she whispered, and the sound seemed to alert the flies to her presence. They scattered from the door, landing on her sweaty face and neck, getting caught in her hair. One flew into her mouth and she choked, spitting it onto the ground. Rowan yanked her t-shirt over her mouth.

"Quinn!" she screamed, slamming her shoulder against the door, yanking the knob from side to side.

A fly lodged in the corner of her eye. She tried to blink it away, but it seemed to burrow deeper. She released the knob and swiped at her face, flicking the fly out.

Crying, Rowan turned and fled down the stairs onto the back porch where Garrett's ax rested against a porch railing.

She grabbed the ax, ran back up the stairs and slammed it into the door. The wood splintered and the ax dug in, sticking in the wood. She tried to jerk it back out, but couldn't, it was in too deep.

Down the hall, her phone shrilled again. Why hadn't she changed that ringtone? It rang in her head, making her head and blood pound in tune.

The phone sat on the bedside table and she snatched it up. An image was on the screen, a picture Garrett had sent moments ago. It showed him and Quinn at the park they'd driven by days earlier. Quinn grinned from a baby swing, eyes huge and sparkling.

Rowan's hand shook as she clicked on the message that accompanied the photograph.

*Just finished up playing at the park. Stopping for pizza, unless you prefer something else? Subs, maybe. Let me know. Home soon.*

Sweat and tears streamed down Rowan's face. Her breath came in ragged gusts and the phone was slippery in her hand. She nearly dropped it, but tightened her grip, searching her foggy thoughts for a suitable response.

*Either is great. Love you,* she typed and hit send.

The thought of eating made Rowan want to gag.

The flies. The ax.

On stiff legs, she moved back into the hallway and toward the closed door.

The flies had disappeared, but the ax remained embedded in the wood. Trembling, she reached for the knob. It no longer felt icy as she turned it. It shouldn't have turned. It should have stuck in place, locked, as it had been minutes before, but now it swiveled to the right and the door swung in revealing the empty room. No Quinn trapped inside. No hordes of flies scrambling to get out.

As she stood in the room, she imagined Garrett's face if he saw that ax sticking from the door. He'd be terrified, maybe angry, but she didn't think so. Not angry. No, he'd look at Rowan with fear-filled eyes.

She had to get the ax out. She'd create a story, she was good at that, but no story could include that ax. Nothing could justify that ax hanging from the door.

Gritting her teeth, Rowan grabbed the handle and pulled. It didn't budge, and she leaned far back, jerking from side to side. Finally, it pulled loose, and she fell back, nearly smacking her head on the opposite wall. Hurrying, she took the ax back outside and propped it where it had been, moving it twice to ensure it leaned exactly as it had before she'd picked it up.

Back in the upstairs hallway, she gazed at the door and tried to find the story that would explain the gash.

What if she said nothing?

She reached into the hole and pulled the caved wood out. Some of it held, though pieces had splintered away. Most of Garrett's work was on the ground floor. He might not even notice the door, especially if she propped it open and...

Rowan ran into a guest bedroom and dug a comforter out of the closet. She returned to the door and threw the blanket over it.

"Oh, I washed some blankets," she mumbled to herself. "This one didn't come dry."

It was a reasonable story, just fine, unless he pulled the blanket off. At some point he would. At some point, the hole in the door would be revealed and then what?

She didn't know, but the blanket would buy her time. The fog in her mind hadn't lifted. She couldn't come up with a better story at that moment.

Rowan returned to the master bedroom, stripped off her wet t-shirt and underwear and stuffed them beneath other clothes in the laundry basket. She carried a clean pair of blue terrycloth shorts, underwear, and a white t-shirt to the bathroom and turned the shower on. Icy water sluiced down her feverish body, and she cringed, refusing to turn the knob toward hot. The cold water blasted away some of the lingering stupor.

They ate on the back porch, Garrett talking excitedly about Quinn's upcoming birthday party and Rowan doing her damnedest to act normal.

She didn't tell Garrett about the flies or the ax. The omission felt like a lie, but it wasn't, not really. What spouse told the other every mundane detail of their day? Every glass of water drunk. Every phone call made.

*But this isn't mundane.*

She ignored the thought as she returned to the kitchen to put their leftover subs in the refrigerator. She sang along to the song playing on the radio. "I'm free, free falling."

Tom Petty's *Free Falling*. It was a song she used to sing to, sometimes loudly, as she cut vegetables for dinner or mopped the floor.

Rowan hummed it now, barely forming the words, trying unsuccessfully to calm the jitters that reached up every time she got too quiet. Mostly she hummed it to hide the truth from Garrett. Same old Rowan singing along to one of her favorite songs—nothing to see here.

## 21

The morning of Quinn's birthday dawned with a sunlit sky and clouds as frothy as marshmallow fluff. It was the kind of day that made every little problem seem all right, except for Rowan, who'd woken to the gorgeous day filled with dread.

The thought of greeting their guests, all family and close friends, had Rowan's guts twisted into braids. The awareness that she should have been rejoicing only amplified her anxiety. Instead, she drank her coffee as Garrett danced around the house singing happy birthday to Quinn and taping decorations to every bare surface.

Rowan searched through the canvas bags tucked in the master bedroom closet. She'd bought the wrapping paper and bow months earlier when she'd seen them at a children's boutique in Gaylord, but now she couldn't find them anywhere.

"I know I packed them," she murmured, casting aside a bag filled with an array of shoes she hadn't worn from beach sandals to high heels. Another bag contained paperback books and magazines she'd envisioned herself reading while she and Quinn sat on the beach. They'd done little playing at the beach and the realization of the previous days, the day before especially, rose ugly and looming in her mind.

Their summer together had turned into Quinn's summer with Garrett or getting lugged around behind Rowan as she hunted for the last moments of a woman who'd likely packed her bags and fled to

California just like the police thought. Rowan tossed another bag, this one empty except for three more of Garrett's bandanas, aside and pounded one fist on the floor.

"Goddamn it," she swore, tensing at the tears trying to crawl up and take hold. She would not cry, would not break down, would not think of all the ways she was failing as a mother and a wife, as a human being.

"Row?"

She stiffened at Garrett's voice, swiping at her face before turning around. "Hey, what's up?" she asked, falsely chipper.

"What's wrong, babe?" He stepped into the room, concern crinkling his face.

"I'm just..." Her voice cracked, and she paused, catching her breath. "I bought all that pretty wrapping paper for Quinn months ago and I can't find it anywhere."

"I put it in the living room yesterday. I knew you'd need it so I took it downstairs."

She pursed her lips, fresh tears threatening. "Oh, okay. Guess I should have thought of that before I raided the closet."

He walked in and offered his hand. She took it and stood and he pulled her close, rubbing her back. "What can I do, Rowan? How can I help?"

The tears rushed out and shook her head against his shoulder. "I'm okay," she murmured. "I am. I swear I am."

"Let's sit down after the party or in the morning, okay? And make a plan. I know you're strong, honey. You are. You always have been, but this year threw you some curve balls and I think..."

"I need a bigger bat?" she whispered.

He laughed and released her, looking into her face. "Maybe a better umpire."

"That's the guy who calls the plays?"

He grinned. "I'm getting lost in my own metaphor. Someone who could offer guidance. That's what I meant." He kissed the tip of her nose. "Better get the presents wrapped. The Cortes crew will roll in any time and once they're here, all hell will break loose."

She nodded and followed him from the room.

Rowan wrapped Quinn's gifts while Garrett distracted her in the kitchen. The paper was yellow and dotted with pink and silver hippos. Rowan ran her fingers over one shimmering silver hippo and smiled.

She secured pink satin ribbons around the presents and then arranged large white and pink taffeta bows on each. Rowan tucked the gifts into a hallway closet.

"Wow." She laughed when she stepped into the kitchen. Garrett had strung yellow, red and blue streamers in loops from the corners of the ceiling. Quinn sat on the floor playing with a spool of red streamers. "What do you think, birthday girl? I'd say Daddy outdid himself."

"Wait till you see the back porch." Garrett pointed to the glass doors.

Quinn dropped the streamers and struggled up to her feet, waddling to Rowan and holding up her arms to be held. "Mmmaaa," she said.

Rowan picked her up and walked onto the back porch.

A huge banner that stated 'Quinn's First Fiesta' hung down from the long folding table draped in a bright red tablecloth. A colorful kids' sombrero read 'Uno' in pink letters. Bright red, blue, and yellow balloons streamed from the railings around the porch.

Quinn reached for a balloon and Rowan walked closer so she could bat at the colorful orbs.

Rowan showered and put on a long-sleeved silk blouse. It was light enough that she could wear it despite the heat, and she wanted to be covered—an added layer between herself and the guests soon to arrive. She loved Garrett's family, envied their loudness, their closeness, but also struggled to comfortably merge into the boisterous cocoon. Now more than ever she feared they would sense that she was not one of them. She pulled on heather-gray linen pants and added silver hoop earrings that used to disappear softly into her hair and now stood out, big and shining beneath her short blonde strands.

"Look at what you get to wear, Quinnie," she told her baby daughter, who'd been watching her from her playpen. Rowan held up a full-skirted white dress decorated with enormous red flowers. It had been a gift from Garrett's mother and the instant she'd opened it, Rowan had known Quinn would wear it on her first birthday. Wear it and ruin it most likely.

"My parents are here, babe!" Garrett called up the stairs.

Rowan finished zipping up Quinn's dress, not bothering with the white shoes she'd bought. She'd just kick them off, anyway.

She held her daughter on her lap for another moment, gazing into her curious eyes. "Happy birthday, my angel," she whispered, kissing Quinn on the top of her head.

Quinn grabbed hold of one of Rowan's earrings, but Rowan pulled her hand away before she could yank.

~

"Hola, cariño. How are you?" Antonio, Garrett's dad, asked Rowan when she stepped outside with Quinn. He wrapped an arm around her and squeezed, leaning down to kiss Quinn's head. "And how are you, cumpleañera? Uno today!"

Rowan smiled and pulled at the collar of her blouse. "We're good. How are you, Antonio?"

He smiled, releasing her, and watched Yolanda speaking quietly with Garrett by her car. Rowan wondered fleetingly if they were talking about her.

"I am well. Though I miss you and Garrett and my little princesa. Uno! Goodness, how the time does fly. It was only yesterday that our last baby was toddling across the floor, rattle in his hand. And now he is a man with a wife and a child of his own." Tears came to Antonio's eyes.

Rowan squeezed his shoulder. "It goes fast," she murmured, feeling the tightening in her chest, the quickness of her breath. It happened when she thought of Quinn growing up, outgrowing her in much the same way she'd outgrown her onesies and footie pajamas.

"Dad!" Garrett announced, grabbing his dad in a full hug and patting his back. "Are you crying already?" He laughed.

Antonio nodded, eyes sparkling. "It is a day for joyful tears, mi hijo."

"Oh, let me see that beautiful girl!" Yolanda said, reaching for Quinn. "The dress fits her perfectly, so bella." Yolanda kissed Quinn's nose and cheeks as Quinn giggled and grabbed at Yolanda's long gray-black hair. "Do not pull out your yaya's hair, nieta. I've got so little left."

"You look lovely, Yolanda, such a great dress," Rowan told her.

Yolanda looked down at her long turquoise and pink dress. "The girl at Kohl's called this a maxi dress. Twelve dollars! Can you believe that? Here, feel, it's so soft."

Rowan touched the satiny fabric. "It's nice," she agreed.

"How are you holding up, honey?" Yolanda asked, her gaze turning serious as she stared at Rowan.

Rowan widened her smile, though her cheeks ached from the effort. "Pretty good. A bit drained. I've been having some trouble sleeping."

Yolanda's face creased with worry. "Have you been to see Doctor Ewing?"

"Not since our last well-child visit. We're due to see him in a few weeks. I'll let him know about the sleep then."

"Good girl." Yolanda squeezed her elbow. "And you cut off all your beautiful hair." She touched the short strands and Rowan tried not to cringe.

Over Yolanda's shoulder, Rowan saw the concerned expression on Antonio's face and knew Garrett had told his father about the gum in Rowan's hair. She hadn't expected him not to, but… it bothered her, anyway.

"Oh, boy, here comes Ava and her troop," Garrett said.

A black SUV parked behind Antonio's car and Garrett's older sister climbed out of the driver's seat. "Hey!" she yelled, waving.

Garrett and Antonio walked over to greet her. Garrett's aunt Rosa climbed from the passenger seat as kids flooded out of the back. Ava had eight-year-old twin boys, a four-year-old daughter, and Calvin, just six months old.

Ava unstrapped Calvin from his car seat. "Slow down," she yelled at her other three children, who'd sprinted through the yard toward the half-moon deck.

Antonio guided Rosa toward where Rowan stood on the front steps. "You remember my sister, Rosa?" Antonio's arm was wrapped around a short, slim woman who looked more like his mother than his sister.

Rosa, from what Garrett had told Rowan, had been born in Mexico to Antonio's father and young girlfriend before his family immigrated to California and later to Michigan. Garrett's grandfather had been unaware that the woman was pregnant and only learned of the child years later when the woman wrote him a letter and included a picture of Rosa. She was fifteen years older than Antonio, who was nearly sixty himself.

"Yes, I remember. How are you, Rosa?" Rowan took the woman's thin hands that clutched her own with surprising strength.

Rosa's eyes left Rowan's and slipped beyond her to the house. She frowned and pursed her lips, but said nothing as Yolanda grabbed her in a hug, crushing Quinn between them.

A moment later, a huge, lifted white pickup pulled up beside the line of cars and then drove into the yard. Garrett's brother Tyler jumped out. He opened the tailgate on his pickup to reveal two cases of beer, a huge piñata, and a jumble of presents.

"Row, check this beauty out," he called when he spotted her. He leapt onto the tailgate and held a huge rainbow-colored donkey piñata in the air. "I drove all the way to Detroit to get this thing."

Rowan gave him a thumbs up as Garrett bounded across the yard, much like his nephews and niece had done moments before.

"Yes!" he shouted. "That is awesome. Here, hand me the beer. I'll get it in the cooler."

Rowan sat on the back porch as a stream of guests arrived for Quinn's party. Rowan's mother and sister arrived next, carrying gift bags with images of *Sesame Street* characters on the side. Garrett's friend Alan appeared with his wife Leah. Another of Garrett's siblings, his sister Emily, appeared with her boyfriend Mark, stating they could only stay for a little while because Mark had a gig playing keyboard in Traverse City that evening.

Rowan watched Quinn get passed around, the oohs and ahhs as they admired her dress and peppered her with kisses. Rowan herself stayed tucked in her chair, making polite conversation when necessary, but feeling as if she were out of her body, watching the day unfold through a pane of colored glass.

She finished her wine and stood, slipped back into the house for a refill. As she poured, she watched the dark red, nearly purple, merlot swirl into the bottom of her glass.

"Are you okay, honey?" Rowan's sister asked, startling her.

Rowan jerked the bottle and spilled wine on the counter. Rowan wiped the crimson liquid with her sleeve, realizing too late what she was doing as the dark stain bled across her cream-colored material.

"Oh, darn it," Olivia said, grabbing a wad of paper towel and mopping at the stain on Rowan's shirt.

"It's fine," Rowan murmured. She moved to the sink and rinsed the sleeve.

Olivia leaned one hip against the counter and studied her. "You seem a little detached."

Rowan shrugged and took a sip of wine. "I'm tired."

"Is that all?"

"Mm-hm. How's Alex holding up?" Rowan changed the subject.

Rowan had seen her younger brother briefly at their father's funeral. He'd flown home from L.A., where he was struggling to make it as a screenwriter doing coffee runs for executives who barely registered his existence. Rowan and Alex had never been close. Rowan felt as if they competed for their father's attention, though Morgan had never been a man who withheld affection from any of his children. Still, he'd had a special relationship with Rowan and her siblings knew it.

Olivia had never seemed to care. She was closer to Emily. The mother and daughter had often taken solo shopping trips or took cooking or craft lessons together. They invited Rowan now and then, but she rarely enjoyed the cooking or crafting. Instead, she'd grill the instructor to see if she could write up an interview for her college newspaper.

"He's okay, I think. I've tried to call him a few times, but his room-mate says he's always out. Mom's only getting in touch with him once every couple of weeks, too. He's obsessed with that new job."

"Guess that's what it takes out there."

"Yeah, maybe," Olivia agreed. "I don't see the perks. Traffic, smog, an endless parade of people with nicer bodies, nicer cars and bigger bank accounts. Seems like a recipe for low self-esteem."

"I doubt Alex struggles with that," Rowan said.

Olivia laughed. "Yeah, he's never met another person he believes is more qualified than himself."

Their younger brother wasn't arrogant exactly, just confident, some-times to a fault. Rowan had often envied the trait.

"There's the vixen I'm looking for," a voice announced from the doorway. Mona swept in, her dark dress swishing around her tanned legs. "Sorry we're late. Caleb decided it was a good idea to schedule a business call on a Saturday." She rolled her eyes.

Rowan leaned forward as Mona stood on tiptoe to kiss her cheek.

"Hi, Olivia. How are you?" Mona asked, smiling at Olivia.

"I'm great. Envying this gorgeous house my sister's spending the summer in."

"It is pretty fabulous," Mona agreed, brushing a hand over the decorative doorway trim. "Are you going to give me a tour?" she asked Rowan.

Rowan swallowed and took another sip of wine. "Olivia, will you do the honors? I should make sure everything's good out back."

"Absolutely," Olivia said. "Garrett showed me the house earlier. It's enormous."

Mona blew Rowan a kiss as she followed Olivia out of the kitchen towards the living room.

Rowan didn't open the glass doors to the porch, but walked instead out the front door, where she encountered Rosa and Yolanda talking in the driveway.

They both looked up when Rowan appeared. Yolanda smiled. "There's the mama of our gorgeous birthday girl. Do you need any help in there?"

Rowan shook her head. "Garrett's grilling out back. I was just... going to walk out to the platform."

Rowan walked stiffly across the yard, aware that Yolanda and Rosa watched her. She bypassed the half-moon deck and took the stairs toward the beach, stopped near the bottom and sat on a step. She watched the waves roll onto the shore and sweep away.

She remembered the story Wilma Kaminski had shared the day before about Piper, the little girl who had gone into the lake, maybe at this exact spot where Rowan sat, only to wash up five miles down the beach days later.

As Rowan walked back toward the house, she spotted Garrett coming around the side.

"There you are. I was looking for you. Are you okay?"

"Yeah, just thought I'd take a walk."

"Well, food is all set up. I figured we'd eat, do birthday cake and then presents?"

"Sure, sounds great."

Everyone had gathered on the back porch and lawn, talking and laughing. Rowan sat between Mona and Olivia, who were deep in conversation about a series of books they were both reading called *Outlander* by Diana Gabaldon.

"I'd marry Jamie," Mona said. "Point me to the big stone things and I'm outta here."

Olivia laughed. "Agreed, though I'm not sure I'd want to live in the 1700s even for a sexy Scot."

Rowan stood and walked to Quinn, who sat on a blanket beside Ava's daughter. "Hi, Trinity, how are you?" she asked the little girl happily shoving potato chips in her mouth.

"Goob," she said, chips falling into her lap.

"I'm going to steal the birthday girl for a minute," Rowan told her, picking Quinn up. "How's my Quinnie girl?"

Quinn happily rattled off a response, grabbing hold of Rowan's earing.

"Oh, no, you don't," Garrett said, coming up beside them. "Here." He reached behind Rowan's ear and unhooked the earring Quinn had been going for. He released the other and stuck them in his pocket. "Good?" he asked.

Rowan smiled. "Thank you. I don't know why I put those on."

"Because they look nice on you." He kissed her neck before turning back to the group. "Save some room, people. It's birthday cake time."

They sang happy birthday twice, first in English and then in Spanish. Rowan and Garrett helped Quinn blow out her birthday candles. Garrett brought out Quinn's highchair and set her in it while Rowan cut her a chunk of the bright yellow and pink frosted cake that Garrett's mother had made.

Garrett attached the pink bib they'd bought for the occasion, which featured a giraffe in a birthday hat, around Quinn's neck as Rowan set the cake on the tray. Quinn stared at it and then patted it with her hand as if trying to gauge what kind of toy they'd put in front of her.

"You can eat it, polliwog," Garrett told her, dipping his finger in the cake and putting it in his mouth.

Quinn grabbed a glob of cake, but instead of putting it in her own mouth, she shoved it toward Garrett's, missing his mouth and smearing it across his eyebrow and forehead. Their guests erupted in laughter.

Rowan pulled off a bit of cake and rubbed it over Quinn's lips. Her eyes went wide as she tasted it. She grabbed a handful and shoved some of it into her mouth and dropped half of it into her lap. Their friends and family clapped and cheered.

After the cake, the kids destroyed the piñata, and then it was time for gifts. It was barely four o'clock, but Rowan was exhausted as she watched Garrett and Tyler haul the load of presents out of the house. She slid past them and headed for the closet where she'd hidden Quinn's gifts that morning.

She opened the closet door and froze.

"No," Rowan murmured.

Quinn's gifts lay in a heap on the floor, the wrapping ripped away, the taffeta flowers strewn and crushed.

## 22

"Holy crap, what happened?" Garrett asked, moving Rowan aside.

Rowan felt a mix of rage and anguish. It bubbled and rolled, and some of the wine streaked into her throat, acidic in her mouth. She swallowed it back down, bracing a hand on the doorframe.

"It's okay," Garrett said, catching the expression on Rowan's face. "Just go sit with everyone. I'll re-wrap them quick. Ava's boys must have got into them. I'll talk to her about it afterwards."

Trembling, Rowan walked through the glass doors and found a chair close to her daughter.

"You okay, doll?" Mona asked, leaning into Rowan's chair and giving her a one-armed hug.

"I'm fine," Rowan murmured, not looking her friend in the eye.

Garrett appeared with Quinn's gifts, no longer wrapped in the beautiful paper she'd purchased months before. He'd hastily wrapped them in newspaper and looking at them made Rowan want to scream.

Rowan sat on the edge of her seat. She should have been down on the blanket with Garrett and Quinn, wanted to be, but she couldn't make her legs move, couldn't get the grimace on her face to turn into a smile, and she knew everyone saw it, saw a mother acting like a petulant child on her daughter's first birthday.

But it wasn't petulance that kept Rowan rooted to the chair. Fear had a hold of her. Fear about what had happened to the gifts, fear about what lived in the house. Fear that nothing lived in the house, that the demon lived in her own mind.

Garrett sat beside Quinn, helping unwrap her gifts. Quinn paid more attention to the ribbons and wrapping paper.

"Oh, look what Grandma Emily got you, polliwog. It's a ball pit. This thing is going to be fun!"

"Open it," Ava's son Max shouted. His twin, Cody, joined the chorus. "Yeah, open it, open it."

"Hush," Ava scolded them, shooting an apologetic look towards Garrett. "Why don't you boys go see if you missed any candy from the piñata." She gestured beneath the tree where remnants of the colorful donkey remained.

The boys stood and ran back to the tree, their little sister trailing behind them. Ava had Calvin, the baby, tucked beneath a nursing cover on her lap.

Rowan watched the parade of gifts from stuffed animals to musical instruments. Every time something that made noise appeared, Garrett called out, "Better have included the receipt with this one."

Garrett and Quinn sat in a sea of wrapping paper and toys.

"One extra one from us," Alan said, handing Garrett a rectangular box wrapped in plain red paper.

Garrett tore off the red wrapping paper to reveal a porcelain doll tucked in a clear plastic box. Glassy blue eyes gazed out from the smooth white face. The doll had a wave of blonde curls that fell over her deerskin vest.

Rowan took in the rest of the doll—the tie-dye shirt, the flared jeans, the red beaded band around her forehead. Rowan's stomach lurched. She gripped the edge of her plastic chair and before she could stop it a violent scream erupted from her lips.

Garrett leapt to his feet as everyone else who'd been chatting fell silent. "What?" He scanned Rowan as if searching for an injury.

"That... that doll. Where did you get it?" Rowan demanded, staring at Alan, unable to shake the accusation from her voice.

Alan's face paled, and he looked toward Garrett and then back at the doll. "It was here in the house. I... I found it when I bought it. I thought Quinn would like it. I'm sorry, Rowan."

"What's wrong, honey?" Mona asked, face concerned as she watched from her own chair.

"It was... it was Amy Prahm's doll. The woman who disappeared from this house. It was hers," Rowan sputtered.

Alan looked uncomfortable. His wife Leah stepped closer to him.

"It's just a doll, Rowan," Garrett said. "I'm sure they left it when they sold the house."

Rowan shook her head from side to side. "No, no, because Colleen said that was Amy's favorite doll and it was missing. She searched for it herself."

"Who's Colleen?" Garrett asked.

"Amy's sister," Rowan murmured, quietly now, registering everyone's eyes on her. Their alarmed expressions, their stiff postures. Only Quinn did not look at her mother, too engrossed in the doll beneath the plastic box.

~

Rowan heard the clanking of dishes, the sound of occasional laughter, all of it drifting up to her bedroom from Quinn's birthday party as the day wound to a close.

The sun burned orange through the slats in the half-closed blinds and lit streaks of amber on the opposite wall.

She didn't want to face them, any of them. Her own family, Garrett's family. Most of them had left, but not Garrett's parents. She listened to Antonio's boisterous laugh, the thump of his heavy boots on the wood floor.

An hour earlier Mona had tried to come talk to her, but Rowan had feigned sleep, not responding when Mona called out her name.

Eventually she heard the last voices murmuring beneath her.

Rowan crept to the top of the stairs and listened. They were at the front door now, speaking in urgent whispers.

"She needs to see a doctor, mi hijo," Antonio said.

Rosa spoke, but she mixed Spanish and English and Rowan could make out only two words, 'espíritus oscuros.'

"Tía Rosa," Garrett said, "I hardly think that's—"

Rosa interrupted him, speaking fast again until Antonio spoke over her.

"Rosa, we are not in the habit of believing brujerías."

"Antonio," Yolanda cut in, "not everything can be explained away with the science of the new world. You've heard the stories. What would it hurt to burn some copal here at the house? I agree with Rosa, this house feels... heavy."

"Well, Mom, it's made of bricks," Garrett cracked.

"Mi hijo," Yolanda said sternly, "do not take what is happening to your wife lightly. There is something very wrong, and she needs you to be strong now."

Rowan could imagine Garrett's face, his desire to sigh and roll his eyes. Instead, she heard him speak low, and with a tone that unnerved her.

"I know. I know it's serious. I just don't know what to do. I thought coming here would help, but it's like it's made her worse."

Rowan tiptoed back upstairs to a window and watched them leave. Rosa turned back toward the house and made a hand gesture with two fingers extended and the other three folded in. Rowan wasn't sure what it meant. It wasn't the usual sign of the cross she'd witnessed Yolanda make on many occasions. This had looked more like the casting of a curse.

Rowan's legs trembled as she stood and walked back to the bed. She sank down on the overly soft mattress and put her head in her hands.

"Row." Garrett stood in the doorway.

She looked up.

"My mom wants to take Quinn for a sleepover. Is that okay?"

On Quinn's first birthday? Rowan should have said no, insisted that she wanted to keep her daughter for the entirety of her first birthday.

"That's fine," she said. Quinn was safer with Garrett's parents.

# 23

A half hour passed before Garrett reappeared.

"I made some tea," he told her. "Can you come downstairs so we can talk?"

"Sure," she said. "Let me change."

She stripped off her blouse and pants, wrinkled from having lain in them the previous two hours, and pulled on lightweight blue pajama pants and a plain white t-shirt.

When she stepped into the kitchen, Garrett waited at the table. He held a cup of tea in his hands and another cup, steam rising from the black liquid in tendrils, sat opposite him.

Rowan relaxed into a chair and wrapped her hands around the mug.

"Cinnamon spice tea," he told her.

"Thank you." She lifted it and inhaled, not taking a drink yet. It was still too hot.

"What happened today?"

"That doll," she said. "Alan shouldn't have had the doll, Garrett."

"What does that mean?"

"It's one of the items that was missing with Amy Prahm. Her sister searched the whole house for it—"

"Rowan, Alan bought the house years after that woman went missing. The doll was in the house. It almost sounds as if you're implying he was involved in her disappearance."

"Well," she sputtered, "I feel like he gave that to Quinn on purpose to upset me."

Garrett gaped at her. "That's..." He didn't finish the sentence, but she knew the word he'd held back—'crazy.' "Why would he do that?"

"He's never liked me."

"Come on, Rowan. That's not true. And even if the two of you haven't been best friends, he'd never intentionally hurt you. You're my wife. You're Quinn's mom. And the truth is, there's more than this thing with the doll today and you know it."

She lowered her gaze, looking into the tea rather than her husband's eyes. "I'm still having a hard time, Garrett. My dad and... I haven't been myself for some time and I know it scares you. It scares me. I want so much to feel normal again."

"What can I do? Do you want me to make some calls? See if I can find someone you could meet with, talk to?"

"What does 'espíritus oscuros' mean?" she asked Garrett.

Garrett's eyebrows knitted together. "Why?"

"Your aunt Rosa was saying it earlier. I heard you guys talking."

Garrett frowned, and Rowan sensed he didn't want to tell her.

"Oh, come on. Do I need to Google it?"

"It means 'dark spirits.'"

"Here? Did she say she felt that here?"

Garrett flopped his head back and closed his eyes, his signal to her that he didn't want to go there. "My aunt has funny ideas sometimes. She's lived her entire life in a very superstitious world. My dad has said losing Beverly changed her."

"Beverly?"

"Yeah, I told you about her. Remember? Rosa's granddaughter. She lived in Baldwin. She went missing in 1998, when she was fourteen. They think she got lost in the woods and had some kind of accident, but they never found her body. That's when Rosa moved from Mexico to Michigan. She moved in with her son Francisco and his wife Carrie. It destroyed their family in a way. Remember my cousin Collin? You met him at Ava's wedding in Port Huron?"

"Vaguely," Rowan said. They'd attended the wedding within the first couple years of dating, over a decade before, and what she remembered most about the night was getting so drunk on tequila Garrett had had to carry her to their hotel room.

"Collin was Bev's little brother. Rosa is his grandmother."

"And they never found out what happened to Bev?"

Garrett shook his head. "So anyway, that's why Rosa is... a little paranoid."

"What about this? What does this mean?" Rowan made the hand gesture she'd seen Rosa perform earlier, lifting her pinkie and index finger and folding the other fingers in.

Garrett rolled his eyes. "Good grief. She was warding off the evil eye."

"The evil eye?"

"Evil in general. Believe me, she throws those out like confetti at a wedding. This house is not evil, Rowan."

"Maybe not," Rowan said. "But listen... I know you're angry I've been investigating Amy's disappearance and I get it. I've lied, and it's unforgiveable. I'm sorry. But you know what I found out? Amy Prahm isn't the only person who disappeared from this house. A little girl named Robin vanished almost forty years ago. Vanished! Never found, nothing. And two other little girls who lived at the house ended up dead."

Garrett crossed his arms over his chest. "And?"

"Two people disappeared from this house. Completely vanished. No trace found. Doesn't that scare you?"

Garrett released his arms and tucked his hair behind his ears. "My sense is that it's a coincidence—a creepy one, yes. But if you hadn't started peeling back all these layers, this would just be a house, Row."

"What does that mean? I'm making it up? I'm creating something that's not there?"

"No, not that exactly, but you have to admit if you'd never met that woman in the bookstore who mentioned the girl who'd gone missing, we'd be having a very different summer."

"That's not true."

"Isn't it? Our first week here was great. We swam, enjoyed the view. You were laughing. You cooked for the first time in months."

Rowan glared at him. "So that's what you're upset about? I've been slacking on my quota of pot roasts?"

He almost smiled, but Rowan's expression soured the joke he might have made. "You know that's not what I'm saying. You're so quick to start a fight again."

Rowan stood and took her tea to the sink before dumping the rest in.

"It's time to drop this, you looking into that woman's disappearance and the house stuff," Garrett said. "Especially if we're going to stay here. You can't keep digging into all this stuff. It's making you—"

"Crazy?" she snapped.

He said nothing.

"I'm going to take a walk."

"We could go back to Gaylord. I'll commute the rest of the summer. It's not that far."

"Not that far? It's almost two hours. Which leaves me home twelve to fifteen hours a day with Quinn alone."

"You're not alone. My parents would love to take Quinn a couple days a week. Your mom—"

Rowan held up a hand, fighting tears. "I'm taking a walk."

"Don't leave mad, Rowan."

"I'm not," she said, not turning back to face him. "I need some fresh air, okay? Please, just… I'll be back soon."

∾

Rowan walked along the narrow path in the forest, leaning to the left as the steep hill sloped off to her right.

She'd ruined Quinn's birthday party, not been present, missed one of the most important days of her daughter's life. She'd embarrassed herself in front of Garrett's entire family and a part of her wanted to scream and beat her fists against a tree in frustration. She'd meant to apologize to Garrett, to beg his forgiveness for the way she'd acted. Instead, she'd picked a fight.

As she walked, she looked down through the trees and stopped, catching sight of a wooden plank suspended high above the steep ground.

"The treehouse," she whispered, remembering the story of Winnie.

The treehouse was treacherously located a few yards down the bluff. Any path that once led to it had been long obliterated by fallen trees and forest growth. Rowan had to hang onto branches and dig her heels deep to keep from sliding as she made her way down to the rickety tree house.

The worn planks remained suspended twenty feet above the steep earth. Rowan couldn't imagine how a group of girls had built it to begin with. Boards were nailed into the side of the tree. Hanging halfway down, swaying in the lake breeze, was a tattered cut rope. Its end was a spray of loose fibers.

Had it been the rope wrapped around twelve-year-old Winnie's neck thirty-six years before? Rowan thought so, and the gruesome image that accompanied the thought made her mouth turn dry and sticky.

Had police collected evidence? Checked the rope for fingerprints? Recreated the scene to ensure Winnie's death had been an accident? Or had she been another forgotten girl, an unwanted girl whose death they'd chalked up to the recklessness of those wayward girls at Helme House?

Rowan sat heavily on the hillside, twigs and leaves biting through her sweats and into her backside. She had to push her feet into the ground to keep from sliding forward, plunging down the hill into the trees.

It wasn't fair. What had happened to the girls wasn't fair. Why was it always the world's neglected who went without justice? The orphans, the prostitutes, the drug addicts. The people who'd often been abused from the beginning, unwanted from the beginning. Why weren't they the ones who most deserved justice?

Because there was no family pushing police, no mother sobbing on the news, no father demanding action. To the rest of the world the unwanted were shadow people. They lived over there, on the fringes. You didn't have to see them if you didn't want to.

Rowan herself could have ended up as one of those girls. If Morgan hadn't chosen her. Morgan and Emily, but really Morgan, her father. It had been him who had recognized something special in her. She remembered it well, remembered the way Emily's eyes fell upon all the children and perhaps looked most kindly upon a little dark-haired boy, just two years old, who smiled and laughed a lot. Rowan had smiled little in those days. She'd already surrounded herself with imaginary walls, big and brick and topped in spikes, but Morgan had seen through them as if they were glass rather than cement.

He'd only been Morgan that first month and then he'd been Dad and eventually it was if he'd always been Dad.

She wanted to be that for Quinn, the rock, the parent who helped her believe she could be and do anything, but she feared she was failing. Failing Quinn, Garrett, herself. And when she tried to imagine how to make it better, how to make herself better, a black void appeared in her head as if there were no hope at all.

Rowan's shoulders shook as she cried. She picked up a twig and stabbed it into the ground again and again as if she might transmute the grief. But she couldn't give it away. It was hers now and it would be forever.

Neither Rowan nor Garrett slept well that night. Though she'd apologized when she returned to the house, their embrace had been stiff. Rowan had climbed into bed alone while Garrett claimed he wanted to work for a while tearing out a wall in the laundry room that needed to be replaced.

Rowan lay in bed listening to the hammering. When he came to bed, she felt him toss and turn throughout the night. She thought of touching him, kissing him, but stayed on her side of the bed, pretending to sleep.

## 24

In the morning, Rowan woke to find Garrett in the laundry room, clearing the last of the plaster from the wall he'd ripped out the night before. A blue bandana caught the line of sweat running from his hairline. His dark eyes appeared hollow, the skin beneath tinged blue.

"I thought I'd go for a drive, maybe run up to a bookstore I read about in Glen Arbor."

Garrett barely glanced up. "Okay. I'll be here."

Rowan parked on Front Street in Traverse City. She walked along the shops watching people stream in and out of the stores laughing, carrying colored bags, eating ice cream cones. In the popular tourist town, the world appeared blissfully shrouded in the simplicity of summer. Bikini-clad girls on bicycles rode by, boys on skateboards, middle-aged men cruised down the street in their convertible sports cars.

Rowan walked, distracted by the window displays and fighting the voices in her head that wanted to talk about all the things she didn't want to think about.

She passed a window with a sign that read 'Traverse City News.' On a whim, she turned and pushed through the glass door.

A young woman sat behind a half-moon reception desk. "Can I help you?" she asked.

"I'm looking for a reporter, Duncan Leach?"

"He's not in. Did you have an appointment with him?"

"I'm a fellow journalist and wanted to get his insight into a case I'm working on."

"Well, he's covering the Beach Bums game today. You can find him at the baseball field. He'll have the press badge on. Follow US 31 south about seven miles and take a right on Stadium Drive. You can't miss it."

"Thanks."

Rowan returned to her car and drove to the Turtle Creek Stadium. Like the tourists on Front Street, the baseball game attendees drifted in a haze of beer and hot dogs and oblivion. Rowan imagined Amy Prahm's family and wondered if a single one of them had enjoyed a hot dog, a baseball game, a sunset, a movie since Amy vanished. Did such a tragedy turn down the color of the world, mute every joy?

Rowan spotted the only man wearing a press badge. He sat in the front row to the right of the dugout.

"Hi. Are you Duncan Leach?" Rowan asked the pudgy man watching the game. Nacho cheese had spilled down the front of his blue, too-tight v-neck shirt. He'd combed his sparse red-blond hair over the shining bald patch on the top of his head.

He eyed her before lifting his extra-large cup and slurping whatever soft drink it contained. He set the cup down, licked his lips and nodded. "Yep."

"I'm Rowan Cortes, a journalist in Gaylord."

"The *Daily?*" He smirked.

"That's the one."

"And what brings a reporter of your high esteem to these parts?"

"I'm looking into the disappearance of Amy Prahm."

He eyed her again, his top lip twitching. "And you fancy that's your big break? An unhappy twenty-five-year-old splits town? Or do you intend to paint something more sinister at play?"

"It looks sinister to me. A twenty-five-year-old woman vanishes from an isolated house and leaves behind a trail of blood."

"Appearances can be deceiving."

"Because she was reading books about people going missing?"

"Have you read any of those books? The ones police found in her house?"

Rowan tried to ignore his mocking tone. "Are you implying if you disappeared and police found a bunch of books about disappearances, they should abandon their investigation and assume you set it all up?"

He chuckled. "Is this the part where you throw my drink in my face and yell foul play? The police dropped the case because the evidence pointed to an unhappy woman with a possible drug problem who wanted out of her life. A woman with a history of avoiding conflict, who also had a mentally unstable mother."

Rowan's eyes widened. Duncan caught the look.

"Not a scuba diver, Miss Cortes? Don't like to dive deep to get to the truth? I've met reporters like you, a dime a dozen, who want the most sensational story so long as they can pluck it off the surface, the floaters. Well, the real story always lies in the deep. If you don't want to get your hair wet, I suggest you get out of the water."

"I can't see how her mother's instability would have anything to do with her disappearance."

"Then my suggestion to you, that is if you care as much as you're putting on, is to get the facts and then come to your conclusions. If you'll excuse me, I'd like to get back to the game." He dismissed Rowan with a look and returned his focus to the field.

Rowan called Colleen's cell as she drove out of town. The woman answered on the first ring.

"Colleen, hi, it's Rowan Cortes. I spoke with Duncan Leach today."

Rowan heard the woman take in a sharp breath. "Now I have a headache," Colleen muttered.

"I'm sorry. I didn't mean to upset you."

"No, it's not you, it's him. Every interaction I had with him left me wondering if our species truly is doomed."

"Colleen, he mentioned your mother having some... umm... health issues."

Colleen said nothing, and when she spoke again, Rowan heard the fury in her voice. "That snub-nosed, pencil-dick bastard. He spent months digging into my family just so he could paint my parents like drug-addled idiots and Amy like their directionless love child."

"Do your parents take drugs?"

"Of course not," she snapped. "Did they take drugs in the 1960s like the rest of the western world? Yeah, sure. Has my mom had a handful of diagnoses over the years? Yes. Depression, bipolar disorder, though the docs never agreed on that one. She spent a month in a psychiatric facility in 1987. Amy was four. She didn't even know it happened until I told her as an adult. Leach wants people to think mental illness runs in the family."

"What happened with your mother? I'm sorry to pry. It's just... Well, he's the one who has written the most about Amy. If I'm going to start a counterattack, I need to know everything that he knows."

Colleen sighed. "It looks suspicious, but like I said, Amy never even knew what happened with my mom. My mother lost a baby in 1984. She was eight months pregnant and had to give birth to her dead child. It devastated her. I was nine. I remember it well. One day, I got home from school and there was a letter. An abduction letter, I guess. It was written in her own handwriting. She'd barely disguised it. She said, 'I've taken your mother. You'll never see her again. Don't look for her.' The police got a call two days later. She'd been sleeping on a park bench in Grand Rapids, she'd shown up at a shelter for a few meals, and she kept asking if anyone had seen her son. The baby who died was a boy. She'd named him Roger even though he had died. My dad went and picked her up. He committed her."

"That must have been hard for you," Rowan said, her mind reeling from the information. No wonder Leach had run with it.

"It was hard. But what's really hard is seeing the lowest point of my mother's life used against her, used to imply that she passed on some genetic dysfunction to Amy that caused her to fake her own disappearance. Essentially, Leach blamed my mother for Amy going missing. It's not true, Rowan. I swear on my life, it's not. Amy did not run away."

"I believe you," Rowan said.

After Rowan ended the call, she considered Colleen's story of their mother. It was unusual, but it hardly pointed to Amy faking her own death. Rowan wondered if Duncan secretly hated women. She didn't know where the idea came from, but when it settled, she felt oddly sure it was true.

As she drove M-72, the long stretch of road that connected Traverse

City and Empire, she passed a sign for Maple City and abruptly turned, thinking of Eddie, the man she'd met at the cemetery. She passed through the little town that largely consisted of a gas station and convenience store and a couple of small businesses, turned left on Burdickville Road and followed it out of town. She had plenty of time to change her mind. Rowan had no intention of stopping at the man's house. That was an absurd thing to do, and yet another betrayal of Garrett's trust.

Four miles along, Rowan spotted the large charcoal pole barn Eddie had described. She recognized the pickup truck in the driveway as the same one that had been parked at the overlook two days before.

Hands slick on the steering wheel, and silencing the voice in her head, Rowan parked behind the gray truck and climbed out of her car.

Eddie emerged from the pole barn. He shielded his eyes from the sun as he approached her.

"Eddie. Hi." Rowan waved, suddenly nervous.

"Oh, hey." He appeared surprised to see her, but not displeased. "I'm glad you stopped by. I put those books aside. Let me grab them."

"I'd love to see some of your paintings, if that works right now."

He glanced at the barn and nodded. "Sure. Okay. I'm in the middle of some stuff in the barn, but I can show you a few I have in the house. Come on in."

Rowan followed him through the dark garage. It was chilly and Rowan ran her hands over her bare arms. As Eddie opened the door into the house, Rowan paused, glancing back at the quiet street. She didn't know this man, and here she was following him into his house. She almost turned back, but sheer embarrassment at backing out propelled her forward.

## 25

He held the door open, and she walked into a dimly lit kitchen, the drapes pulled closed as if to block the day's heat.

A metal fan whirred from the corner of the kitchen counter. A square table stood against one wall. No pictures hung from any of the walls, not in the kitchen or the hallway as he led her toward a shadowy sitting room with oddly feminine and antique-looking furniture.

He grabbed a stack of three books from a claw-footed coffee table. Rowan's eyes fell on a pink and white floral couch sheathed in stiff plastic. A china cabinet to the right of the couch shelved glass angels in varying sizes.

Eddie followed her gaze. "It was my mom's stuff. I need to get rid of it, but… I never seem to get around to it. I have a few paintings in here." He moved from the sitting room and pushed open another door, revealing a room so dark Rowan could not see the contents.

Rowan hesitated as Eddie disappeared into the gloom. He emerged a moment later with a stack of canvases.

He set them on the ground and Rowan flipped through them, pausing at one taken of the forest bluff where Helme House stood as if he'd painted it from the water. Helme House was mostly hidden, but through an opening in the trees, she sensed the dark structure that hulked at the top of the bluff.

"This one," she said, pulling it out. "How much?"

He chuckled. "We can negotiate while we sit out back on the porch and have a glass of wine."

She looked toward the light-filled glass door at the end of the hallway, aware that she should say no and walk right back out through the kitchen, climb in her car and drive home.

The voice in her head grew louder. *What about Garrett?* it murmured. *What about Quinn?*

"Sure," she told him, shutting out the voice and following Eddie onto the porch.

~

Eddie poured her a glass of wine and took a chair opposite her on his shaded back deck. Like his living room furniture, his patio furniture appeared both feminine and old. It included a white cast-iron bistro set with four ornate chairs and a round table.

A wall of juniper trees blocked his yard from passersby, of which Rowan doubted there were many. No other houses sat within sight of Eddie's home. A large firepit surrounded by boulders stood in the center of his yard, and dandelions poked through the grass.

Rowan sipped her wine. "How'd you get started painting?"

Eddie leaned back in his chair and propped his feet on another chair. "I fell into it. I dated a girl a long time ago who took art classes. She dragged me to a few. Turned out I was good at it."

Rowan nodded. "Stories like that have always fascinated me. The natural talent stories. Did anyone in your family paint?"

He shook his head. "None that I'm aware of. You said you're a writer? Nature or nurture?"

She smiled. "Nurture. I never felt naturally good at anything. Writing helped me to process things when I was young. My dad nurtured it. He started sitting with me at the breakfast table and opening up the newspaper. We'd read the articles out loud and talk about what the writer did well, what they didn't. Eventually, writing people's stories became natural. I joined the newspaper in high school. Ended up as the editor in college."

"You're a reporter?"

"Yeah. I'm on an extended leave for the summer, though. Garrett and I wanted to live in the house in Empire while he worked. Plus, I needed a break after the death of my dad."

"Makes sense."

She didn't mention the other things. How the birth of her daughter had changed her as a person. How she couldn't cover stories about kids anymore, at least not dark stories. How she'd gone months barely sleeping, how she still felt like half a person. How she wasn't sure if she was living in a haunted house or a haunted body.

"I'd love to paint you. Your structure, it's unique. You're very beautiful."

Rowan blushed and lifted her glass to her lips. She'd been complimented by men plenty of times in her life, but this man's compliment sounded different in her ears. The last two years, pregnancy and then motherhood, had shifted her perception of herself. She didn't feel beautiful anymore. Sometimes she didn't even feel like a woman. "That's very kind of you to say, but—"

"I'm not hitting on you." He cut her off. "I'm telling you the truth. I know you're married. It's not a sexual thing." He caught her eye and held it. His expression told her another story. *It's not a sexual thing unless you want it to be.*

Rowan swallowed and took another sip, more warmth crawling from her neck into her face. She had to be the color of a chili pepper by now.

"What do you say?"

"I'm sorry, about what?" She rested her wine on the chair and broke his intense stare.

"About painting you. Give me…" He cocked his head. "An hour. I'll sketch you. The painting I'll do on my own later. We'll call it even, my painting of the bluff in exchange for one of you."

"Umm…" *Say no,* her brain barked, the tiny voice of reason that still had some space in her head. She pushed her hands through her hair, once long and golden, and wanted so much to remember the woman she'd once been. The woman who recognized herself when she looked in the mirror. "Okay," she whispered.

Eddie studied her for a long moment and then stood and walked back into the house. He emerged several minutes later with an easel, a canvas, and a box of charcoal pencils. He sat and faced her.

Rowan fiddled with her hands. "Do I just sit here?"

He appraised her and then smiled. "Yep. And we'll talk. It might help you to relax a bit. I feel like your shoulders have risen two inches since I suggested this."

Rowan tried to force her shoulders down, invite some tension release, but failed. She knitted her fingers together, the bulk of her diamond wedding ring biting into her hand, which caused her stomach to plummet.

"How did your dad die?" Eddie didn't clarify the question with 'I hope this isn't too harsh, too direct,' and she found she preferred it that way. A simple question not cloaked in pity.

Rowan didn't look at him, though she heard his pencil scrape across the canvas. "He went in for knee surgery and developed a staph infection, which led to sepsis. He was gone in a week."

Rowan heard the hollow words, words that couldn't possibly contain the anguish of that week. The long days and nights pacing hospital hallways, the purple bags beneath her family's eyes, the way her mother seemed to shrink each day closer to his death as if the cost for another twenty-four hours was an inch off her already diminutive frame.

After hours in the hospital, Rowan had returned home, drunk with grief, exhausted but unable to sleep. There would be her infant daughter waiting to be nursed, the plastic bottles waiting to be filled, her husband's tentative touch as if he didn't know her anymore. Her dad had lasted only one week, but a year seemed contained in those seven days.

On the last day, the final day, when Morgan slipped from a coma into the void, Rowan had walked from the hospital, climbed into her car and driven to the Mackinac Bridge. She still didn't know why she'd done it. Garrett had asked a dozen times and then let it go, but his voice had been filled with fear. *Were you going to kill yourself?* That was what he'd wanted to say. Sometimes Rowan thought, *Was I?* but her brain never coughed up an answer.

Rowan had driven to the top of that bridge, two hundred feet above the turbulent Lake Michigan waters below, and pulled to the side of the road. She'd climbed from her car, icy wind whipping her hair and lashing her face, and stood looking into the gray water.

Rowan couldn't remember what she'd thought about—what she felt. She'd stood there for minutes, or maybe hours, until a car with flashing blue and red lights had arrived, and a state police officer had led her to the backseat and driven her to a state police post.

Garrett and Alan had driven up. Rowan still remembered Garrett's ashen face. The way his body shook when he hugged her. They'd driven home in silence, Alan following in Rowan's car. She hadn't even asked about Quinn. The awareness of that thought brought such shame her face grew pink at the memory.

"My mom died in a home," Eddie said. "Alzheimer's. She didn't know me anymore."

"I'm sorry," Rowan murmured. She glanced at him, but his eyes remained fixed on the canvas and yet in some far-off place. They sat on the porch together, but they were both in other worlds, worlds come and gone, worlds they could never retrieve unless they'd been properly encoded first in the prefrontal cortex and then in the hippocampus.

Rowan had once done an interview with a researcher at the University of Michigan who'd been studying the effects of sleep on memory. At the time, Rowan had finished been finished with graduate school and sleeping the best she had in years—unmarried and childless. The researcher's findings had been intriguing, but they were mostly fodder for her article.

Years later, after Quinn's birth and the death of her father, when insomnia had invaded her life like a plague she could neither treat nor cure, Rowan lay awake often and thought of the man's findings. *Lack of sleep reduces the brain's ability to code short-term memories into long-term memories,* he'd said. Would Rowan forget the first months of her daughter's life? Would she struggle to recall Quinn's first words or her father's last?

During those long dark nights, the thoughts would propel her overwrought brain into panic mode, and she'd slip from bed to the kitchen to furiously scribble everything she could remember from the previous days into a notebook. She had three of those notebooks shoved in a closet at her home in Gaylord, hidden beneath shoeboxes as if they held dirty secrets rather than the mundane details of her daily life.

"I was adopted," Rowan said. "I was seven and living in a foster home in Flint."

"A good home or a bad one?"

Rowan sighed. "Not as bad as some, but not good. There were six of us kids living there. The dad yelled a lot. Then one day Morgan, that's my adopted dad, and Emily, my adopted mom, showed up to meet the kids. They took me home the next day."

"And how was that?" His pencils scratched.

"Good. Better, but... hard to adjust to. They'd been trying to have children for years. Emily couldn't conceive, then poof, a few months after they brought me home, Emily found out she was pregnant. She had Olivia, my younger sister, and then three years later she had Alex."

"And that was hard on you because you were the adopted kid and they were the blood kids."

Row hadn't spoken much about those feelings to anyone. She and Garrett had covered it all in the early years, but she couldn't remember the last time she'd told someone new that she was adopted. In a way, she wanted to forget—she wanted to be Morgan and Emily's daughter, nothing more and nothing less. "Yes. It was hard. Less so with my dad. He and I had a special connection. But my mom and I were more distant. She was pregnant or had a new baby during the first four or five years of my life with them, so we just never... clicked like me and my dad."

"Do you like your siblings?"

"Yes, of course."

Eddie chuckled.

"What?" she demanded.

"I don't believe you. I heard something else just now, and I think you're giving me a rehearsed answer. That's okay, your prerogative, but you can tell it like it is. It's never going to leave this porch, and you know what else? The image changes the more honest the subject becomes. A realness starts to come through..."

Rowan looked at him. He'd lifted his eyes from the picture and they bore into her.

She blinked and looked away. "I do like them. When I was little, I hated them at first. I was terrified my dad would love them more and he and Emily would get rid of me." She bit her lip. She'd never told another soul that she'd felt that way.

"I get it. You'd already been abandoned once, right? Hard to get over that shit. What happened to your birth parents?"

Rowan pulled at the hem of her t-shirt. "I don't know. I've never asked."

"Why not?"

Rowan frowned. "I guess... I was afraid if I asked it would remind my parents that I wasn't their real daughter." She laughed dryly. "Stupid, huh?"

He didn't answer. Several minutes of silence lapsed, the only sound his pencil moving over the canvas.

"I have to use the bathroom," Rowan said, feeling her bladder suddenly heavy on her pelvis. Since Quinn she'd gone from zero to now on the need-to-urinate scale in about two seconds. She stood quickly, fighting the urge to shove a hand between her legs to stop the need to go.

Eddie tilted his head toward the door. "First door on the right. It's across from the bedroom."

Rowan pushed open the sliding door and hurried back into the dim hallway, shoved into the bathroom and barely got the door closed before she whipped down her pants and fell onto the toilet. Her urine rushed out in a long, loud burst and she closed her eyes, relief loosening the previously taut muscles in her legs. "That was a close one," she murmured.

She stepped back into the hall, her eyes catching on the stacks of paintings in the opposite room. Glancing back toward the deck, she noted Eddie's hand still sliding across the canvas.

A painting directly in front of her depicted the Leelanau shoreline with a red and gold sunset kissing the mirrored water. It was lovely and yet made her feel sad, as if the fading daylight signaled not only the death of day, but the death of life itself. She slipped closer to the image and then turned to look at other paintings stacked along the walls and draped across the bed. Another caught her eye, this painting in shades of black, purple and blue. It was a surreal painting with a tall claw-footed mirror, but within the mirror stood a doorway that looked into a closet and within that doorway stood another doorway that peered into a tiny candle-lit room.

Somewhere in the house an alarm beeped and Rowan jumped, spun away from the painting and hurried back to the porch.

Eddie glanced up. "Found it?"

"Yeah, thank you." Rowan settled back into her chair and took a sip of her wine.

"How long have you been married?" Eddie nodded at the gold and diamond ring on Rowan's finger.

Rowan blinked at him, pushed off-kilter by the abrupt change in conversation. "Umm… eleven years. Garrett and I met in college. We both attended Saginaw Valley."

"Love at first sight?"

Rowan touched the ring on her finger and shook her head. "I met him at a party one of my friends dragged me to. Garrett was loud. He and another friend had these big lifted trucks they were racing up and down the road. I took one look at him and decided he was a jerk."

Eddie's eyes stayed fixed on the portrait, hand moving faster now.

"He cornered me that evening and said, 'I see you on the fringes, always on the outside looking in. You can't see it yet, but I'm there with you.'"

"And what did that mean?" Eddie asked, though Rowan sensed he only half-listened now. He'd gotten lost in the work beneath his hands.

"Garrett's never met a stranger, but being Mexican in a small northern Michigan town means being different. Even if your family has been there for decades and everyone, mostly, sees beyond your differences, you're still forever on the outside of that very bubble. I'd felt that way my entire life, like I was looking in on a club that I could never join, and not because they wouldn't let me in, but because I couldn't ever truly feel like one of them."

Eddie paused and looked up, gray eyes locked on hers, and she saw something in them, a piece of herself reflected there. "I know exactly what you mean."

She started to ask more, but he spoke again. "Your husband's from Mexico?"

"His family is, but he's lived in Gaylord his entire life. His father, Antonio, moved there with his parents when he was just a boy. Garrett's grandfather started a home remodeling business, which his father inherited and then passed to Garrett, though technically they own and run it together."

"And you work as a reporter in Gaylord?"

Rowan nodded.

"Doesn't seem like there'd be much to report on in northern Michigan."

She shrugged. "There's not, but I make do. I write a few bigger pieces for magazines every year. Not this year though."

"Because of your dad?"

"And Quinn."

"Your daughter?"

"I had a hard time. Maybe I'm having a hard time." Rowan chuckled and swiped at the hair that had fallen across her forehead. She'd unburdened her soul to this stranger, and though guilt niggled at her, she also felt lighter. Suddenly Mona's urging she get a therapist for the previous year made sense. "I'm sorry to unload all this on you."

He didn't smile. "I'm asking the questions. If anything, you might say I'm prying. That's what my mother would have said."

"It doesn't feel that way. Maybe because we don't know each other. It's hard to tell the people who love you you're not okay. That you're fucking falling apart." She laughed, and a sob cracked through, startling her.

Eddie watched her, unmoved. He didn't smile to make it more comfortable or ask if she was okay. There was something comforting in his indifference, his not needing to console her, his not stumbling over kind words.

"Sorry," she murmured, though she knew it was unnecessary.

"I've never seen anyone all that together," he said. "Not on the inside. People do an outstanding job of projecting the image, painting on the façade, but when it comes to the guts and bones, everyone's a mess."

She smiled. "Sounds morbid, but yeah, I guess there's a lot of truth in that."

# 26

Rowan climbed into her car. Thick clouds marred the sky. She grabbed her cell phone to check the time. It was dead. She'd forgotten to charge it the night before. She backed out of Eddie's driveway, knowing she should have called Garrett and checked in hours before.

Rowan hit the gas, accelerating towards Empire. The dashboard clock read seven p.m.

As Rowan turned onto the darkening road, an orange light appeared on the dash of her car.

*Check Engine Soon.*

"Shoot," she muttered, thinking back to her last oil change. Garrett had taken her car into a quick lube shop in Gaylord several months before. Squinting at the sticker attached to her windshield, she saw she hadn't yet surpassed the mileage for the future oil change. She rounded a curve and the car engine sputtered and shook. Despite her foot pressed on the gas pedal, the car decelerated. The engine died.

"No..." she murmured, closing her eyes and sucking in a breath. She shifted into park, switched off the key and waited to a count of five. "Please start," she whispered, turning the key.

The engine didn't start. It didn't even sputter. She waited, counted to sixty seconds and tried it again. Nothing.

"No," she moaned, picked up her cellphone and tried to power it on. The screen stayed blank.

She was probably a mile away from the long driveway at Helme

House. She'd have to walk it. There were no gas stations nearby, no businesses at all, and if she waited much longer, it would get dark.

Rowan grabbed her bag and stuffed her dead cell phone and her car keys inside, hitting the lock button before closing her driver's door. She stuck to the edge of the road, not wanting to risk cutting through the woods and getting lost. As she walked, she chastised herself for not charging her phone, for not looking into a new vehicle, for going to Eddie's to begin with. She wanted to cry. The emotional upheaval seemed always standing by, waiting for some minor inconvenience to push her over the edge. She hated it. Hated how vulnerable it felt, hated how unstable it made her feel.

Her mother Emily had always been a frequent crier, Olivia too. Infomercials about starving children, soap operas, sappy greeting cards sent both women into regular crying jags. Not Rowan. She'd been the tough one with her thick skin and her detached persona. Now she was none of those things and as she walked, tears started streaming down her cheeks.

She thought of Quinn spending the night of her first birthday with her grandparents instead of her mom and dad. She thought of Garrett and the way he'd always chosen her, striven to make her feel welcome in his family, gone above and beyond to prove to her his loyalty. She imagined her dad with his bright blue eyes and the laugh lines around his mouth. The terrible jokes he told at every party, the way animals gravitated toward him, the way she could tell him anything and he'd listen without judgment.

The sobs grew louder and Rowan stuffed her hands over her mouth, though there was no one to hear them. In front of her, an engine rumbled and a car shot around a bend in the road, its headlights sweeping over her. Rowan wiped at her face, gulping in air. She glanced over her shoulder and saw the car's brake lights glow red.

They were stopping, turning around.

Impulsively, Rowan turned into the trees, shoving branches out of the way, her tennis shoes crunching across twigs and leaves. She heard something behind her, a rough breath as if someone had followed her into the forest.

Her guts turned fiery and thick bile rose into her throat. She tasted the wine she'd drunk at Eddie's house, a poisonous reminder of her betrayal.

Off to her right branches crunched underfoot, and she froze, searching the shadowy forest, but unable to discern a person amongst the crowded trees.

A gust of wind lifted a swirl of leaves and sent the trees writhing and groaning. Another branch cracked, and Rowan took off. Her feet pounded on the soft forest ground and she ran with her arms held out, slapping away branches as they tore at her hair and face.

Something cool and slick grazed the back of her arm. Fingers, dead corpse fingers. Rowan shuddered away, slapping a hand back, though she found only air.

Breath exploded between her lips as she sprinted uphill, dodging saplings and leaping over tangles of bush. Rowan had never been a runner, and a stitch wound into her side, twisting the flesh along her hip and lower back into a coil of fire.

The uphill climb sent her thighs spasming until she had to turn and run sideways, parallel with the road, but too deep in the woods to see it. Her ankle, which had felt better that day, awoke and sent shocks of lightning down into her foot and up into her knee.

Out of breath, ankle throbbing, she lost speed until she was hobbling, sweat-soaked, and nauseated. When she broke from the trees at the edge of the long driveway to Helme House, she gasped and turned, shoes slapping the asphalt driveway as she limped toward the house.

When the house loomed before her, she spun around, sure whatever chased her had merely allowed her a glimpse of salvation before it dragged her back into the darkening woods. The driveway stretched empty, the woods beyond silent save the wind whistling through the branches.

Rowan stumbled through the front door, gritting her teeth against the drumbeat in her ankle. No sounds emerged from the bathroom, but laughter spilled from the kitchen. She staggered down the hall, stopped hard, her torso pitching forward as her feet ground to a halt.

Mona stood in the kitchen next to Garrett. They leaned over something on the counter, their heads too close, intimately close.

Rowan watched, sick in her stomach, a thousand tormented muscles and ligaments and pains chorusing from her body. Garrett murmured something, but Rowan couldn't part out the words from the rush of sound in her ears.

*They're having an affair.*

A part of her wanted to scream at them—that part that wanted to implode her life, throw her baby off a balcony, wade into Lake Michigan and float away. She put a hand against the wall to steady herself, gulping for breath, but as the thought detonated in her head, all the sounds of her body oozed out in a guttural cry that startled her husband and best friend.

Garrett whirled around, eyes expanding.

"Rowan?" In two strides, he was with her, touching her, brushing the damp hair from her forehead.

The suspicion she'd had moments before evaporated.

"Oh, my God, Rowan," Mona boomed. "What happened? Your hair is full of leaves."

Rowan closed her eyes, felt Mona's hands plucking at her hair and Garrett's arm snaking around her waist. Tears poured over her cheeks, equal parts relief and desperation.

"Come on, babe. Here, let's get you to a chair." Garrett helped her, Rowan biting her lip against the pain in her ankle.

She collapsed into a chair. Garrett knelt in front of her.

"Water," Mona announced, hurrying to the cupboard and taking out a glass. She filled it with water and handed it to Rowan, who spilled half of it down her shirt as she lifted it to her lips.

They watched her and after another drink, Rowan found her voice.

"My car… it broke down."

"And you walked home? Why didn't you call?" Garrett demanded.

"My cell died."

"Jesus, Rowan. I looked up and saw you in the doorway and thought… shit." Mona shivered. "I don't even know what I thought."

"I've been calling you for two hours," Garrett murmured. "I was starting to panic, and Mona was telling me to chill out."

Mona smiled, but her eyes looked troubled. "Is that it, honey? Your car broke down? Or did something else happen?"

Rowan pushed hands shakily through her hair, drawing out a twig. "I got spooked in the woods."

"Where's your car at?" Garrett said, standing up.

"Not far. About a mile south of the driveway."

Garrett sighed, the worry lines in his forehead deepening as he stared at her. Rowan looked into her lap, wishing she could unsee the fear in his eyes.

"I'll drive down there. See if I can get it fired up. If I do, I'll come back for you, Mona, and you can drive my truck up."

"Happy to," Mona said, pulling out a chair and sitting next to Rowan.

They waited, listening to Garrett walk out the front door, and a moment later his engine turned over.

Mona took Rowan's hand and squeezed. "I came by a couple hours ago, picked up Chinese food, thought you might like some company out here."

"Thanks," Rowan murmured.

"What spooked you in the woods, honey?"

Rowan shivered as the memory of that slippery touch feathered down her spine. "I saw a car stopping after I stalled. I ran into the woods and... I don't know. I heard footsteps. I was afraid they'd followed me."

"Not to help you?"

"Maybe... I panicked."

"I don't blame you. Too many horror movies start with a woman's car breaking down on a lonely road."

"Too many real-life horrors start that way too."

"Let's not go there. I'm happy you ran for it. Did you get hurt? You were limping."

"That happened the other day," Rowan said, not wanting to dredge up her near-drowning.

"I know what we need," Mona said, standing. "A little Tennessee whiskey. Caleb's brother gave him a bottle for his birthday, but Caleb swore off whiskey after our barbecue last summer. He was retching all night." Mona walked to a paper bag on the counter. She took out a bottle of whiskey and a plastic bottle of sour-mix. "Better make mine light. I've got a long drive ahead of me."

"You can stay the night," Rowan said, watching her pour whiskey and sour-mix into glasses.

"No, I better not. It's our last night before the kids come back from camp and I'm expecting to get some." She waggled her eyebrows at Rowan.

"Doesn't Caleb go to bed at nine? Your window of opportunity is rapidly passing."

"No better midnight wake-up than a naked woman sliding into your bed." Mona handed Rowan a glass.

Rowan smiled. "Caleb's a lucky man."

"Don't he know it." Mona returned to her seat and sipped her drink, eyeing Rowan. "So... can we talk about what happened yesterday?"

"You mean how I ruined Quinn's birthday?"

"You didn't ruin her birthday. It was a great day, but... the reaction over the doll. What was that about?"

Rowan stared into her glass, watching the bubbles fizz and pop. "The girl who disappeared from this house, Amy. That was her doll."

"And Alan found it here when he bought the house?" Mona asked.

"I mean, that's what he said, but Colleen Prahm, Amy's sister, said that doll was not in the house. Other than Amy's cell and her purse, it was the only thing missing. Colleen searched for it."

Mona frowned. "Could she have missed it?"

Rowan sighed. "Maybe. That's the reasonable explanation."

"But you don't buy it?"

Rowan sipped her drink. "I overreacted. I know that. It's just... seeing that doll was like seeing..."

"A ghost?"

Rowan remembered the girl crouched in the bedroom upstairs, watching her in the dark. She clenched her eyes shut and took another long drink and emptied her glass.

"Here." Mona took the glass. "And don't tell me not to refill it. After the evening you've had, you're on a two-drink minimum."

"I don't seem to have control of my emotions," Rowan continued. "Since Quinn was born really, but losing my dad amplified it. I'm like a volcano of emotion constantly erupting all over the place."

"Have you called a therapist? I know you're not sold on the idea, but... why not give it a shot? What'd you have to lose?"

"I will. I'm going to, but I'd rather wait until we move back to Gaylord. What's the point of starting up with someone over here when we'll be moving back home in six weeks?"

Mona gave her a skeptical look. "Because you need help now, not in six weeks."

"Is that what you think?" Rowan asked quietly, unable to hide her hurt feelings at the comment, which too was an overreaction that she couldn't quash.

Mona returned with another whiskey sour, handing it to Rowan. She scooted her chair closer, taking Rowan's hand and twining her fingers through Rowan's. "I love you, Rowan. I think you are one of the most spectacular, brilliant, beautiful people I've ever met. When I say you need help, I'm not saying you're broken. I'm saying you've been through a shitshow this last year and it's going to take a power washer, not a garden hose, to get you cleaned up. Caleb and I went to couples' counseling less than a year after we got married. It saved us. We would have been divorced otherwise. We all need help navigating the hard parts."

"Yeah, okay. I hear you. I'll make some calls."

"How about the house? Is this place still getting to you?"

A stream of memories surged across Rowan's mind. The ghostly face of a child, flies on the door, Quinn dead in the lake... "A little, but... I'm afraid it's me. I'm not sleeping and the emotional bedlam has me all over the place."

"You don't think the house is haunted?"

Rowan bit her cheek. She didn't want to lie to Mona, but if she said yes, it might get back to Garrett and fuel his fears about the state of his wife's mental health.

"No," she said at last. "I think it's all in my head."

The front door banged open, and a moment later Garrett appeared. "No luck on the car, Row," he said gently, perhaps knowing it would crush her if the car her father had bought for her was unsalvageable. "I called a tow company and they're picking it up tonight and taking it to a mechanic in Empire. Hopefully, they'll be able to fix it."

"Whiskey sour?" Mona asked.

Garrett nodded. "Yeah. Thanks, Mona. And let's dig into that Chinese food."

After Mona left, Rowan took a long shower. Standing beneath the hot spray, she watched flecks of dried leaves swirl down the drain. She toweled off and pulled on worn sweats and a t-shirt.

She found their bedroom door closed. Assuming Garrett had already fallen asleep, she eased it open softly.

Tall glass candles depicting images of Jesus, Mother Mary or another Catholic saint glowed from surfaces around the room.

Garrett sat on the bed watching her with hopeful eyes. He wore plain white boxer shorts and his black hair was loose on his shoulders.

"Don't tell my mom I'm using her candles for seduction," he said, standing and moving to Rowan.

Rowan glanced down self-consciously at her sweats and the t-shirt.

Garrett leaned in and inhaled, pushing his hands up into her wet hair and pulling her face to his. "You smell so good, baby."

They hadn't made love since their first days in the house, and Rowan's body responded to his touch with desperation as she helped him to yank off her shirt and shove down her pants.

Rowan lay naked beside him and rested a hand on the small of his back, leaning over to kiss him between the shoulder blades. A surge of emotion swarmed in her belly. Gratitude for this man who'd chosen her, guilt at the lies she'd been telling, fear that she would lose him forever.

When he stood and started toward the candles, leaning over as if to blow one out, Rowan stopped him.

"Can we leave those burning? Please?" she asked.

He glanced up and grinned. "Yolanda Cortes would cry tears of joy."

Rowan patted the bed. "Come back and spoon me."

He returned and curled himself around her, tucking his knees behind hers and wrapping one strong arm across her ribcage. She watched the glow of the candles and listened as Garrett's breath turned slow and silky. Comforted by the faces of the saints, she fell into a dreamless sleep.

# 27

The next day, Garrett got started early, stripping the wallpaper in the downstairs bathroom. Rowan tried to busy herself with other things. She did two loads of laundry, walked down to the beach and flipped through a copy of *Oprah* magazine she'd been carrying around in the diaper bag for months and hadn't read.

Relaxation eluded her, and she returned to the house, which seemed altogether different during the day with sun streaming through the windows and Garrett's music at max volume.

"Deadly mimicry," she murmured, surprised that her mind had jumped to that place.

She'd interviewed a Detroit zoologist years before who'd described the snapping turtle's means of finding of food as deadly mimicry. He'd float in the water, appearing much like a rock, his tongue lolling as if it were a worm, and wait for a fish to approach and then snap, fish gone, snapping turtle satiated.

Rowan walked to the second floor and paused outside their bedroom, her eyes drawn to the attic access in the ceiling halfway down the hall. Garrett had opened it their first day, cussing when he got a faceful of dust. Rowan hadn't inspected the space with him, not interested in the spiders and mouse droppings that would live over their heads for the next two months, but now she eyed it curiously.

She slipped downstairs and grabbed the small stepladder Garrett had leaned against a wall in the laundry room. Black Sabbath blared from the bathroom.

Rowan returned to the second floor and set up the ladder, climbed up and pulled the ring. The door creaked and then picked up momentum, swinging fast. She yelped and jumped off the ladder before the door bashed her in the head.

Dust floated down, twinkling in the sunlit hall. It took a moment to clear, and Rowan stared up into the dark space. She didn't know if there was a light in the attic, but she didn't feel like crawling around in the darkness trying to find one.

She grabbed one of the saint candles from the master bedroom, glancing at the serene image of Jesus Christ, heart blazing from the center of his chest. Rowan lit the candle from the book of matches Garrett had left on the dresser.

Candle in hand, she crept up the ladder into the attic.

It was a long narrow space, the peak of the roof in the center, which slanted toward narrow dark crevices on either side. It was also packed with stuff. Rowan climbed all the way in, holding the candle out to reveal sagging boxes overflowing with clothes, a wicker basket of dolls —some missing their hair and eyes—and boxes of yellowed children's books.

Alan had likely found Amy's doll in the attic, tucked away. Somehow Colleen had missed it, buried with the older stuff that Rowan was confident had been left behind by Doris Helme whenever she'd left the house. The explanation was logical enough, but still didn't sit right with Rowan. Why would Amy have added her own belongings to the junk-filled attic? In particular, her beloved doll?

A tall object hidden beneath a black sheet stood near the wall. She had no intention of peering beneath the sheet and yet, even as she tried to ignore it, her feet stepped closer and closer. She grabbed the corner of the sheet and yanked it off, cringing away from the grit that blew into her eyes and nose. A distorted face stared at her and she jumped, realizing she gazed into a tall cracked mirror, her own face reflected in the spiderwebbed glass.

"Holey baloney," she muttered, using one of her father's signature phrases and feeling an immediate pang of sadness that she'd never hear him utter it again.

Rowan continued through the room, peeling back the mildewed flaps on boxes to find more clothes, toys, dishes and school workbooks.

Shoved against the sloping ceiling to one side stood a gray metal filing cabinet. Rowan set her candle on the top and squatted down. The drawers weren't labeled, and each had a lock, but when she tugged at the topmost drawer it pulled open with an ear-splitting metallic screech. Rowan cringed, but continued. A row of yellowed files occupied the drawer. She read the labels printed in neat black marker.

*Rice, Dorothy. Lambert, Justine. Hamilton, Winifred.*

Rowan paused, finger on the folder for Winifred Hamilton. Winnie, the girl who'd died the last summer Helme House was operational. Rowan pulled out the folder and set it on the ground, picked through in search of the other two girls.

Behind her something sighed and Rowan stood and spun around, searching the corners, the hidden spaces.

Nothing stirred and, setting her unease aside, Rowan turned back around, squatted in front of the file cabinet. She flicked through the files.

"Piper and Robin," she whispered, squinting at the names. *Rothwell, Piper,* the file said. Rowan dug it out and added it to Winnie's.

She closed the top drawer and started on the next down, discovering Robin's folder in the far back, stuffed so tightly in the row it had been partially crushed. "'Underwood, Robin,'" Rowan read.

Once she'd grabbed the files and candle, Rowan stood, starting toward the hole in the floor where the slant of natural light appeared like a beacon out of hell. That thought creeped her out further still, and she shuddered. Behind her that sigh came again, but this time it sounded less like the settling of an inanimate object and more like a human sound, the sigh of a person.

*Don't turn around,* her brain shouted, but she was already twisting, looking back.

The tall cracked mirror caught the light of Rowan's candle, but another face leered out from the glass. A child's bloated face, eyes soft and bulging, watched her. Wet limp hair fell over swollen cheeks. Something moved near the corpse-child's eye. It squirmed and fell out, a fat white maggot on the attic floor.

Rowan screamed and stepped back, smacked her head on the eaves and dropped the candle and the files. A glob of hot wax poured from the glass and snuffed out the flame.

Paralyzed, Rowan stood in darkness, the back of her skull throbbing. She peered toward the mirror. A muted light trickled in beneath the curtains covering the attic windows, not enough to reveal if the decayed face, eyes oozing like soft-boiled eggs, still watched her from the glass.

Rowan gritted her teeth and touched the tender spot on the back of her head. She broke her gaze from the shadowy glass and bolted forward, snatched the sheet from the grey wood floor and tossed it over the mirror.

For several long moments she watched the dark shape beneath the black shroud, imagining the moment she turned her back it would slide off and the thing in the glass would step out and lumber on sodden split feet across the room toward her.

Rowan bit back her rising scream as the seconds ticked by and the heat in the attic grew oppressive. A tear of sweat rolled between Rowan's shoulder blades, and she willed her feet back to where she'd left the files.

In a single quick motion, she plucked the files from the floor and fled from the attic, backing down the ladder steps before shoving the ladder back into the ceiling with a crash.

Trembling, she made for the stairs.

∼

After fifteen minutes of standing in the kitchen gulping water, and squeezing and releasing Quinn's rubber giraffe, Rowan calmed down. It didn't matter if the child had been in the mirror or in Rowan's head. She had to dive in, go deeper, all the way to the black cold depths if that was what it took.

"Otherwise this house will never let me go," she whispered, and rings of cold sweat leaked from beneath her arms at the thought.

Smoothing back her hair, Rowan made her way to the bathroom and pushed the door open.

"I'm going to take the truck and drive to a coffee shop," she called to Garrett over the blaring song of AC/DC screeching from his ancient boombox. "The internet is terrible here, and I'd like to send some emails."

Garrett gave her a thumbs up. "Last night was great," he shouted.

She blew him a kiss and walked out.

∼

Rowan drove away from Helme House, avoiding looking in her rearview or sideview mirrors, terrified she'd see that face reflected in the glass.

She opted for Glen Arbor, a little tourist town north of the house, and found a coffee shop with outdoor seating. She sat beneath an umbrella and took the yellowed folders from her bag.

Before cracking the files, she had another call to make, compelled by the face in the mirror. After unzipping the side pocket of her purse, she withdrew the napkin Dan had given her.

Sally Mitchell answered after two rings. "This is Sally Mitchell. How may I be of service?"

"Hi, Sally, this is Rowan Cortes. I'm Dan Webb's cousin."

"Ah, yes, hi, Rowan. I had a sense Dan was thinking of me."

"You did?"

"I did. But now I see he was thinking of me for someone else. What can I do for you, dear?"

"Well—"

A young man in a t-shirt that said 'Coffee by the Lake' paused at her table. "Did you want to order something?"

Rowan had the distinct impression that the cafe tables were for paying customers. "Yeah, sorry, Sally. Can I have you hold on for just a sec?"

"Go ahead, dear."

"A black coffee, thanks," Rowan told the guy, who looked mildly irritated at her order.

"If you want black coffee, there's a pumper pot inside the door. It's self-serve." He walked away before she could say more, and Rowan rolled her eyes at his back.

"Sorry about that, Sally."

"No trouble for me. I'm on the back porch watching the hummingbirds without a care in the world."

"I'm calling because… well, Dan gave me your number because…."

"Go on, dear. Believe me, I've heard it all before."

"Okay, yeah. I think I'm staying in a haunted house. A woman who lived there went missing and has never been found. I thought maybe you could come to the house. Do you do that? Make house calls?"

"I can and I do. Where are you located?"

"Empire, Michigan. Dan mentioned you were in Buckley. I think that's pretty close."

"It is, and Buckley is a lovely drive with all that shoreline and sand dunes. When would you like me to come?"

"I think my husband is going back to Gaylord to pick up our daughter tomorrow. Does that work for you?"

"It does. Shall we say ten-thirty in the morning?"

"That'd be great. Thank you."

Rowan gave Sally the address and then described how she could find the house. When she hung up the phone, a calm that had eluded her in some time swept in and she stood, drifting in to get a cup of coffee. When Rowan returned to her chair, the stack of discolored folders overshadowed her relief at speaking with Sally. Each bore the name of a dead or missing child.

Rowan opened Piper's file first, trying not to think about that face in the mirror. The face of a child who looked as if she'd drowned.

*Name: Piper Lynn Rothwell*

*D.O.B.: 05.16.1965*

*Birth Mother: Bernadette Rothwell*

*Birth Father: Unknown*

*Place of Birth: Pontiac, Michigan*

*Illnesses/Ailments: Hay fever*

*Previous placements:*

*Mary Mother Home for Children, Cadillac, MI 1968-1971*

*Home with biological mother, Cadillac, MI 1964-1968*

The other pages in the file included handwritten notes and progress reports, as well as a few standardized tests Piper had taken.

Rowan studied one note written in cramped cursive.

*Piper is a mild-mannered child with a dull personality and a tendency to become too attached to other children (i.e. Robin Underwood).*

In the back of Piper's file, Rowan found a certificate of death. Rowan skimmed it, searching the space for cause of death. Two words were listed: *Accidental drowning.*

Rowan set Piper's file aside and opened Winnie's.

*Name: Winifred Pearl Hamilton*

*D.O.B.: 04.04.1963*

*Birth Mother: Eloise Hamilton*

*Birth Father: George Smith*

*Place of Birth: Hart, Michigan*

*Illnesses/Ailments: N/A*

*Previous Placements: Various family members—see list provided.*

Doris had written only a single note in Winnie's file. It read, *'Acts like a boy.'*

Like Piper's death certificate, Winnie's death certificate contained two words beneath the cause of death: *Accidental hanging.*

Rowan opened Robin's file last. This one contained half a dozen handwritten notes.

*Name: Robin Kay Underwood*
*D.O.B.: 1.13.1963*
*Birth Mother: Stella Underwood (deceased)*
*Birth Father: Unknown*
*Place of Birth: Sarah Fischer Home*
*Illnesses/Ailments: N/A*
*Previous placements: Sarah Fisher Home for Children, Farmington Hills, 1963-1969.*

It also included a handwritten note on letterhead from the Sarah Fisher Home for Children in Robin's file. Rowan read it.

*To Whom it May Concern,*
*Robin Underwood was a child of incest. It is possible this will lead to future complications in her physical and mental faculties. She is prone to occasional outburst and frequent attempts at running away. At times, she develops unhealthy relationships with other children. Be advised.*
*Best,*
*Nancy Courtright*
*Social Worker*

Rowan opened her laptop and typed Nancy's name into the search engine. She discovered several Nancy Courtrights in Michigan and clicked each page, trying to identify age ranges that would fit the woman she looked for. Robin had been transferred to Helme House in 1969, forty-three years before. Her social worker could very well be dead or senile.

Rowan dialed the first phone number she found for a Nancy Courtright in Novi, Michigan who was sixty-eight years old. The line was disconnected.

She tried another Nancy. This one had an address in Lansing, Michigan and an age of sixty, which would have made her only nineteen when Robin was sent to Helme House. Unlikely.

A woman answered.

"Hi, is this Nancy Courtright?"

"Yes, may I help you?"

"I'm wondering if you ever worked at the Sarah Fisher Home for Children?"

"No, I'm sorry."

"Oh, okay. Sorry to bother you." Rowan hung up.

She clicked on a Nancy Courtright with an address in Flint. Courtright appeared in parentheses with the new surname, Tisdale. This woman's age was listed as sixty-eight. Rowan dialed the phone number.

A man answered. "Tisdale residence."

"Hi. I'm looking for Nancy."

"Yep, hold on, who's calling?"

"My name is Rowan Cortes."

"Mom! Phone for you. Rowan Cortes."

Several moments later, a woman's voice came on the line. "Yes?"

"Hi, Nancy? My name is Rowan Cortes. I'm wondering if you ever worked at the Sarah Fisher Home for Children in Farmington Hills."

"Well, I surely did, but that was… forty-some odd years ago. I hadn't even had children of my own yet."

Rowan grabbed her pen and notebook, flipped to a blank page. "I can imagine the memories are a bit faded, but I'm looking into a child you worked with. Her name was Robin Underwood. Do you remember her?"

"Robin…" the woman murmured. "Yes, yes, I do. I remember her because she was one of the last children I placed before I met my husband. After I got married, I stayed at Sarah Fisher in a secretarial capacity, but I ended my career as a social worker. I needed a position that kept me close to home so we could start our family."

"Did you know Robin disappeared from Helme House in 1975?"

# 28

There was a silence on the line before Nancy answered. "No. I was never informed of that."

"Doris Helme never contacted the Sarah Fisher Home?"

"She did not."

"What about inquiries about Robin's birth family? Did anyone ever reach out in that regard?"

"Not that I'm aware of."

"What about Robin's parents? Did they ever try to find her?"

"Sadly, no, but I can tell you they wouldn't have. Robin was a child of incest. An adult family member had raped her mother. Her parents sent her to us at Sarah Fisher. We had a separate home for unwed mothers to give birth."

"But… still, Robin's mother might have wanted to know—"

"She died in a car accident three months after the birth. I know because I kept tabs on certain mothers. By that time we knew deformities could result from incest. Any child who might exhibit such traits was more closely monitored. But when the mother died… well, that was that."

"Did Robin know she was a child of incest?"

"No. We would never have shared that. It's painful enough to be an orphan. There were people in the system who told such things to the children, sometimes as punishment, despicable people, but I would never have—"

"What about Doris Helme? Did she know that information?"

"Absolutely. A copy of Robin's file went with her to Helme House on the slight chance she'd ever get adopted, though by that age she was out of the likely pool of children who'd find a permanent home. But Doris Helme still had the file."

"What if she told Robin? Do you think that would cause Robin to run away?"

"Robin was a runner, there's no doubt about that, but I don't see why her birth story would have caused her to run unless it was being used against her in some way, such as to isolate her or embarrass her in front of the other children. I don't believe Doris Helme would have done that. I met several girls who lived in Helme House. They described it as a mostly positive experience. Doris was firm, but fair. Girls ran away from the home, but at no higher rate than from any other homes."

"Where would she go though? A twelve-year-old girl in northern Michigan? There's not exactly a population of street kids to disappear into. Did she have any friends she might have reached out to? Made her way to?"

"You're asking me to remember people I barely knew of forty years ago." She paused. "There was one boy. They'd been at Sarah Fisher together. A family adopted him before we transferred Robin to Helme House. Let me see if I can track him down. I'll send you an email if I can find his name and contact information."

"Nancy, why was Robin moved to Helme House? If she was born at Sarah Fisher, why didn't she stay there?"

"We were at capacity and Doris Helme was seeking children. She chose Robin. It was very exciting for Robin to live in a new place. She'd never left Farmington Hills unless we took a special trip to the Detroit Zoo or to visit the Henry Ford Museum in Dearborn. She wanted to go."

"Had you placed girls at Helme House before?"

"Yes, twice, I think."

"And after they left Sarah Fisher, would you check up on them? Would Doris Helme give updates?"

Nancy sighed. "I wish I could say yes, but the truth is no. We worked long thankless hours. I remember falling into bed most nights with my feet and heart aching in kind. There were too many forsaken children, there were too few resources.

"I can do some digging into the old files. I don't work at Sarah Fisher anymore. The home has been closed for ages, but they still serve the community with after-school programs and classes. I volunteer there every other week. I'll pop in and see what I can find."

"Thank you, Nancy. I appreciate that."

"My son set me up the email last year. I'm a novice, but I can send a message. You tell me your email and anything I find, I'll send to you."

Wilma had told Rowan that Doris Helme lived at the Cordia assisting living facility in Traverse City, a space that had once housed a mental institution. Rowan had read about the area over the years. The Northern Michigan Asylum had popped up in the news at an alarming rate back in the 90s when Rowan was just starting her career. She'd imagined a time or two digging deeper into the stories coming out of the former asylum, but never got around to it.

Now she turned down a sunny road lined with tall oak trees on either side. The former asylum rose before her, massive and pale with red turrets pointing toward the cobalt sky. There was nothing sinister about the space. The former asylum, now a menagerie of condos, restaurants and boutique stores, lay ahead, the parking lots full. People milled about on the long stretches of bright lawn. She turned and drove through the medical complex, passing the hospital, cancer center and other medical facilities. She turned, winding back toward the former asylum, and spotted the sign for Cordia.

Like the other asylum buildings, it was big and built of pale yellow brick. Wide balconies and tall windows framed in white colonial grids jutted from the exterior. Rowan walked up the wide cement steps and pushed through the large glass-paned door.

Gleaming mahogany floors and brick walls stretched before her. A woman at a reception desk glanced up and smiled.

"Welcome to Cordia," she said. "How can I help you?"

"I'm here to visit Doris Helme. I read online that visiting hours are between one and three."

"Right you are. Doris will love to see a friendly face. Are you family?"

"Umm… yes, a cousin. I'm on vacation in the area and wanted to say hello."

"Lovely. And you're aware that Doris is... largely uncommunicative? She's had three strokes and Alzheimer's has set in."

"Yes, so unfortunate," Rowan lied, wondering if she'd made a mistake visiting Cordia.

"Well, then." The woman stepped from behind her desk, red-gold hair swishing as she walked. "I'm Courtney and I'll be happy to show you the way."

Rowan followed Courtney to a tall, wood interior elevator.

From the speaker, a soothing woman's voice announced the various happenings at Cordia, including a concert in the park the upcoming weekend.

"This place seems nice," Rowan said.

"Yes. It is," Courtney told her. "Most of our residents are very happy here."

The elevator stopped on the second floor. Another long hallway stretched before them; streams of sunlight poured through the tall windows, casting the paintings on the opposite walls in shades of red and yellow.

Courtney knocked on a door and then turned the knob. "Miss Doris, you have a visitor," she announced, easing the door open.

An elderly woman sat slumped in her reclining chair, her feet tucked into pink satin slippers. Her hands were curled into claws in her lap and her head drooped forward, eyes staring unblinking at the little television playing silently across the room. Dark hair framed her sagging face, and Rowan wondered if Cordia had a beauty shop where the residents could color their grays and whites.

Soaring windows invited a flood of natural light into the room, and yet it seemed dark and claustrophobic as Rowan stepped into Doris Helme's little apartment.

Rowan paused, inhaling the familiar scent wafting from a ceramic pot on the bureau. "What is that?" Rowan asked, gesturing at the sinewy stream of pale smoke winding out of the pot.

"Frankincense and myrrh in those little incense cones. Doris just loves those. She gets a bit agitated on the days we forget to light it."

Rowan swallowed, staring at the smoke and thinking of the nights she'd woken at Helme House to the smell of incense, the same incense burning in Doris Helme's room.

"I'll leave you," Courtney said, pausing in the doorway. "If you need anything, I'll be at the front desk or you can find nurses and other staff in the halls."

"Miss Helme?" Rowan asked, approaching the woman.

Doris blinked, but she didn't turn to look at Rowan.

"I hoped we could talk about Helme House." Rowan sat in a stiff little blue chair that sat diagonally from the sofa.

Doris Helme's home was pleasant enough, but Rowan still pitied her. She lived in a mental prison where any memories she still had arrived in fleeting bursts and then disappeared, assuming she had any at all.

"I'm staying in the house," Rowan said, bracing her palms on her knees and following Doris's listless gaze to the silent television that played a rerun of *The X-Files*. "It's beautiful, your house, or former house. But..." Rowan watched as a woman on the screen stared into a mirror and a monster appeared behind her.

Doris pulled in a sharp little breath, and Rowan flicked her eyes toward her, half-expecting the woman to have sat up and started paying attention to her. But no, Doris remained slumped over, eyes tilted toward the television.

"I wonder if something's going on in the house." Rowan stood and stepped away from the woman, walking toward a bureau decorated with knickknacks. A dozen or more glass angels stood on a green silk runner. Some were fat little cherubs and others were tall, slender angels with wings made from real feathers. "These are pretty," Rowan said. "Do you collect them?"

Doris said nothing, and Rowan felt foolish for asking.

On the screen, Agents Mulder and Scully stood talking with their heads close together.

"I don't know if it's the house or if it's me." Rowan moved around the little apartment. A small kitchenette stood against one wall. A single bowl, spoon, and coffee mug sat drying in the plastic dish rack. "You see, I had a baby last year and then my dad died and I've been... I've been..."

The woman made a little hissing sound, and Rowan stared at her. Still the woman's eyes hadn't left the television, where a scraggly-haired monster held Agent Mulder beneath the water in a bathtub, then fled when it saw its own reflection in the water.

"Do you want me to change the station, Miss Helme? Is this show...

bothering you?" Rowan stood next to the television, but still Doris said nothing.

Rowan sighed. "Okay. I'm sorry for bothering you. Thank you..." Rowan slipped into the hallway, glancing back a last time at Doris's slouched form.

Courtney wasn't at the reception desk when Rowan passed by. Outside the sun warmed her face and Rowan smiled at two wrinkled men sitting at a little table playing checkers.

She walked down the steps and stopped at Garrett's truck, glancing up at the building. A woman stared down at her from the second floor. It took Rowan a moment to realize it was Doris Helme standing, her stature much larger, more like the photo Rowan had seen of the woman with broad shoulders and a square face.

Rowan couldn't see the woman's eyes clearly, but she felt them fixed upon her. Rowan stared back at her, having half a mind to run back into the building, to burst into the woman's room and demand to know how she was standing there when moments before she'd seemed incoherent. Old Rowan, tenacious Rowan, might have done just that, but seeing the woman there caused a trickle of ice to slip down her spine.

Rowan didn't want to confront the woman. She didn't even want to look at her. Hands shaking, she unlocked the truck and climbed inside.

Rowan threw the truck in reverse, backing up so fast she nearly hit a white-clad orderly striding through the lot behind her. She slammed on the brakes as the man jumped out the way, shaking his head at her as she sped past.

In the twisting of roadways that led through the former asylum grounds, Rowan got turned around. She gazed out her window, seeing another side of the renovated asylum. These were the old buildings with barred windows, the glass smashed from their frames. Graffiti marred the faded brick. A door boarded shut had a sinister message spray-painted across it: *Welcome to Hell.*

## 29

Rowan didn't know why she drove to Eddie's house, and as she turned on his road, she hoped he wouldn't be home.

His truck stood in the driveway, the passenger door flung open. Eddie emerged holding a stack of blank canvases.

Rowan let her foot off the gas, knowing she should drive by. Eddie looked up, frowning at first and then smiling when he recognized Rowan behind the wheel of the truck.

"Hi," she called through her driver's window. "Here I am again showing up unannounced."

"Hard to announce yourself when I didn't give you a phone number."

She climbed from the truck. "I wondered if, umm..." She didn't have an answer. Fortunately, he provided it for her.

"If I finished your painting? I did, in fact. Want to see it?"

"Sure, yeah. Thanks."

She followed him, much as she had before, through the dark garage and into the dim interior of his house. The kitchen smelled like scorched toast, and she saw the remnants of his breakfast plates in the sink.

"Coffee?" he asked. "Or beer if you're a day drinker? I'm out of wine."

"I'll have a cup of coffee," she said, moving towards the half-full coffee pot.

Eddie slipped behind her, his hand brushing against her lower back as he leaned forward and opened a cupboard. "Mugs are in there," he said. "I'll grab the painting."

Rowan stared at the shelf of mugs, the trace of his fingers on her back still palpable. She exhaled the breath she'd been holding and grabbed a mug with a gray wolf howling at a full moon painted on the side. She filled it halfway with coffee.

"Come into the living room," he called out. "Better light in here."

She stepped through the doorway into the living room with its plas-tic-sheathed furniture, struck again by the peculiar furnishings in the home of a man who appeared to be a bachelor.

He set the painting on an easel and pulled open the curtains to allow a burst of sunlight into the room. The sun briefly blinded Rowan, whose eyes had accustomed to the dark interior. As they cleared, she gazed upon Eddie's rendering of her.

It was not a flattering painting. Rowan looked sickly. The word that popped into her mind was 'haunted.' Her short pale hair framed her gaunt face. Two charcoal smudges depicted the shadows beneath her eyes. The bones of her chest stood out above her low-cut black shirt.

Rowan said nothing, hand paused at her lips, which in the image looked too red as if rather than lipstick she'd smeared them in blood.

"Wow," she said finally. "Is this how you see me?"

"It's a version," Eddie said. "We all have many faces. I notice the darkness in people, the pain. It's my niche. And probably the reason I haven't become a commercial success."

"Is that what you want? To be a commercial success?" she asked, studying her eyes mirrored in the painting. Not only haunted, she looked hunted.

"And have my art picked apart by critics or, worse, replicated on cheap canvases and sold as home décor in Walmart?" He laughed coolly. "No. It's a sickening aspect of our culture. This need to distort everything we love into money."

"Yeah." Rowan dropped her hand and turned from the painting. She didn't want to look at it anymore. It was too ugly and maybe too real. She sipped her coffee, but it tasted suddenly bitter.

"How's the house going? Your husband making progress?"

Rowan turned back to him, avoided looking at the painting, and nodded. "Yeah. He's getting there."

"And you? Are you enjoying the house?"

She bit her lip, glanced at the painting, noticing Eddie had captured the small birthmark just below her left collarbone. It consisted of two parallel strips of discolored skin. Her father had called it a kiss from God. Rowan reached a hand to the mark, noticing how Eddie had added definition to the blemish so it did almost appear as a tiny pair of lips.

"Do you believe in ghosts?" she asked.

Eddie lifted the painting from the easel and leaned it, face down, against the wall. "You think the house is haunted?"

"Why do you ask that?"

"Because I asked if you were enjoying the house and you asked if I believe in ghosts. Simple deduction. And don't forget I'm well aware of Helme House. She's an old one. Let me guess, you're hearing whispers in the night, ominous creaks in the floorboards."

Rowan sighed. "Among other things."

"Like what?"

The air conditioner kicked on and an arctic breeze flowed from the vent in the wall beside her.

She shivered and rubbed her arms. "Can we sit outside? I'm chilly."

"Yeah, sure. Let me grab something out of the kitchen. I'll meet you on the back porch."

She walked down the hall and out the back door. She noticed an ashtray that hadn't been there days before filled with cigarettes, many of which had lipstick on the butts.

Rowan sat in the same chair she'd occupied before, wondering if another woman had been sitting in the chair the previous night and simultaneously ashamed at her curiosity.

"Okay, Rowan Cortes, if you're going to spill all your secrets, we should have a drink." He held up a bottle of bourbon and two glasses.

"Makes the tongue loose, right? Why not?" She took the glass he poured and sipped it, wrinkling her nose. "Don't you have some soda water to make this more agreeable?"

He winked at her and sat down, resting his glass on the arm of his chair. "Better if it's disagreeable. It will distract you from your fears."

"My fears?"

He stared at her. "You're afraid, aren't you? You saw my painting. There was fear in that woman's eyes."

Rowan laughed, a flush rising, in part from the whiskey but largely from the way he gazed at her. She thought of Mona, how her best friend would encourage a little healthy flirtation, but Rowan had never been one to flirt. She tended toward the loyal-to-a-fault personality type, which had worked to her disadvantage twice in her younger years when she caught boyfriends cheating on her. "Can't we talk about something civilized like the weather?"

Eddie stared at her, eyes glittering. "I don't do small talk."

Rowan swept a hand through her hair, tucking it behind her ear. "Our first night in the house, I smelled incense. It was a little thing. I sort of played with the idea in my mind that the woman who owned the house before us still lingered there. It didn't scare me. But then I found out the previous owner vanished mysteriously. She's still missing."

"And that has you up at night?"

"That's the least of it. I woke one night and saw..." Rowan wrinkled her forehead, wishing she could describe the entity without seeing it. "I saw this person, a child crawling on the floor toward the bed, except not like a baby, an older child. And then there was this terrible pressure on my chest."

Eddie lifted his glass to his lips and drank. She noticed the lift of his Adam's apple, the tendons in his neck that snaked down to his broad shoulders.

She looked at her own glass, swirling the liquid around. "Something put gum in my hair. I used to have long hair," she murmured.

"I'm sure it was beautiful."

There was an invitation in his voice, and Rowan didn't look at him for fear her own mixed emotions would show in her expression.

"I think someone was murdered in that house, maybe multiple someones," she went on. It was strange the conversation, the darkness of it, all churning with the desire, the heat of that and the heat of the whiskey and the heat of her shame.

"What were their names?" His voice dropped lower, quieter.

"Amy and Robin."

He said nothing, but she felt him watching her. If he leapt from his chair and kissed her, she wasn't sure she'd say no. Something animal existed between them, something raw and reptilian, something that wanted to override her prefrontal cortex, her loyalty, her love for Garrett.

She stood abruptly, her glass tumbling to the deck and spilling bourbon across the wooden planks.

"I have to go," she blurted.

Eddie didn't get up. He didn't stop her and she was grateful for it. If he had, she might not have resisted him.

Back in the truck, the wheel beneath her hands, Garrett's smell invading her senses, Rowan felt sick. She hadn't cheated on Garrett, but fury at her yearnings made her want to slam the gas pedal to the floor, do something crazy. She let out a howl, pounding her hands on the wheel.

"Stop fucking your life, Rowan, stop!" she shrieked. Tears blurred her eyes and a car horn honked when she drifted across the center line.

When she spotted a gas station, she whipped the truck in and parked in the back near the air pump. She turned off the engine and let the silence grow, the warmth spread through her. She rested her head against the seat and swiped fingers beneath her eyes, sucking in breath.

"I'm sorry," she murmured, not sure who she spoke to, but a line of people marched across her vision: Garrett, Quinn, her dad, her mom, herself. "I'm sorry…"

# 30

Garrett barely questioned what Rowan had been up to that day and with each lie she told another boulder of shame settled on her shoulders. When they went to bed, Rowan listened to Garrett breathe as she cried silently.

In the morning, fog rolled in off the lake, obscuring the ground in front of Helme House. It crept through the trees and turned the distant lake into an endless rolling white void.

Rowan blinked at it as she drank her coffee, remembering once as a girl running into the early morning fog with her father and scattering the frothy, damp air like smoke. Her sister had not joined in the game, insisting it would soak her new shoes, and it would have, for Rowan's own purple sneakers had been heavy and wet by the time they'd stumbled back into the house.

Now she tried to envision rushing out in the thick white clinging to the grass and trees, but felt rooted to the stool beneath her. She hadn't slept well, and the coffee did little to revive her.

She'd dreamed of Eddie, a dream where they'd been together in a dark room, too close, and Garrett had stepped in and flipped on the lights. Except Garrett shapeshifted in the dream and became Rowan's last foster father, the man she'd lived with before Morgan and Emily had rescued her from his probing eyes and wandering hands. It had never escalated beyond those two things, but it had been headed that way and even at seven Rowan had known it.

When Rowan had awoken from the dream to Garrett snoring softly beside her, she'd wanted to touch him and reassure herself she had not ruined their marriage. Instead, she'd rolled over and lain awake for an eternity, listening to the wind pushing against the windowpanes.

Garrett had left an hour before to make the two-hour trek back to Gaylord to run some errands and pick up Quinn. Rowan longed for her daughter, to hold her in her lap, to hear her laughter. The house grew darker, gloomier without Quinn, and Rowan herself felt that way as well.

She stood, refilled her mug and grabbed her laptop, waiting for her emails to load. A message appeared near the top from Nancy, Robin's former social worker.

Rowan clicked the email.

*Rowan,*

*I found some records for Robin Underwood. The name of her friend was Jonah Bellinger. I have a former address, but considering this was forty years ago, he's likely moved. That address was 948 Bishop Lane, Farmington Hills, MI. Good luck tracking him down.*

*Best,*

*Nancy*

Rowan searched Jonah's name and found a listing for a restaurant in Howell, Michigan, called Break Time—the owner's name was Jonah Bellinger. She took out her phone and dialed the number for the restaurant.

"Break Time," a cheerful woman answered.

"Hi, I'm trying to reach Jonah Bellinger," Rowan told the woman.

"Sure, he's cooking. Probably be a few minutes, hon. What's this regarding?"

"It's kind of a long story, but it's about someone he knew as a child. My name's Rowan Cortes."

"Okay, Rowan. I'll grab him."

Several minutes passed and Rowan wandered from the kitchen to the back porch and sat on the top step, scribbling doodles in her notebook. The sun pierced the clouds, cutting through the fog.

"Hi. This is Jonah," a man said.

"Hi, Jonah. I'm sorry to call out of the blue. My name is Rowan

Cortes and I'm a reporter in northern Michigan. I'm actually looking into the disappearance of Robin Underwood."

"I'm sorry, who?"

Rowan's shoulders slumped forward. He didn't remember her. "Robin Underwood. I believe you guys knew each other at the Sarah Fisher House in Farmington Hills."

"Oh, Robbie! You're talking about Robbie. Did you say 'disappearance?' When did she disappear?"

"The last confirmed sighting that I'm aware of was in 1975."

Jonah said nothing for several seconds. "That was over thirty years ago."

"I know. I'm kind of hoping she didn't actually disappear then. Maybe she ran away. I'm trying to track down anyone who might have had contact with her after June of 1975."

"Damn, wow, umm... Jeez. I have letters somewhere, not here, but at my parents' house. My adoptive parents. I don't usually call them that, but... technically. Anyway, I can get those and give you an exact date for our last communication. Offhand, I'm just not sure."

"That would be great. I'm wondering though, do you remember any correspondence where she said she'd run away from Helme House? Did she ever try to get to where you were, ask for help or anything like that?"

"No, definitely no on that. Things weren't great there, I remember that. But she never mentioned running away. It was pretty isolated, that place. I kind of had the feeling she couldn't run away unless she was going to, like, live in the woods or something crazy. Robbie was tough, but, well, she wasn't exactly a survivalist. What twelve-year-old is?"

"Is there anyone else she would have contacted for help if she ran away? Anyone besides you?"

"I was her only friend. I really was. Other than one girl she chummed around with up there. When we were at Sarah Fisher together, we only had each other. Robbie got picked on a lot. The other girls threw gum in her hair, shoved her, ruined her clothes. She was a tomboy, and they didn't like it. Makes me grateful I've only had sons. If I'd had a daughter who was treated the way Robin was... well, I won't go there. But we were in the same boat. I was scrawny, looked about three years younger than I was. Freckles and bowed legs. Sometimes I still can't believe my parents adopted me." He chuckled, but his words pierced Rowan like an ice pick in her chest.

Rowan knew it too well, that sense of not being pretty enough, talented enough, smart enough. What parents would choose her?

"I'm sure your parents are grateful to have you," Rowan said, murmuring the same words more than a few friends had told her over the years when she'd briefly revealed her own deeply rooted feelings of inadequacy.

"Yeah." He laughed in that slightly embarrassed, slightly hopeful way that she also knew too well. "They seem to, anyway. I got lucky. Robbie never did. She was great. I never understood why no one adopted her, but… shoot, I don't know. I haven't thought about this stuff in years. Makes me think I'm going to take my kids out to play putter golf tonight after all, make sure they know how much I love them even when they're driving me nuts on summer break."

Rowan smiled and reached for a plastic puppy, one of Quinn's toys discarded on the patio table. She missed her daughter.

"In a way, Break Time, my restaurant, started with me and Robbie," Jonah continued. "We'd both spent so many years hungry, we loved to sit around and fantasize about food. The Sarah Fisher Home was all right—they fed us—but we'd both been in fosters where if you got a slice of bread in a day it felt like you were eating like a king. We'd pass notes sometimes. 'If you could have anything to eat right now…' Robbie always had the sweet tooth. Banana splits and chocolate-chip cookies and milkshakes. I opted for the savories myself. Mashed potatoes, mac 'n' cheese, Italian subs." He laughed. "All stuff on the Break Time menu now. Nothing like starving as a kid to make you pack on pounds as an adult. I thought of Robbie when I first opened this place up. My son, also a sweets kid, kept saying we needed chocolate-chip pancakes on the menu. Those were Robbie's favorite—chocolate-chip pancakes."

"It sounds like you guys were really close."

"We were until we weren't. It's terrible, but we both understood that nobody stays for long. When I never heard from her again, I kind of hoped she had gotten adopted. I realize that right now. That when her letters stopped coming, I figured some family adopted her, and she was living the good life up there, skiing in the winter, swimming in the summer. I sent her a few more letters, but by then I was in a new house and new school and just… I guess I kind of forgot her."

"It happens," Rowan said. "It was different back then. No internet, cell phones. You couldn't exactly send her a message on social media."

"Yeah," he agreed, though his voice had fallen. "Did something happen to her? Is that why you're looking into her disappearance? Something bad?"

Rowan sighed. "I honestly don't know. I have very little information. I'm trying to put things together as best I can, but it was a long time ago."

"Yeah, a lifetime ago. I'd like to help, but I'm not sure how."

"If you could find the letters you had from Robbie, anything she sent you, especially in 1975, that would go a long way."

"Absolutely. I'll go to my parents' house tonight. My mom's a neat freak, so she can probably pin that stuff down in a few hours."

"Thanks so much, Jonah. Do you have a pen? I'll give you my email address. You could take pictures of whatever you find and email it to me."

"I can do one better. I've got a scanner."

Rowan showered and shoved into a pair of cut-off jeans and a t-shirt and paced around the house looking at the clock. Sally Mitchell had said she'd be at Helme House by ten-thirty a.m. It was nearly a quarter to eleven and no sign of her.

Rowan poured another cup of coffee and then, noticing her jitteriness, walked it to the sink and dumped it out. She walked to the garage and peeked out. No sign of Sally Mitchell, but as she started to close the door, she heard an engine chugging up the driveway. Rowan walked outside as a two-toned Buick emerged from the trees.

A woman with bright white hair cut pixie-style stepped from the car. "I wasn't sure this old beast was going to make it up that driveway," the woman said, beaming at Rowan. "You must be Rowan." She strode across the driveway and extended her hand.

"Yes. Hi. You're Sally?" Rowan shook the woman's hand.

"Yes. And this is the house..." Sally gazed up at Helme House, nodding. "It's... imposing."

"Yeah." Rowan chewed her bottom lip and tugged at her short hair.

"You're nervous," Sally said.

Rowan stopped fiddling with her hair. "My husband's in Gaylord getting some tools and picking up our daughter, but... he's been worried about me."

"Which means he could suddenly appear to check on you?"

"He never has before, but… this has been a year of firsts for both of us. Not good ones, either."

Sally smiled and reached into her purse. She handed Rowan a card that read 'Sally's Home Décor.' "Or"—she reached back in and pulled a little plastic box out, flipping it open and thumbing through a dozen more cards—"Sally's Baked Goods, Sally's Upholstery, Sally's Floral Design. Take your pick."

"Cover cards?"

"Yes, indeed. Psychics are called upon for all sorts of things, but nosy neighbors abound and I'm always ready with a backup story. The cards work for spouses too."

Rowan frowned. Yet another lie. Too many had piled up to count.

"If it gives you some peace, I don't think he'll be coming back early."

"How do you know?"

"Beats me." She grinned. "I gave up trying to understand the mechanism long ago. I simply enjoy the output and try not to get in its way."

Rowan took a deep breath and led Sally up the front steps. Sally paused, closing her eyes and tilting her head slightly.

Rowan had told the woman nothing about the house, but Rowan couldn't discount the possibility the woman would be familiar with it somehow. The history wasn't exactly secret information.

"I sense children here," Sally said. "Several of them, more than that, six or more children."

As they walked across the threshold into the house, Sally's appearance changed. The color drained from her face and she pulled her arms close, hugging them across her body. Her expression grew pinched, but she said little as she followed Rowan up the stairs.

Rowan's heart thudded behind her ribs as they walked down the hall toward the nursery.

When Rowan pushed open the door to the nursery, Sally recoiled and put a hand to her nose. After a moment, she lifted her hand away and inhaled as if trying to catch the scent that had initially assailed her.

"Did you smell something?" Rowan asked.

Dark grooves had appeared between Sally's eyebrows. Rowan could see goosebumps lining her forearms.

"Decomposition," she said after a moment. "That's what I smelled when you opened this door. An odor so powerful I expected to see a hunk of rancid meat lying on the floor."

Rowan sniffed the air but detected no such scent. "We have noticed a weird scent in here a few times. I don't notice anything now. What does it mean?"

"I think someone died in this room."

Rowan looked at her sharply. "Really? Well…" She almost said there were several girls from the home who'd died, and there had been, but none had died in the room. Amy, on the other hand…

"Not a natural death. I sense a violent death in this room, a terrifying death."

"Do you have a sense of who? If they were old or young?"

Sally put a hand on the wall, a long shudder starting at her shoulder and rolling out through her palm, but she didn't move her hand away. "There's a lot of… input. I sense girls who were young, but… a woman too, not the head mother, a younger woman, but not a child. I keep hearing her singing, as if she's singing to herself as she cleans."

"Is she the woman who died here?"

"If she is, she's not making that known." Sally drew her hand back to her body, wiping it on the leg of her jeans. "This room is… black. I am seeing black shadows at the corners of my eyes. Let's leave this room. But first"—she moved to the window and pushed it open—"I would leave this open all the time while you're here."

"Okay, why?"

"Energy needs to move. You want this energy to go out." She gestured at the open window.

Rowan stepped from the room, Sally following.

"Close that door, please," Sally said.

Rowan pulled the door shut, but the blanket hanging over it blocked it from closing. Rowan blinked at it. If she took the blanket down, Garrett would see the hole in the door. She'd replace it before Garrett returned, she decided, quickly yanking the blanket off and shutting the door.

Sally eyed the hole in the door where Rowan had buried an ax in the wood. "I suggest you keep that door closed all the time. While you are in this house, I would not re-enter that room and I would especially keep your child away from that room."

# 31

"I get the creeps from that room too," Rowan admitted. "But... do you see more?"

Sally took in a breath, rubbing something between the fingers of her right hand. Rowan studied it for a moment, realizing Sally held a black stone with flecks of red in its polished surface.

"It's bloodstone," Sally told her. "The properties of certain stones and crystals can provide a layer of protection, though I dare say what's going on in this house will not be subdued by a handful of healing stones."

Sally stepped into the spare bedroom across the hall from the former nursery. "This was a young man's room. The only male energy I've encountered. He spent a lot of time in this room," Sally closed her eyes. "Shades drawn, in the dark. He preferred to sit in the dark and sometimes I think the sound of the girls in the hall, their feet running up and down the wood floor, that bothered him. Maybe it gave him headaches. I think..." Sally reached a tentative hand out to touch one wall painted a deep maroon. "This was an orphanage of some kind, but this child... he was in the family bloodline. He was the blood child of the woman who oversaw the children."

Rowan almost said no, the head mother had had no children, but she closed her mouth and wrote it down instead. She was determined to give nothing away to this woman and to record everything she said.

Still, it was a startling revelation if Sally Mitchell knew nothing of Helme House.

They walked through the rest of the house, but after they left the second floor, Sally relaxed, her jaw loosening. By the time they stepped out the front door, her calm demeanor had returned.

"Let's go out there and speak," Sally suggested, pointing to the half-moon deck that overlooked Lake Michigan. "We can discuss your plan of action."

They walked to the deck overlooking the lake.

"It's a beautiful place, but I have a powerful impression that you're not safe here, Rowan."

Rowan put both hands on the rail. "Why?"

"That's not how this works. I know that's frustrating to hear. I can't give you a why. But… it's not just a feeling coming from me. It's coming from there, that house, and whoever still occupies it. They want you to leave, your family, especially your girl."

Rowan sighed and slumped into a plastic chair.

"Your dad wants you to leave too."

Rowan started. "My dad?"

"He's been coming in and out, keeps showing me a daisy. His wishes are very clear when he comes in. He wants you to go back to your home."

Tears bubbled up and streamed from Rowan's eyes. "You can… you can see him?"

Sally put a comforting hand on Rowan's arm. "I can feel him."

"We put daisies on his casket," Rowan murmured. "Garrett bought them at the grocery store on our way to the cemetery. We'd all forgotten, been so consumed by our grief that no one brought any to take to the graveyard."

"Is your mother gone as well?"

Rowan frowned and shook her head.

"Someone else then," Sally said, cocking her head.

"It's real? What's happening to me? What am I seeing? Why me? I mean, why isn't Garrett seeing this stuff?"

Sally laughed. "I've been asking that question since I was five years old. Why me? Some people are born more open, more susceptible to the other stuff, the stuff that most people block out. Maybe we evolved to ignore it because it was too distracting from the necessities of life—food, water, shelter. I can say this, many times when it comes up suddenly, it's combined with other... emotional distress. Your father passed recently; I know that for sure. There's more, though. You're a new mom, right? A new baby, a first-time mom?"

Rowan nodded. It wasn't a groundbreaking observation. The house was littered with evidence of Quinn.

"Giving birth changes a woman," Sally continued. "You literally become a conduit for a spirit. A soul enters your body and is birthed through you. A doorway that was closed is now open. After I had my first child, Rodney, I became so sensitive to spirits and other people's energies and intentions that I stopped leaving my house. With my second and third child, I stayed for six months at a little cabin my husband and I have out in the woods in the Upper Peninsula. I simply could not handle all the input. Before becoming a mother, I had more control over what I let in. Afterwards"—she moved her hand in a sweeping gesture—"it all just flooded in. Not only could I not close the door, I couldn't find the door. As I've grown older, I've found some of that control again, but let me tell you, menopause was another shock to the system. Three years of madness."

Rowan gazed out at the lake where waves frothed and rolled. "I've thought I was crazy these last few weeks."

"On some level, our culture associates such sensibilities with insanity. That's why so few of us who have the ability from childhood ever see it as a gift. Just down the road in Traverse City, they had an institution filled with psychics and mediums and sensitive individuals who were labeled crazy for their ability to perceive that which is not perceivable to most. At least we've surpassed those dark days, though I wonder if humanity evolved or the people with the gift merely learned to hide it."

"I can't imagine a lifetime of experiencing this stuff," Rowan said faintly.

"It's not all bad. Most of it, in fact, is lovely. I cannot tell you the joy it brings me to tell someone in grief that their loved one is standing beside them, touching their hair, visiting them while they sleep. What exists here though"—Sally cast a troubled glance back at Helme House —"is very dark. I wonder, Rowan, why you have stayed."

Rowan swallowed and interlaced her fingers. "I guess because... well, Garrett is working here for the summer and I didn't know if—"

"It was real?"

"Yes."

"It is real. And now that you know that, it's best to advise your husband that working on this house is not safe and you all need to leave."

"I don't know how to say that without... alarming him."

"Alarm him. Alarm is a protective response, a safe response, Rowan. There is cause to be alarmed."

"Okay..." Rowan sighed, though she still couldn't imagine demanding that Garrett pack up their stuff and quit with his work half-finished because she was seeing things.

"It's easy for me to say these things," Sally continued. "I know that. If you need to lean on a nervous breakdown or some other excuse, then so be it. Find a way to get out of this house."

When Garrett and Quinn returned, Rowan was so excited to see her daughter she forgot, for a short while, about the unnerving experience she'd had with Sally that morning.

The three of them walked down to the lake and swam and sat on the sand helping Quinn build sandcastles, laughing when she squealed as the water washed up and licked her toes.

When they returned to the house, Rowan stripped out of her sandy clothes and tossed them in the washing machine along with Quinn's and Garrett's.

"How are your parents?" Rowan asked, watching as Garrett made turkey sandwiches and piled his own plate with a mound of barbecue chips.

"They're good," he said, shoving a handful of chips in his mouth, chewing loudly and losing more than a few crumbs.

Quinn laughed and pointed at the fallen chips.

"Daddy's a pig," Rowan told her.

"Oink, oink," he said, leaning toward Quinn and snorting into her dark curls.

She laughed and reached for his head, getting ahold of his ponytail and yanking him closer.

"A little help?" he asked Rowan as Quinn held him hostage by his hair.

"Let go of Daddy's hair, Quinnie," Rowan told her, smiling and loosening Quinn's fingers. "Here." Rowan spooned out a glob of smooshed peas and put it to Quinn's mouth. She ate it and then plucked the spoon from Rowan's hand, clacking it against her tray.

"Mo..." she announced. "Mo... mo..."

"More peas? Here they come." Rowan took the spoon back and fed her another spoonful.

"I'm going to chow this and then get back to work. Okay?"

"Okay," Rowan said.

She finished feeding Quinn, taking turns spooning peas into Quinn's mouth and taking bites of her own sandwich. She hadn't figured out how she intended to tell Garrett they needed to leave, but she felt better at the prospect.

After they finished lunch, Rowan washed Quinn's face and took her to the living room, settled into a chair and rested Quinn, whose eyes had grown sleepy, on her chest. She crooned to her daughter, a song her own mother had sung to Rowan's siblings when they were babies. "'Swing low, sweet chariot, coming for to carry me home...'"

As she sang, Rowan watched Quinn's eyes drift closed and her lips soften and part. Everything about her was perfect. Perfect dark lashes resting on her cheeks and a perfect little rosebud mouth.

Rowan listened to Garrett sanding the study floors and tried to imagine suggesting they leave Helme House. He'd agree to her and Quinn returning to Gaylord. That wouldn't be the problem. The problem would arise when she insisted he stop working on the house. She couldn't puzzle out how to justify her position.

If they were going to leave, there was work to be done. Laundry to wash, stuff to pack. Rowan eased Quinn off her chest and laid her in the rocking bassinet. She turned it on so that it gently rocked from side to side.

Rowan passed Garrett in the study, humming to himself. She pulled clothes from the dryer into a hamper and switched their beach clothes from the washing machine before filling the machine with another load of laundry. She hadn't done laundry in a week and it had piled up.

Laundry in hand, Rowan walked back through the house and up the stairs, deposited the basket on the bed. She picked up a pair of Quinn's pants and froze. Dark red blotches speckled the bedspread. As she lifted her gaze, she saw more red. It ran down the opposite wall in sinewy trails.

She gasped and dropped Quinn's polka-dot pants, then stepped back and slipped, her feet streaking through a puddle of red. She could smell the fumes of blood, pungent and coppery.

# 32

"Garrett!" she screamed, spinning around, slipping again and landing hard on her left knee. She shot back to her feet and burst from the room, tore down the stairs and slammed into Garrett on his way up.

"There's... there's..." she sputtered, but couldn't get the words out as her body had begun to shake.

"What is it? Someone upstairs? Get Quinn and go to the truck." He shoved past her and took the stairs two at a time.

Rowan lurched to the ground floor, pulled a sleeping Quinn from her rocking bassinet and ran out the front door, leaving it yawning wide open. Her mind reeled with the sight of the blood. When had it happened? How had it happened?

"You're okay," Rowan murmured to her sleeping daughter, chasing away the momentary fear that the blood had belonged to Quinn.

Why hadn't she dragged Garrett from the house, insisted they both leave, drive away and call the police from some safe distance?

After an excruciating amount of time, though only two minutes had passed on the dashboard clock, Garrett emerged.

"Rowan..." Garrett tapped on the window, startling her. She'd been in a daze, staring through the window but seeing only walls streaked with blood. She looked at him, expecting horror reflected in his face, but his expression held something else—puzzlement.

She eased open the door, Quinn miraculously still asleep in her arms. "Did you see it?" she asked.

"See what? I didn't see anything. I searched the entire upstairs. There was no one. Please don't tell me you flipped over a spider."

She gaped at him. "Did… did you go into our bedroom?"

"Of course. I searched the closet, under the bed, everywhere."

Rowan began to shake again. Her knees clacked painfully together, the left knee already tender and likely swelling from her fall.

Garrett's eyebrows pulled together. "Baby, what? Jesus, your lips are blue. What's happening?"

"I saw… there was…" She pushed Quinn toward Garrett and climbed from the truck, limping now as she hurried back toward the house.

Garrett followed her, grabbing her arm and trying to pull her to a stop. "Rowan, stop. Why are you limping? What did you see?"

She ignored him, walked back through the open door and, wincing, half-ran up the stairs into the bedroom.

The laundry basket she'd carried up sat on the bed, Quinn's black and white polka dot pants lay discarded on the floor. Nothing looked amiss. Not a speck of blood dotted the pale grey bedspread. Clean eggshell walls stood opposite her. When she looked, stunned, toward her feet, no mess of blood-smeared footprints marred the wood.

Garrett touched her again, and she jumped, shrieking. The shaking started again. Her teeth bumped and clattered, but she could do nothing to still them.

Garrett looked terrified now, but it was not because of the blood, because there was no blood.

Rowan allowed him to lead her to the truck. Her knees clacked and her hands shook though she'd folded them together. He buckled Quinn into the car seat, retrieved the diaper bag, and then they were driving. Rowan didn't know where. She didn't ask. She tried to close her eyes, but the blood-spattered room appeared and she shook her head so violently to rid herself of the image that she knocked her skull on the passenger window glass.

Garrett gasped and grabbed her hand, squeezing it. "Just… hold on, okay? Hold on and breathe."

Sometime later she watched as they passed a large sign with the words 'EMERGENCY ROOM' in red block letters. Garrett unstrapped Quinn, who'd woken up and called out for Rowan, reaching toward her mommy, but Rowan didn't move. Garrett disappeared inside, returned several minutes later. He walked next to a man in blue scrubs pushing a wheelchair.

～

Rowan shivered, the thin hospital gown barely covering her to mid-thigh. The purple-black bruise on her knee pulsed. It looked like the eye of a hideous monster glaring at her.

The nurse had put the cold metal disc of the stethoscope to Rowan's heart and listened. She'd wrapped a blood-pressure cuff around her arm and watched the monitor, exclaiming Rowan was in the 'normal range.' She'd touched Rowan's neck, peeked in her ears and eyes, but she didn't ask the normal questions that nurses ask. "What brings you in today? How are you feeling?"

Instead, she cooed at Rowan as if she were a baby and Rowan knew Garrett had told them that something was wrong with his wife, but it seemed to be happening in her head.

～

"Hi, Rowan. I'm Dr. Flores. How are you?"

Rowan gazed at the man, short and thin, with rectangular black spectacles and a surprising head of thick red hair. He didn't wear the attire of the other doctors, blue pants and white coats. This man wore black slacks and a short-sleeved charcoal button-down shirt.

"I'm okay. I'm ready to go home."

He sat, crossing one leg over the other, pen and notepad resting on his knee. "I don't blame you. Impossible to get a moment's peace with people barging into your room every fifteen minutes. You are expected to be discharged this evening, but I would like to speak with you first. I'm not a medical doctor. I'm a psychologist. I've been asked to evaluate you before release."

Rowan sighed and leaned back against the stack of pillows. "Okay. Go ahead."

"For starters, do you feel you need to be evaluated?"

She looked away, concentrating on the white sheet that separated her half of the room. "I don't know. I understand why everyone else thinks I should."

"And why is that?"

"Because I've been... having a hard time and yesterday thought I saw something that wasn't there."

"Yes, that's noted here, though what you thought you saw is not recorded. Can you tell me about that?"

Rowan closed her eyes, saw the blood-splattered room and flung them open again. A shot of bitter half-digested oatmeal rose up, and she swallowed it back down, grimacing.

"Blood," she said finally. "I saw blood on the walls and comforter in our bedroom."

"Blood? Did you have any idea where the blood might have come from?"

"In the moment, no."

"But now you do?"

"Maybe, but if I tell you, instead of signing my discharge papers, you're going to want to commit me."

He chuckled, tapping his pen on the metal spiral binding of his note-book. "Doubtful. People aren't committed willy-nilly these days, so please release that as a fear in our conversation. I'm genuinely here to help you so that when you leave, you feel good about walking out of here."

Rowan picked at a string on the blanket draped over her legs. "Garrett and I—that's my husband—are staying in a house in Empire for the summer with our little girl, Quinn. We found out about a week after we moved in that a woman disappeared from that house four years ago. They never found her."

"Okay..." Dr. Flores waited.

"I think the blood was hers."

"Your husband did not see the blood. Correct?"

Rowan nodded.

"Was the woman's disappearance investigated?"

"Yes, but they only found a small amount of blood, a few smears. This was a lot of blood. She couldn't have survived that much blood loss."

"So you believe you were seeing something that was once real in that room. All this blood. You think the woman was killed then?"

"Yes. I think someone murdered her in that room."

"Why do you believe you saw the blood rather than your husband?"

"Because I've… I've seen other things since we moved in."

"Like what?"

Rowan sighed and pushed her hands through her hair, remembering the gum and wondering how deeply she should go with this doctor. She hadn't even told Garrett these things, and now she was telling a man who could put her in a padded room for her statements. "Our first day in the house, there was blood on the door handle leading to the back porch, but when I looked again, it was gone. I woke one night to see someone in our room, a ghost-child, I think. I saw a face in a mirror. I've heard sounds."

Dr. Flores tilted his head slightly, lifting his pen up to tap on his bottom lip. "And you think these instances are related to the woman who vanished from the house?"

"I think the house is haunted. I think it's haunting me."

"Why you?"

She blew out a frustrated breath. "I don't know. I wish it wasn't. It's driving me…" She halted before saying the word 'crazy.' "It's creating a lot of tension."

"Between you and your husband?"

"Between me and everyone. Between me and myself."

"Have you spoken to anyone else about the stuff you've been experiencing?"

"A little, but not all of it. There's just so much. It's overwhelming and… well, before we moved in, I was having a hard time. I think I had some postpartum depression with Quinn and then my dad died and…"

"This all occurred before you moved into the house?"

"Yeah."

"Did you ever seek any treatment for the postpartum depression?"

"No. I thought it'd go away on its own."

"And has it?"

Rowan laughed dryly. "Beats me. There's so much going on I don't know what's in my head and what's out there."

He lifted an eyebrow. "Some women who suffer severe postpartum depression, which is sometimes referred to as postpartum psychosis, experience hallucinations, delusions, paranoia, inability to sleep. Have you considered the possibility that everything you're seeing is a product of this condition?"

The anguish started rolling about, waking up, wanting to send her into a fit of sobbing. "I don't think it is, though," she murmured.

"Okay. I understand that. Let's try some medicine for the postpartum, one thing at a time. Maybe something for grief. And in one week, you come back and visit me, not here at the hospital but at my office next door. We'll reevaluate."

"You think I'm hallucinating it? That it's all some hormonal imbalance?"

"Not necessarily. But that's the easiest place to start. We tackle one thing at a time rather than everything at once."

Rowan gazed out the window as they drove home, the little white paper bag with her prescriptions nestled in her lap. Garrett's eyes flickered toward her, but she avoided him.

Her left arm snaked awkwardly into the backseat to hold Quinn's hand. Quinn had been saying her name on repeat since they'd discharged Rowan from the hospital.

"Mmaa... Mammaa! Mmmaaa," she called, occasionally maneuvering one of Rowan's fingers into her mouth and slobbering on it.

"Did you miss your mama while she was in there talking to the doctors, polliwog?"

Quinn continued her mama babble, and Garrett reached for Rowan's knee, giving it a squeeze. Rowan winced, and he blanched.

"Oh, shit, Row. I'm sorry. That's your sore knee." He patted higher up on her thigh.

"It's okay," she promised, giving him a tight smile.

When they reached Helme House, Rowan stared at the formidable structure and wondered why it hadn't crossed her mind to insist that Garrett drive them back to Gaylord. The thought of an additional two hours in the truck brought a wave of exhaustion that tempted her to recline the truck seat and go to sleep.

Garrett swung the driver's door open and hopped out, releasing Quinn from the back and coming around to Rowan's door. He opened it and offered her a hand.

"You've got your hands full," Rowan told him. "I'm good, don't worry."

She followed him into the house and up the stairs. Garrett walked into the bedroom, paused and looked back at Rowan, who'd stopped in the hallway. She stared into the bedroom, eyes grainy, so tired she wasn't sure she could take another step, though it wasn't the exhaustion that kept her rooted in place.

"You coming, babe?" Garrett asked, leaning down to sit Quinn on the bed.

Rowan swallowed and took a leaden step into the bedroom. No blood on the bedspread. No blood on the walls. Relief rippled through her and she crawled heavily onto the bed, allowing Garrett to help her out of her pants. He drew her shirt up, and she shook her head.

"I'll sleep in it. I just need to sleep now."

# 33

Garrett woke Rowan with a tray that included a glass of orange juice, a cup of coffee, a bowl of Frosted Wheats and three little white pills. "Breakfast in bed?" he asked.

Rowan pushed herself up and stared at the pills, reaching first for the coffee.

"How are you feeling?" he asked.

Rowan took a sip and tried not to remember what the bedroom had looked like the day before. All of her elation that Sally had confirmed what she'd witnessed had been obliterated by the previous day's events. "I'm okay. Whatever they gave me to sleep knocked me out cold, so that's nice at least."

"Good." He lifted the blanket and peered at her bare legs. "Knee looks pretty swollen. Does it hurt?"

Rowan shook her head. She could feel the dull pulsing in the knee, but it barely registered. What hurt was the careful way Garrett was treating her, as if she might crack at any moment.

She sniffed at the air, wrinkling her nose at an odd piney odor. "What's that smell?"

Garrett flushed and glanced at the dresser where a wooden plank held a stick of incense releasing a tendril of smoke. "It's copal. My mother sent it home with me when I picked Quinn up in Gaylord. It's meant to…" He threw up his hands. "I don't know, purify the energy of a place."

Rowan bit her lip, watching the smoke for another moment. "Where is Quinn?"

"Downstairs with Alan. He's showing her some paint swatches. Very entertaining stuff."

"Alan's here?"

"Yeah, he came early this morning. We went into town and picked up your car. Nothing wrong with it, the mechanic said. So that's good news, right? He thinks an air pocket in the fuel line caused it to stall."

"That's a relief," she murmured.

"Alan's going to come around more for the next week or so, to help me get this place done. I thought maybe you and Quinn—"

"All three of us," she interrupted. "All three of us need to go back to Gaylord."

"I agree. I'll come back during the day to get finished up—"

"No!" She turned her face away, tears starting.

"Hold on, babe, just... It's okay. We don't have to figure it all out right now. Have some breakfast, take the medicine, a shower and then... this afternoon we could talk about our next step."

Rowan closed her eyes and jerked her head once, not able to look at him without crying. She wanted to demand he leave with them and never return, but the emotion rolled and swelled and she knew she couldn't say it without sobbing, which would have him looking at her like a vase he'd just dropped on the floor.

He stood and walked to the door, paused. "It's going to be okay, Row. I know it is."

He disappeared, and she stared at the tray. She wasn't hungry, couldn't imagine trying to take a single bite, but she forced down some of the orange juice and popped the pills in her mouth.

The shower beckoned and Rowan put the tray on the floor, grabbed a pair of shorts and a t-shirt and slipped into the bathroom. She turned the shower on scalding and stood beneath the water, wincing when the hot water hit her scraped knee. The familiar scents of her shampoo and Garrett's sandalwood soap soothed her, and by the time she stepped from the shower, she felt vaguely human again.

Her shorts hung on her hips when she buttoned them, and she frowned at herself in the mirror. She'd lost too much weight in the previous weeks. The bones on her face and neck stood out. Rowan grabbed her brush from a vanity drawer and slid it through her wet hair. She needed to visit a salon and get an actual haircut.

"Fire!"

Rowan heard the shout and dropped her brush in the sink.

"There's a fire in here." The bellow came a second time. Alan's voice.

Rowan burst from the room into the hallway. Smoke billowed from the nursery at the end of the hall. She started toward it and stopped when Garrett's hand closed on her arm. "Get back. Go outside. I put Quinn in the front yard in her playpen."

Rowan ran down the stairs and out the front door, grabbed Quinn from her playpen and ran to the half-moon deck before turning back to face the house. She watched, terrified, expecting to see flames pouring from the windows.

Minutes passed, and she saw no smoke or flames.

Garrett walked from the house, and Rowan hurried across the lawn to meet him. "What happened? What was on fire?"

He looked at her and then looked away as if it was hard to meet her eyes. "That pile of wallpaper on the floor."

"What? How?"

"I don't know. It couldn't have just spontaneously combusted. It makes no sense. You were up there. Did you... were you in the nursery?"

Rowan gaped at him. "No. I was in the shower." She reached a hand to her wet hair as if it offered proof. "Is it out?"

Garrett nodded. "There was a blanket on the door. Alan pulled it down and threw it over top of the wallpaper and stomped it out."

Rowan stiffened. Now it was she who didn't want to meet Garrett's eyes.

"There's a huge hole in the door, Row. Do you have any idea how it got there?"

She searched her brain for the lie she'd created, that she'd rehearsed again and again. Her mind was blank.

"I... it... I fell into it when I was cleaning one day, or I hit it with the broom... or..."

"Which is it?" he asked quietly.

Rowan rested her cheek against the top of Quinn's head, fighting the tears swimming up. "I don't remember," she whispered. "I didn't light that fire, Garrett. I didn't. I mean, Alan was up there—"

"You think Alan lit his own house on fire?"

"You think I did it!"

"No, of course not. I just... I don't know who did it."

Rowan looked beyond Garrett where Alan had walked out the front door. He stared at her for a long moment, and she sensed the accusation in his eyes.

"I think I'd like to go into town, get out of here for a little while. I'll take Quinn and—"

"Quinn can stay," Garrett said quickly, too quickly, and color rose into his face. "Go do something relaxing. Take in a movie or go for a walk. Quinn's okay here with me and Alan. I'll whip up something for dinner. How about nachos? You like those."

"Sure." Rowan once again blinked back tears, struggling to hand Quinn over when Garrett reached for her.

After hurrying back to the house, Rowan grabbed her laptop, shoulder bag and car keys. She heard Alan moving around in the kitchen, but she avoided him.

Rowan parked at the Glen Lake library, which occupied a small Cape Cod-style house in downtown Empire. After choosing a small round table in the back, Rowan flipped open her laptop and clicked on her email.

Jonah Bellinger had sent her an email the day before. The subject line read, 'Robbie.'

*I found two letters and a photograph. I re-read them, but didn't glean much. I know there were more—unfortunately they probably got thrown out at some point. I've attached scans of the letters and the photo. Please let me know if you find anything.*

Rowan clicked the attachments Jonah had scanned. She read the first two letters Robin had sent Jonah. One was dated March 1975 and the next was from April. The first letter spoke of the bitter northern Michigan winter, snowdrifts as high as the windows and a cold that would freeze the balls off a grizzly bear—Robbie's own words.

The second letter described a long list of things Robbie intended to do the moment the weather turned warm: swim, outfit the treehouse with lanterns, build three forts, beat Winnie at kickball, and talk Doris into weekly trips to the ice cream shop. Rowan searched for any hint of what was to come, a clue that the girl had intended to run away or, worse, a revelation that she was afraid of someone. Nothing.

When she opened the third attachment, Rowan found a faded photograph of Helme House.

Doris Helme, tall and imposing, stood next to four girls. The girls wore plain dresses, their arms linked together. On the opposite end of the girls stood a teenage boy. Rowan studied him, seeing something familiar in his face. He looked like the headmistress, for one, but she'd been a spinster, Basil had said. Rowan thought of Sally's comment about the room upstairs, a boy's room.

Rowan printed the image and the letters, tucking them into the large folder she kept her notes in. She drove to the Kaminskis' house in Cedar, wishing she'd asked for their phone number during her previous visit so she could call ahead.

No Basil in the garden as Rowan turned into the driveway and parked. The scent of lilacs enveloped her as she hurried up the wooden porch stairs to the front door. The screen door was closed, but the inner door was open and Rowan heard voices from inside. She knocked on the frame, waving when Basil poked his head into the hallway.

"Hi, me again," Rowan called.

Basil stepped into the hall. "Two visits in one week. Who'da thunk a reporter would be interested in the talk of a couple old geezers."

Rowan smiled. "I'm sorry to just show up—"

"Nonsense," Wilma called. "Invite her in, Basil. We're just sitting down to second breakfast."

Rowan followed Basil into the house. Bacon and biscuits and something cinnamon wafted in the air. "It smells delicious in here," Rowan said.

Wilma stood at the kitchen counter ladling scrambled eggs onto a plate. "Our grandkids and a couple great-grandkids will come through that door in the next ten minutes and we like to make sure they've got full bellies to start their days. Here, have a seat. Let me make you a plate."

"Oh, no, thank you. I already ate." She hadn't and her stomach grumbled at the smells.

"Poppycock," Wilma said. "Basil, pull out her chair. You might have had first breakfast, but this is second breakfast."

Rowan allowed Basil to steer her into a chair as Wilma plunked a plate heaped with eggs, bacon and biscuits with cinnamon and sugar in front of her.

Rowan's stomach rumbled again, and she picked up a fork. "Okay, a few bites anyway. Thank you so much." She ate a bit of eggs and bacon, closing her eyes at the salty goodness.

"Best hogs in the county right here at the Kaminski farm," Basil told her, dipping the bacon from his own plate into a pool of syrup.

"It is delicious," Rowan said. She reached for the folder in her bag. "The reason I'm here is that I tracked down a friend of Robin Underwood's and he sent me a photo that Robin mailed to him." Rowan laid the printed image on the table. "I'd like to know who this is." She pointed at the young man standing off to the side of the girls.

Basil's face darkened, and Wilma's lips went into a grim line.

"Who is it?" Rowan asked.

"It's Samuel," Basil said. "Doris Helme's son."

"I thought they converted the house to a girls' home because Doris was a spinster," Rowan said, puzzling at the solemn face of the boy.

"Sure. That's true in a sense," Basil agreed. "But the actual truth is that Doris got pregnant out of wedlock. It would have been a terrible scandal, so the family pretended the boy came from distant relatives who'd died tragically."

"Old-fashioned folks making weird decisions based on the opinions of total strangers," Wilma muttered.

"Samuel lived at the girls' home?"

Wilma nodded. She reached a callused finger to the girls and touched their faces. "I haven't seen those faces in forty years. I'd forgotten that funny little cleft Piper had in her chin."

"What happened to Samuel?"

Basil shook his head. "Odd kid, not altogether friendly either. He sulked a lot, rarely made eye contact. Honestly, we always felt it was inappropriate having a teenaged boy in the house with all those girls, but—"

"He drifted away," Wilma said. "Doris moved out of the house in 2000 after her first stroke. She sold it in 2008, that was to the Stilts family. We heard Samuel wanted the house, maybe even fought her not to sell, but that came outta the rumor mill, so might not be an ounce of truth in it."

"She didn't give it him?"

"Oh, no. Their relationship was… difficult," Basil explained.

"We suspected him," Wilma said suddenly, clasping her hands in her lap. "Do you remember, Basil? You saw him walking in the woods the night that Winnie… that Winnie died."

"Wait, you thought he might have been involved in her death?"

"Maybe we were in the wrong," Basil said. "I don't know, but we took our fears to Doris and she... well, she wanted none of it."

"It wasn't just that though," Wilma said, sitting up higher. "After Piper drowned, do you remember, Basil? The footprints on the beach?"

Basil scratched at his jaw. "There were two sets of footprints on the beach," he agreed. "Small ones and bigger ones, like Piper and Samuel."

"Did you tell the police?"

Basil flushed and shook his head. "Doris forbade us from doing that. Samuel would never have hurt the girls, she insisted. How dare we accuse him? We'd be ruining his life forever, ruining the reputation of Helme House. The house would close, we'd lose our jobs, and a dark shadow would follow Samuel for the rest of his days. How could we be so cruel, so malicious..."

"But Helme House did close."

"That it did," Basil agreed, "mostly on account of little Delilah up all hours of the night shrieking and crying and running through the house like the devil himself had invaded her dreams."

# 34

"This is Delilah?" Rowan pointed to an angular, dark-haired girl clutching a mangy stuffed bear.

"That's her," Wilma said. "Sweetest little thing, always following me in the kitchen back then. She ran with the older girls now and then, but she clung to me like a cub to its mama. Course, Basil and I had our own cubs back home here, two girls and three boys. Once in a spell, I'd bring Delilah home with me. That's how she met the Binkowskis, the family who eventually adopted her. They'd been trying and trying…" Wilma trailed off, picking at the biscuit on her plate.

"She started having night terrors?"

"Seems so, though we didn't sleep at Helme House," Wilma explained. "Mornings used to be busy times at the house. They changed. We'd arrive to find Doris sitting at the kitchen table with bloodshot eyes, Delilah asleep in Doris's own bed, and let me tell you, that was most unusual. Doris had never allowed a child in her bed in all the years Helme House operated. A month after Piper drowned, Bonnie got adopted, and that really pushed Delilah over the edge. She kept saying she was the only one left, she was next, but she didn't mean next in line for adoption, she meant next in line to die."

Rowan shook her head. "That's so sad. She was only six?"

"It was a blessing for the Binkowskis," Basil cut in as if hoping to lighten the mood. "They cherished Delilah—cherish," he corrected. "They've got a big family farm just like us. Delilah married Peter

Nowark, another Cedar, Michigan, lifer, and now the Binkowskis and Nowarks share land and meals and lives. It's a beautiful story, even if it started out a little rocky for Delilah."

"She lives nearby?"

"Just down the road," Basil said. "She runs the Nowarks' farm store with the help of her two youngest. Freshest milk you ever tasted. Not pasteurized of course, and the government crooks are always trying to come down on them with their regulations, but they've got the community behind them."

"Do you think she'd be open to speaking with me?" Rowan asked.

Basil and Wilma exchanged a look. Basil nodded. "Yeah, she prolly would, but... it's been a long time ago."

"And like I said," Wilma added, "she mostly hung around me. I'm not sure if she'd even remember much from those last months at Helme House."

Rowan studied the pictures, eyes flickering again to the boy, Samuel. "And you don't have a clue where he ended up? Did you stay in contact with Doris after the house closed?"

"We did off and on. I'd run eggs out that way once in a while, but Doris became a shut-in, one of those ladies who almost never left her house, or even her bedroom after a while."

"Samuel was seventeen in 1975. He left that next year for somewhere out west. I saw him once, maybe in 1990, something like that. He'd come back to town to see Doris."

"Was he married? Have children?"

"Not that he mentioned to me," Basil said, "but he didn't have much to say to me at all. Barely took off his sunglasses, muttered a few words about northern California and how even twenty-five hundred miles away Helme House could reach out and drag him back."

"That's what he said?" Rowan asked, chilled.

"We figured he'd gotten involved in drugs," Wilma said, still working the biscuit into crumbs.

"Nana, Papa!" a child's voice shouted from the front of the house.

The screen door banged, and the sound of a child's feet clattered down the hallway. A little boy wearing a Spiderman t-shirt and bib overalls burst into the kitchen, a black and white cat wriggling in his arms.

"Danny, you're not supposed to bring the barn cats inside," Wilma chastised, reaching to free the cat.

Basil grinned and opened his arms for the little boy to jump in them. "Nana made sweet biscuits and bacon and eggs," Basil told the boy.

Rowan stood and gathered her papers. "Wilma, Basil, thank you both so much. I appreciate everything you've told me."

She didn't wait for them to respond as the door opened and more children rushed into the kitchen followed by several adults, the Kaminski clan gathering for breakfast. Rowan slipped out the door and walked to her car.

~

The Nowark Farm Store occupied a red barn with a white awning over the door. A large fruit and vegetable cart stood outside.

Rowan parked and walked through the heavy door. The store included only a small front portion of the barn. Dark wood floors gleamed from beneath shelves of jams and baked goods. A tall cooler was filled with milk, butter and yogurt. A dark-haired woman stood stocking a shelf with bags of homemade breads. She turned when the bell above the door tinkled.

Rowan stared at Delilah, now a grown woman, but still reminiscent of the child she'd been.

"Hi, there, welcome to the Nowark Farm Store. Looking for something in particular?"

Rowan smiled and pushed her hands into the pockets of her jeans. "I'm looking for you, actually. You're Delilah, right?"

Delilah's smiled widened. "I am. Are you Monica with the children's books?"

Rowan shook her head. "No, my name is Rowan. I was just visiting Wilma and Basil."

"Oh, well, silly me. A local author reached out to me this morning to see if I'd be willing to sell her kids' books on consignment. She's got a whole series about farm animals."

"Those sound fun."

"They do," Delilah agreed. "How can I help you, Rowan?"

"I hate to spring this on you, and I understand if it's not a good time, but I'm staying at Helme House."

Delilah's smile melted away, and the color drained from her face.

"Gosh, I'm sorry," Rowan said, holding up a hand. "I didn't mean to upset you."

Delilah put a steadying hand on the shelf and shook her head. "No, it's not you." She fanned her face. "I… well, it's the strangest thing. I dreamed of that place last night for the first time in… years. I don't even remember the last time. You caught me off guard there, a bit of déjà vu straight to my heart."

"You dreamed of Helme House last night?"

"Yes, not a pleasant dream either, not that many of them ever have been."

"Would you mind speaking with me about Helme House, Delilah? About the summer of 1975."

Delilah crossed her arms over her chest and blew out a puff of breath. "Okay, yes. You know what I thought when I woke up from that dream? I thought, 'The house is calling to me.' Isn't that a weird thing to think? That a house can call to us. It's a house." She laughed and shuddered at the same time. "Let me grab my daughter Katie and ask her to come watch the register. There are some picnic tables out front. Go pick a spot and I'll join you."

Rowan picked a table beneath the shade of a maple tree. When Delilah emerged from the barn, she'd put on a white knit sweater despite the warm day.

"Blackberry lemonade?" Delilah set a plastic cup with a lid and straw in front of Rowan. "My daughter makes it fresh."

"Thank you," Rowan said, tilting it to her lips. "Mmm… it's good."

"Katie's my little Julia Childs. That's what I call her. She's always creating new dishes and drinks. She makes all the unique jams. Vanilla peach, lavender plum. Her creativity astonishes me."

"I've never had a knack in the kitchen," Rowan admitted. "I'm still amazed every time my scrambled eggs aren't full of shells."

Delilah laughed, shaking the ice in her cup before taking a drink. "I've always loved to cook. Wilma got me started at Helme House. The kitchen was the only place that felt… safe."

"Why is that?"

"Oh…" Delilah's eyelids fluttered. "Well, the other girls were older than me, louder. Miss Helme was cold. And then there was…"

"Samuel?"

Delilah's eyes darted to Rowan's. She nodded. "Yes, Samuel. He could be mean, but mostly he was… weird. I'd catch him watching us sometimes, us girls, from the trees, from a crack in a bedroom door or even a closet." She wrinkled her nose. "The kitchen smelled good. Wilma was motherly. I stayed there most of the time."

"Did anything happen that last summer, Delilah? Anything that explains what happened to the girls?"

Delilah wrapped both hands around her lemonade. "Something did happen. At the time… I… forgot, I guess. After Winnie died, we all went into shock. It only got worse from there."

"What was it that happened?"

Delilah made an odd face, as if she were in pain. "Robin called it the summoning."

"The summoning?"

"We did it on one of those stormy spring days in May. Tornado weather, Wilma called it. Hot and sunny and then all of a sudden high winds and black clouds. I can still hear things hitting the windows, leaves and twigs and stuff. That wind was just roaring outside.

"Robbie drew a pentagram in the center of the kids' room floor with pink chalk. It was the only color we had. Then we brought in this big oval mirror on legs, a wardrobe mirror. It belonged to Miss Helme, but she almost always had a sheet thrown over it. Robbie and Piper used to giggle and say it was because she was so ugly."

Delilah's mouth turned down. "I feel bad about that now. The way we treated her. We were so used to being on opposing sides, us versus them. Anyway, we brought in that mirror and then we melted candles and poured the wax on the floor. We had to carve the spirit we wanted to contact in the melted wax. Robbie wanted to bring back Mr. Helme, the one who built the house, because Samuel told us when the house first opened, Mr. Helme gave the kids candy and did a carnival every year where they hired clowns and little ponies for the girls to ride. I didn't care who we summoned.

"Honestly, I hated the idea from the word go, but Robbie could get me to do just about anything in those days, me and Piper both. Winnie wanted to conjure her dead grandmother. The woman had been raising her and then got sick with tuberculosis and died. That's how Winnie ended up in the system. Robbie and Winnie fought about it for three or four days before and then finally agreed we'd try for Mr. Helme first. He was most likely to be in the house, anyway. If that worked, we'd summon Winnie's grandmother.

"We pricked our fingers with a needle from Miss Helme's sewing kit and smeared blood on the mirror. That was our payment for the spirit to come through. Then we had two candles, one with the word 'yes' carved in the side and the other with the word 'no.' We turned off the lights and sat around the pentagram facing the mirror.

"The 'yes' candle kept growing and flickering, but the 'no' barely moved. The scariest part was when we heard this creaking and my eyes popped open and I saw Samuel in the doorway behind us, watching. I screamed and scared the whole group. I pointed at the mirror, but he was gone. It all started the next day."

# 35

"What started?"

"The… bad things." Delilah's voice had dropped lower, and she seemed to shrink into herself. "That's what we called them. We'd let something in, awoken something, and I don't think it was Mr. Helme." She crossed herself. "First, it was the cats. We had two at Helme House. They lived outdoors. Winnie found them…"

"Dead?"

Delilah's lips pressed into a thin line. "Yes. I'll spare you the details. Something had killed them and they were on display. Piper cried for days. She adored those two cats. Then it… it drew something on the wall in the nursery."

"The face?"

Delilah shuddered and nodded. "I can still see it. I can still remember playing outside with Robbie and Piper and walking into the room and just… we all froze."

"And you think whatever you summoned did this?"

"It had to be. What else could have done it?"

Rowan bit back her thoughts that one of the other children or Samuel could have done it. She didn't want to impede Delilah's memories of that time.

"Winnie vanished the next day. Robin found her hanging from the tree house. Even now… even now I can barely stand to remember it. The way we lay in bed at night, awake and terrified. Piper and I both started sleeping in Robbie's bed, even though it was a single and we could hardly fit. We didn't want to sleep in the kids' room anymore, but we couldn't exactly tell Miss Helme what we'd done. And it just kept happening. And Robbie disappeared and two months later... Piper drowned."

"I can't imagine."

"I lived in a waking nightmare. I rarely left Wilma's side during the day and Miss Helme's at night. The nights were the worst. I heard things, saw things. I decided if the demon showed itself to Miss Helme then at least she'd know and we could face it. One day Miss Helme was in her room sewing and I was sitting on the bed trying to read, but I couldn't concentrate because that mirror was in the corner with the sheet covering it. Then all of a sudden the sheet just slipped off. I looked into the glass. Robbie was reaching out for me, eyes big and black, lips peeled back from her teeth as if she were shrieking."

Delilah rubbed her eyes.

"Oh, God, I freaked. I started screaming and crying, pointing at the mirror, but by the time Miss Helme looked Robbie had disappeared and I was... inconsolable. That night the Kaminskis took me home and... I never returned to Helme House. I refused. I cried and begged. I told them I'd rather go to jail than back to that place. They picked up my stuff and a couple months later the Binkowskis adopted me."

"The summoning that you did. It sounds... mature for such young girls. Where did the idea come from?"

Delilah bobbed her head. "We never would have known how to do it on our own. Samuel told us. He read a lot, all the time, and he had this big black book he said he'd found in an antique store. That's where the idea came from. He told Robbie all about it."

Rowan pushed the door open to Helme House, the sounds of music floating down the hallway. She stepped in, kicked off her tennis shoes, and walked down the hall, spotting Quinn standing in her playpen.

"Hey, Quinnie," she said, moving into the room.

Quinn stared blankly, mouth slack. Her hands gripped the edge of the playpen, fists so pale they appeared blue.

Rowan froze at the sight of her daughter.

"Hey," Garrett called, stepping from the bathroom, smile fading at the expression on Rowan's face. He shifted his attention to Quinn and a look of terror passed between Rowan and Garrett so quickly it barely registered. Garrett rushed to their daughter, hands beneath her armpits, sweeping her up. For an endless moment, Quinn's empty eyes gazed and her empty mouth yawned.

"Quinn," he shouted too loud, his own fear preventing him from softening the bellow.

But Quinn did not startle and cry out. She stared blankly. Rowan, terror causing her heart to flap and spasm against her ribs, grabbed Quinn's arm and pinched her skin hard.

Their little girl blinked, mouth opening and closing like a fish dropped on the sand. Her eyes welled and the first glorious sound, a splitting scream, emerged from her purple lips.

"Oh, God, oh, thank God," Garrett murmured, rocking on his feet and patting Quinn's hair.

Rowan too clasped onto her daughter, her own tears pouring unbidden down her face, her entire body trembling as she looked at Quinn, whose lower lip quivered as she continued to cry.

Minutes passed as they stood there, huddled together, the adrenaline seeping out until Garrett, pulling Rowan by the hand, walked backwards to the couch. He sank down, cradling Quinn in his lap. Rowan sat beside them and he wrapped one arm around her, pulling her closer.

"We have to get out of here," Rowan murmured.

Garrett flickered his eyes open and looked at her, the color still gone from his cheeks. Quinn's cries had faded to a whimper, and she'd shoved several of her fingers into her mouth, sucking them.

"Okay, yes. You're right." He looked beyond her as if considering the room surrounding them. In his eyes she saw the first glimmers of knowing, as though he were finally seeing the house for what it was.

"We're not sleeping here tonight," Rowan said.

Garrett nodded. "Alan's upstairs. I need to let him know."

"I'll tell him," Rowan said. "I'm going to pack a bag. We can come back for the rest."

Garrett rested his chin on Quinn's head, rubbing her back. "Okay."

Rowan walked up the stairs, lighter. They were leaving, going home, driving away from Helme House for good.

The sounds of a ball game emitted from a radio at the end of the hall. Alan must be working in the nursery. Reluctantly, Delilah's story of the summoning rolling through her mind, Rowan trudged down the hall.

"Knock, knock," she said, tapping her fist on the wall as she stepped through the doorway.

Rowan stopped, breath stuck in her throat. Red droplets on the floor, smeared across the partially bare walls. She smelled it, felt it as if the entity the blood had fled from lived in each of those tiny crimson drops.

She clenched her eyes shut and held onto the door frame. *It's not real. It's a hallucination or a haunting, but it's not real.*

But when she opened her eyes, the blood glared red and dark.

She didn't scream, refused to create the panic yet again that would end in her convulsing in the passenger seat of Garrett's truck as he rushed her to the emergency room.

Calmly, she walked down the stairs where Garrett and Quinn still sat on the couch, his eyes closed.

"Garrett," she murmured.

"Hmmm?" He sighed, opening his eyes. He looked sad and suddenly very tired.

"I need you to come upstairs."

He frowned, opened his mouth to ask why and then closed it, seeing in her face the things she was too afraid to speak.

"Okay." He stood and rubbed a reassuring hand on her arm. "It's all right, Rowan. Whatever is happening. I promise we'll figure it out."

"Maybe we should leave Quinn," Rowan started, but Garrett jerked his head no.

"I can carry her. She's fine."

"Garrett." Rowan's voice rose. "Please leave Quinn in the playpen."

He frowned and tilted his face to look at their daughter. She'd fallen asleep.

"Please," Rowan said.

Frowning, he laid her in the playpen.

Garrett started up the stairs and Rowan followed, her feet dragging up each step as if they'd become as paralyzed as the scream trapped in her ribcage.

Garrett was halfway down the hall to the nursery when Rowan saw the blood again. Saw it splattering the opposite wall in the former nursery, but this time Garrett saw it too.

Though she'd just seen Quinn moments before, Rowan had the irrational sense it was Quinn's blood. The thing in the playpen was not their daughter. Their daughter had been murdered and hidden by the house and a replica stuck in her place.

"Holy shit," Garrett shouted, breaking into a run. He skidded into the room, slipped on blood and fell on his side, cussing.

Rowan lumbered behind him, seeing the room as if through a smudged lens, as if she were far away.

Garrett struggled to his feet, stared at her as if searching for her wound and then pushed past her back down the hall. She turned, followed him with her eyes, and noticed barely perceptible scrapes of dark red along the hallway wall. Garrett flung open the bathroom door across from the master bedroom.

"Alan," he shouted and disappeared through the doorway.

Rowan leaned against the wall, black spots dancing behind her eyes. She kept trying to come back to earth, to feel the ground beneath her, to draw in a breath that actually sent some oxygen to her brain, but her body had slid further and further into paralysis.

"Call 911," Garrett shouted, but Rowan couldn't take another step, another breath. Her knees buckled, and she slid down the wall.

Garrett reappeared, face grey, blood now on his pale blue t-shirt. More black spots flooded Rowan's vision. It cleared for an instant. She stared past him. Alan lay half in and out of the bathtub, blood covering the side of his head and saturating the right side of his shirt, creating a Jekyll-Hyde appearance, half yellow, the other dark maroon. There was blood on the floor and dripping down the tub.

Rowan rocked forward, tried to put out her hands to protect her face, but had no control over her limbs. She fell, cheekbone smacking the hard wood. An instant of dazzling white pain seared across her cheek, and then the black spots grew and morphed and dragged her down.

# 36

Rowan woke to the glare of bright overhead lights reflected off a shiny white ceiling. She tilted her head sideways to see the tall metal pole of an IV stand, a clear bag of liquid draining through the plastic tube that led to her arm.

When she looked the other direction, she spied Garrett in a chair, face ashen, elbows on his knees, hands clasped together so tightly his knuckles were colorless. He registered her watching him and stood up.

"Rowan..." He stopped closer to her bed, took her free hand and pressed it between his own.

"What happened?" she managed after swallowing the dryness coating her throat.

"Here, have a drink," he told her, grabbing a Styrofoam cup of water and tilting the straw to her lips. Water trickled from the straw onto her neck and she shuddered as a bead of wetness slid toward the back of her neck.

"Sorry," he said, grabbing the little white remote and maneuvering the bed.

She took the cup from his hand and took a drink, welcoming water into her parched mouth. She swished it around and swallowed. "Alan?" she asked.

Garrett's mouth quivered, his eyes filling with tears.

"No..." she murmured. "No, Garrett." She shook her head. "Is he...?"

Garrett took two steps back and sank into his chair, rubbing the sides of his head and staring at her as if it hadn't fully registered for him, as if he couldn't put words to it yet.

"How?"

He opened his mouth to speak, and his lips trembled. He pressed them closed for a moment and seemed to regain his self-control.

"Alan... must have been putting up the light fixture he bought for that room... the nursery room. It broke and somehow he cut himself. It severed his... radial artery, the doctor said. He bled to death."

"Oh, God." Rowan put both hands over her mouth and closed her eyes. "Oh, Jesus. You never heard anything?"

"I had the music on loud and..." Garrett's voice shook. "I never heard a thing. It happened in minutes. He tried to stop the blood loss by pressing his arm against his chest, but..." He shook his head.

"Leah?" Rowan pictured Alan's wife, and her stomach formed into a knot of grief for the now widowed woman.

"She's... umm... gone to her parents. She was here, right after. I called her on my way to the hospital. You and Alan were both in the ambulance, but... I think... I think Alan was DOA."

Guilt roiled within her. She'd never been fond of Alan, had even suspected him of messing with her head in the previous days, and now he was dead. Gone in a freak accident that stole his life in minutes.

"I'm so sorry, Garrett." She held out her hand to him.

He scooted his chair closer and took it, pressing it against his cheek, now wet with tears.

Uncertainty flickered across Garrett's face. "Did something else happen, honey?" she asked.

Garrett leaned forward, gripping the safety bars on the hospital bed until his knuckles turned white. He looked as if his words caused him physical pain. "Alan wasn't dead. When I pulled him from the bathtub, he started mumbling. He kept saying 'the girl in the closet.'"

A cold moan twisted up out of Rowan, and she put a hand to her stomach as it lurched painfully.

"I'm sorry," Garrett said, taking a clammy hand from the rail and putting it on Rowan's arm. "I shouldn't talk about this now. Alan was my oldest friend in the world," he whispered. "I just... It still doesn't feel real."

~

"You don't have to go back to the house," Garrett told Rowan. "I can come back with my brother, get our stuff, pick up your car—"

"No. I... I want to pack my stuff." *And see it one last time,* she thought, but bit back the absurdity of those words. Who in their right mind would need to say goodbye to a house that had brought nothing but misery and terror?

Rowan watched the trees whir by, listening to Quinn, who'd suddenly discovered a new word and spoke it on repeat in the backseat. "Bobby, bobby, bobbin, bobby..."

"What's she saying?" Rowan glanced at Garrett, who stared ahead at the road.

He flicked his gaze to the rearview mirror and smiled at their daughter. "Bobby? Maybe one of the nurses at the hospital. Thanks, polliwog, for coming up with some guy's name before you learned 'Dada.'"

"Dobby, bobby, bobbin." She went on bouncing in her seat and grinning at her parents.

Rowan reached back and rubbed her leg. "It's going to be good to go home."

Garrett nodded his agreement, though she saw the set in his jaw and suspected he'd been fighting tears for most of their drive.

"Are you okay to go back in the house, honey?" Rowan asked.

He didn't look at her. "Yeah. In and out."

They packed quickly. Rowan stuffed boxes and suitcases while Garrett hauled their things to the truck. He didn't walk upstairs at all and twice Rowan caught him leaning with his back against a wall as if trying to catch his breath.

Rowan opened a suitcase on the bed and pulled clothes from the dresser and hangers, tossing them in. She'd worry about de-wrinkling back in Gaylord. After she'd packed everything from the room, she stepped into the hall and walked haltingly toward the nursery, the place where, according to Delilah, it had all begun.

In the doorway, her eyes fell upon the pool of blood, the smears left behind by Alan and further smeared by Garrett. It looked like a crime scene, a horror show. Something tapped against the window, and Rowan saw a huge moth, larger than a monarch butterfly, butting against the glass. It fluttered its brown flaky wings.

For a timeless span, the edges of the room blurred black and indistinct. Rowan smelled not the blood, but the frankincense and myrrh incense burning in the master bedroom, the candle wax melted on the floor, the coppery scent of the girls' blood as they smeared it across the mirror, the damp of wet earth as the rain and wind came. She gazed into the candle-lit room at the four giggling girls who seemed to be playing not in a second-story nursery, but on the edge of a perilous cliff that fell away to stone teeth jutting from a black, turbulent sea. As they dipped their fingers in the wax, the cliff eroded beneath them and none of them noticed a thing.

"Rowan." Garrett's call ripped her back to the present moment and out of the strange portal she'd slipped into. Rowan reeled back, pressing her back against the wall and struggling to catch her breath.

"I'm coming," she shouted, though her voice sounded weak.

As she backed from the room, she paused and stared at the open door to the closet, Garrett's words in the hospital echoing through her mind.

*The girl in the closet.*

~

"Locked and loaded," Garrett told her, standing at the driver's side door of Rowan's car.

She hugged him, arms tight around his waist, face buried in his hair. "Homeward bound," she whispered.

He pulled away and looked at the house, flipping it his middle finger. "Good riddance, Helme House," he muttered back toward his truck.

Rowan opened the back door of his truck and leaned in to kiss Quinn's cheek. "Love you, Quinnie. I'll be right behind you guys," she told Garrett, climbing into her own car.

She watched the house in her rearview mirror until the driveway curved and Helme House disappeared.

# 37

It was for the best, it was. Rowan wasn't a detective. She had no responsibility to Amy's family, to Amy, to those little girls. Garrett was right. It was time to care for herself. She picked up her cell and called Garrett.

"I'm going to pull off at the rest area here. I have to pee," she told him.

"Okay. I'm going to keep driving. Quinn's zonked out. I'll see you back at home."

"Love you," she said and hung up the phone.

She ran to the double doors that led into the building. It was muggy inside. The moist warmth left an opaque mist on the glass. She walked into a stall and peed. On her way to the door, a flier tacked to a corkboard caught her eye.

*Northern Michigan Carnival. Coming July 10-12.*

*Ferris wheel, zipper, pirate's ship and more.*

*Fair food galore: cotton candy, elephant ears, French fries, coney dogs.*

*Don't miss the Spooktacular House of Delusions, mirrored rooms, secret passages, and thrills and chills to haunt your dreams.*

Rowan climbed back into her car. Something from the carnival poster twitched in her mind.

Her folder with some of her notes from Amy's case had fallen open. Several papers had slid out onto the floor. On the top was the photograph she'd printed of the five girls at Helme butted on either side by Doris Helme and Samuel at the opposite end.

Rowan picked up the photo and considered it, studying the young man's face. Again, she sensed something familiar in his features. But what? She frowned and stared, the awareness right at the tip of her mind, searching for its foothold and then it was there, looming and obvious.

"It's Eddie," she said, the words slipping from her mouth the instant her mind made the connection. She stared at the slightly turned tooth in Samuel's smile, the same quirk she'd noticed in Eddie's face on multiple occasions.

Rowan leaned her head back against the seat, closing her eyes and remembering their first meeting in the cemetery. He'd said he'd been visiting his mother's grave, but it had been a lie. His mother lived in a retirement home.

Why had he lied? Why had he never mentioned living at Helme House? Growing up at Helme House?

Rowan's mind tripped over their encounters, searching for the purpose. Why had he offered her the books? Invited her to his house?

"To find out what Garrett was doing," Rowan said, and then another memory slid into place, the painting tucked in Eddie's bedroom. Eddie had painted the nursery at Helme House. He'd painted the claw-footed mirror the girls had used to perform the summoning. Reflected in that mirror had been the closet, but not only the closet. There'd been another doorway within the closet.

"Secret passages," she murmured, repeating the words she'd read on the carnival poster, but thinking of Alan's final words whispered to Garrett, 'the girl in the closet.'

There was a hidden room in Helme House, something accessible through the closet in the nursery upstairs.

Had Eddie hidden something inside? Something he'd feared Garrett would discover during renovations of the house?

Rowan pulled back onto the highway, but instead of heading for Gaylord, she hit the brakes and took the police access in the center of the highway, jamming the accelerator to the floor as she shot onto the southbound lane driving back toward Empire.

She glanced at her cell phone. Garrett would make it home long before she returned to the house. He'd worry.

She texted him, 'Forgot my wallet at the house. Running back quick to get it. Be home right after.'

The phone rang. She didn't pick it up. He'd demand she come home, that they'd return together, but no. She had to go back now. If Eddie had been watching the house, and she suspected he had been, he'd know they left.

He might seize the chance to go into the house, remove anything he'd left behind. Rowan felt sure he'd left something behind, something that now occupied the room hidden in the nursery closet.

~

The house was quiet and heavy when she stepped in. Long shadows lay down the hallway, and her footfalls on the stairs seemed deafening. Rowan's heart thumped against her ribs as she moved toward the second floor.

The nursery appeared as it had when she'd last peeked in. Blood smeared on the floor, wallpaper in a singed pile in the room's corner. The evidence of her axing the door.

"You wanted us to know," she murmured, not knowing who she referred to—Amy, Robin, the other girls who'd died. She didn't know, but she believed it. Someone had been trying to tell her what lay hidden in that closet.

She opened the closet door, breath catching as she stared into the empty space. There was no obvious sign of a doorway within the space, but she folded her fingers into a fist and started knocking on the walls, listening for the spot that sounded different from all the others. She found it along the far left wall. She knocked and a hollow ping greeted her ears. Rowan ran her fingers along the wall, searching for a seam, but found nothing. She pushed the wall, and it creaked and slid forward an inch. Rowan pushed harder, and the wall swung open, revealing a narrow passage that immediately turned to the right.

It was dark in the space, and Rowan retreated to the master bedroom where one of the saint candles still sat on the dresser. Rowan lit it and walked back to the nursery. She crouched to get into the passage, followed the abrupt turn and stepped into the secret room.

Two stiff-backed chairs occupied the space around a square table arranged with empty plates, two wine goblets that seemed to have a dark, rancid liquid gelled inside of them. Other items littered the table —old toys, candles burned to their bases, and a big black book.

Rowan's eyes drifted to the floor, and her stomach lurched. Two huge rugs rolled up lay side by side on the dusty wood floor. A tangle of dark hair protruded from the top of one rug.

"Amy," she whispered.

## 38

Rowan stood for a long time staring at the two rugs.

Somewhere in the house beneath her, a door opened and slammed and at almost the same moment a whisper stole past her.

"Shhh..."

The sound, like a warning, blew out her candle, and Rowan found herself suddenly cast into darkness.

Terror coursed through her, tried to take hold of her limbs and push her into paralysis, but she forced her feet to shuffle backwards until the wall rose behind her. She slid along, hands groping in the dark, and found her way back to the passage that led out of the room.

Dull light seeped in and she could see as she stepped from the passage into the closet. She paused, hands braced on the doorframe, listening.

If Garrett had entered the house, why hadn't he called out her name? Pounded up the stairs searching for her?

Her stomach twisted. She started down the hall and heard again the door below open and slam.

"Rowan?" Garrett shouted.

Rowan opened her mouth to respond when something below released a dull thwack. Rowan gasped as the sound filled her head and she knew someone had struck Garrett.

Trembling, she continued forward, wanting to hide, but knowing she had to walk down those stairs. If there was any hope for Garrett, for Quinn, for herself, she couldn't freeze.

Hand slick on the bannister, she stepped off the final stair and froze.

Garrett lay sprawled in the downstairs hall, blood trickling from his right ear. Holding her breath, Rowan grabbed Garrett beneath the arms and pulled him toward the hall closet, maneuvered him inside and closed the door.

In the kitchen, she heard the sliding glass door open and close. Rowan stepped through the doorway, facing Eddie across the kitchen island.

"I knew you'd come back," he said, smiling knowingly. "I watched you and your husband today carrying those boxes out, but I knew you'd be back."

"I found the hidden room in the nursery."

"It's not what you think," he told her, his voice oddly flat.

Rowan stared at him, incredulous. "I think you murdered Amy Prahm, Robin Underwood, Winnie Hamilton, and Piper Rothwell."

He shook his head, walking slowly around the kitchen island. Rowan walked as well, keeping the island between them.

"I didn't."

"Then who did?"

"You'll never understand."

"Try me."

"Robin did it."

Rowan widened her eyes. "Your scapegoat is a twelve-year-old girl? How will you explain to police that she rolled herself up in that rug upstairs?"

"I had to do that. The evil had to be contained."

"You're sick."

"They opened the gateway. It was Robin's idea. She was always playing with stuff she shouldn't have been. Once it was opened... there was no closing it."

"You told them about doing that, the summoning thing. I talked to Delilah."

Eddie glowered. "Robbie kept pestering me about the book I was reading, so I said, 'Fine, here,' and showed her the pages. She asked, if I could bring someone back, who would I choose, and I told her Luther Helme. He was the only parent I'd ever known. To Doris, I symbolized the thing she most hated in the world, the man who'd abandoned her."

"You expect me to believe they opened a gateway and... what? A demon came through and killed the girls?"

"There was always something wrong with Robbie, something... vengeful," Eddie said, bracing his hands on the edge of the counter. "That's why it chose her. She killed the cats. It was Robin. She lured Winnie into that tree house and shoved her off with that rope around her neck. Those girls despised me. Do you think I ever could have gotten Winnie to come into that treehouse with me?" He laughed bitterly. "And Piper... Piper was easy. All Robbie had to do was say, 'Let's go for a swim,' and take her out too far. Piper wasn't a strong swimmer."

"Robin had already vanished when Piper drowned."

He shook his head. "She was in the woods, waiting, watching."

"This is very convenient for you considering Robin's dead."

"It was the only way to stop her. Delilah would have been dead too, and my mother and eventually me."

"What did you do to stop her?" Rowan didn't believe a word he said, but she wanted the story. She needed to know.

"I tricked her. She'd been waiting for the right time with me, a time I'd be vulnerable. I went for a walk in the woods. She followed me. I hid and waited and then I pushed her into the cellar behind the graveyard."

"Why bring her back to the house, hide her in that room?"

"Because the house wanted to keep her."

"What about Amy? The house killed her? Or did Robin come back from the grave to kill Amy?"

"There's no distinction anymore between Robin and the house. When she opened the portal, it all bled into one evil. Amy was seduced by it, lured into the attic to get the mirror. She was hauling it down the ladder and cut herself. She was bleeding out. Blood all over the bedroom." He blinked at the counter, drifting away, remembering.

"Then she should have been found there. But someone cleaned up most of that blood and hid her. Are you trying to tell me the house did that?"

"I had to." His eyes drifted up and bore into her. "The house wanted her. If I hadn't put her in that room, it would have taken someone else. And now it has, hasn't it? It's taken someone of yours."

Rowan frowned, not believing him, chasing away the memory of Alan lying bloody in the bathtub. It was the rantings of a madman. But... he believed. He believed his words.

Rowan thought of the two bodies hidden in that secret room. "I don't understand how police didn't find those bodies. They searched this place. There must have been a smell..."

Eddie's eyes glittered. "You don't get it. This house reveals what it wants and nothing more. That alone should prove to you its power. There was never a smell if the police came. They could have let loose half a dozen tracking dogs and they wouldn't have alerted to that room."

Ludicrous, she wanted to shout, but she didn't. The police had never brought dogs. That had to be the reason the bodies were never found.

"And what now? What will you do with me?"

"The house wants you too. Listen..." He cocked his head. "You could have left and never come back, but it called to you, didn't it? It called you home." He rushed at her then, tore around the counter and shot a hand out. If her hair had still been long, he would have caught her, but his hand grasped emptiness as she fled into the house, down the front hallway and burst through the front door.

Rowan raced across the yard. A steady rain had begun and it pattered on the leaves as she dashed into the woods.

The steep hillside was slippery, but Rowan didn't slow down. She snatched at branches and leaned heavily to the side, bracing her tennis shoes to keep from slipping and plunging down the bluff. She couldn't hear Eddie through the pounding rain but knew he was there, back there somewhere, stalking her.

Rowan's body shrieked for attention. Her ankle throbbed, her lungs burned, and even her c-section scar pulsed painfully beneath her shirt. She gritted her teeth and focused on the trail ahead of her.

She reached the cemetery and ducked into the forest behind the tombstones, pressing her back against a wide oak tree. She heard him, the slap of his boots on the wet leaves, and her teeth chattered, but she bit back her fear.

"Rowan..." he murmured. "Rowan, you can't escape it. Even if you get out of here today, it will reach out for you, it will bring you back."

She waited, holding her breath, praying she'd sense the moment when Eddie stepped into place.

*Don't screw this up.* She heard the voice in her mind and understood the consequences if she died in those woods. Garrett would die too and Quinn. Her family would be next in the line of unexplained tragedies at

Helmer's House, and their deaths would be attributed to the wife who'd lost her mind.

"You can never leave, Rowan," he shouted.

*"Now..." An icy breath whispered the word into her ear.*

Rowan ran forward and shoved him toward the dark hole that had once been a cellar. His mouth opened in a howl and his arms darted out, both hands closing on her biceps, but her skin, slick with rain, left nothing for him to hold. He careened backwards, dropping onto the stone floor.

# 39

Quinn wasn't in the truck when Rowan returned, and her muscles seized up as she stared into the empty cab.

Had Eddie taken her? What had he done with her girl?

She ran to her car and fumbled her phone from her purse. Through the spitting rain, she heard the wails of her daughter from within the house.

Soaked and panting, Rowan slammed through the front door. Quinn stood in the downstairs hallway, both hands slapping against the closet where Rowan had shoved Garrett.

"Oh, God, baby, you're okay." She scooped up her daughter, hugging her tight. With the other hand, she wrenched open the closet door.

Garrett lay unconscious, blood spreading out from his dark hair.

Rowan knelt and felt his pulse. It beat weakly beneath her fingers. She dialed 911.

"I need an ambulance right away at Helme House in Empire. And police, send police. There are bodies here."

~

The visitor area at the hospital was quickly becoming a stifling family reunion, with Garrett's parents and siblings huddling about, talking too loud. His brother kept walking amongst the group, adding shots of brandy to everyone's coffee.

"Tyler, no más. This is not a fiesta. Go sit down," Antonio Cortes admonished his son, who smiled sheepishly.

"I'm done. I promise," he insisted, moving to where Olivia sat next to Emily, both fussing over Quinn, who stared up at her grandmother and aunt, grinning.

Olivia batted her eyes at him and held out her coffee. He poured in a generous splash of brandy.

When her cousin Dan appeared, Rowan rushed into the hall, grabbed his arm and steered him back toward the elevator.

"Let's go to the cafeteria," she insisted.

"Garrett's okay? I saw your last text. You said they expect a full recovery."

"Yeah. The doctor said his eardrum was damaged, and he suffered a pretty severe concussion, but he's going to be okay."

"Thank God."

"Yeah. I'm so grateful. The ambulance made it to the house in less than ten minutes. If I'd been out there alone for much longer..." She shook her head. "Did you hear from anyone on the force? Did the police—?"

"Find the guy? Yep. Not in the hole. He'd made it out, came stumbling back to the house while they were inside with forensics."

Rowan nodded. "I'm happy they got him. Did he confess?"

"Not exactly. He said Robin and the house were evil, the house wanted blood sacrifices, all kinds of crazy shit."

"Did they look inside the rugs?"

Dan nodded, pushing the elevator button for the ground floor. "Both female, one mid-twenties, the other younger, pre-teen or teen. Based on clothing and jewelry, the older girl is Amy Prahm."

"The other one is Robin Underwood."

"Who?"

"A twelve-year-old girl who disappeared from the house in 1975."

~

Rowan cradled a sleeping Quinn against her chest, twisted the door-knob and pushed into their home in Gaylord.

The tears came as she walked inside and saw the rocking chair her father had given her, a quilt sewed by her mother lying over the back. Her mother, because that was what she was, not her birth mother, but her one true mother. Rowan and Emily might not have had the intimacy shared by other mothers and daughters, no long talks on the phone or nights vegged out in front of Hallmark movies, but her mother had been the one who'd met Garrett and Rowan when they returned home after Quinn's birth. She'd stocked their refrigerator with food, including bags of chicken salad sandwiches, Rowan's favorite. She'd been the one who'd hustled Rowan into the shower and insisted she nap while Emily sat in the rocking chair and sang lullabies to Quinn.

Rowan touched the quilt, lifted it to her face and smelled it. It held no particular scent, and yet it did. It smelled like home.

A hand touched the small of her back, the soft whisper of Garrett's fingers down her spine. She sighed and leaned against him.

"It's good to be home," she whispered.

"Your mom's here," he said, holding her for another moment.

When Rowan pulled away, her mom was standing in the doorway, a large envelope in her hands.

"I hope this isn't bad timing. I was organizing some of Dad's things this morning and came across it and I thought... well, I thought it was time."

"Time?" Rowan stepped toward her mom, not understanding.

"Your dad put this folder together years ago should you ever ask. It was very important to him, and me, that you know about your birth parents if you wanted to, but you never asked and we didn't want to unnecessarily rock the boat, I guess. But then... these last months, all your suffering. I wondered if not knowing was causing you... pain."

Rowan thought of all the times she'd almost asked about her birth family, found the words on the tip of her tongue when she and her dad were bowling or sitting together reading the newspaper. But she'd always bitten the questions back, afraid... afraid that if she opened the door, a wedge would form between them. He might not say it, might not even know he felt it, but their bond would shift further and further apart. He'd grow closer to his biological kids, the children who came from his own body. Rowan didn't dare invite that in. Without her dad, the person who'd always made her feel the most special, the most included, Rowan would have grown cold and distant. But now she realized he'd never forgotten that she was adopted. He simply hadn't cared. Or maybe he had. Maybe he'd cared so much that he'd pulled her closer to ensure having been adopted left no wounds within her.

"Let me take this beauty so you can have some time to read through it."

Rowan allowed her mother to take Quinn. Emily walked to the rocking chair and sat down, brushing Quinn's curls off her forehead.

"Mom," Rowan said, sitting on a couch near her mother. "Can you just… tell me? Would that be okay?"

Garrett settled beside her, resting his hand on her knee.

Emily gazed at Rowan. "We knew the moment we laid eyes on you, Rowan, that you were meant to be with us."

"You did?"

Emily ran her fingers through Quinn's wispy hair. "You were at the playground down the street from your house. You had those pink and black cheetah leggings on, and your hair was up in a side ponytail with a bright pink scrunchie." Emily laughed. "You were collecting acorns and piling them at the base of a tree for a squirrel."

Rowan gazed at her, surprised. "But… I didn't meet you guys until the next day."

"I know. We just watched you that day. Then we set up the meeting with your social worker."

"When you came to the house, you knew you wanted me? Both of you?" Rowan's voice cracked.

Emily smoothed her hand over Quinn's forehead. "It was love at first sight for both of us."

Rowan pulled in a shaky breath, clasping Garrett's hand tightly in her own.

"Your birth parents died in a car crash. You were six months old. They were young, both seventeen, but trying… trying to do it, be parents, start a life."

"They're dead," Rowan murmured, loosening her grip, her hand falling away from Garrett's.

"Row." Garrett snaked an arm behind her, pulled her closer.

"No, I'm okay," she said. And she allowed the truth to settle in, to slip between her ribs and take up residence in her gut, in the place so much turmoil had lived. It hurt, and yet the truth was a salve against the rawness within her.

"I spoke with your maternal grandmother," Emily went on. "Only one time. I tracked her down through the adoption agency. She was still heartbroken over the loss of Frances—Franny. That was your mother's name. She was a single mother herself and she might have wanted to keep you after Frances passed, but she just couldn't. They loved you, your mother and father. She wanted us to tell you that."

Tears streamed down Rowan's face, and Emily stood, handing Quinn to Garrett. She wrapped her arms around Rowan, holding her so tight that Rowan thought this was the embrace that might finally put her back together.

# EPILOGUE

Rowan sat on the hard metal chair looking through the thick-paned glass where Samuel Edwin Helme watched her.

"I knew you'd come," Eddie said, when Rowan lifted the phone to her ear.

"I almost didn't."

"We're kindred spirits, Rowan. I sensed that the first day I saw you in the cemetery. The unwanted ones have a certain look, a yearning. I saw it in the mirror enough to recognize it. People whispered about me living in that house, I didn't belong there, but the truth is that I did. I belonged there more than anyone. My mother wanted the girls, every last one of them. It was me she didn't want."

"Maybe that's because she knew what you were capable of."

He licked his chapped lips and smiled. "Say whatever you want. I know what you believe. It was happening to you. The bad things."

"You were the only bad thing happening to me," she muttered, trying not to the let the shiver creeping up her spine become visible.

His eyes shone and a knowing look twitched across his face. He smiled slowly, and Rowan tore her gaze away, staring at her hands pressed in her lap.

"You came to me, Rowan. Does your husband know that?"

She forced her eyes to meet his. "You're going to prison, Eddie. That's what matters now."

"Sure. Whatever helps you sleep at night." He leaned close to the glass. "Are you sleeping? Because I am. I dreamed last night that someone bought Helme House and turned it into an inn." His mouth stretched into a wide, wicked grin. "The house always gets what it wants."

~

"How was it?" Garrett asked when Rowan returned home after visiting Eddie.

He sat at the kitchen table with Quinn balanced on his knee. Smashed banana coated the pink plastic tray in front of her. Quinn grinned and waggled her sticky hands at Rowan.

"Weird," she admitted, trying to erase the words that Eddie had uttered, the knowing gleam in his eye. "Hi, baby girl," she told Quinn, bending down to kiss her soft forehead.

"The important thing is that guy is locked up for good," Garrett said. "Leah sold Helme House too, to some investor from downstate."

"What's going to happen to it? Tear it down, I hope?"

"Doubtful. Seems he wants to remodel it and open it as a B&B."

The skin on Rowan's arms prickled. "I'm not sure that's a good idea."

"Not ours to worry about anymore."

"Garrett, how do you think Quinn got into Helme House that last day? You said you didn't take her in. You left her asleep in the truck, still strapped into her car seat."

His face darkened. "Eddie must have taken her inside. I just thank God you led him back out and away from her." He pulled Quinn closer, nuzzling his face into her neck.

Rowan frowned, remembered those harrowing minutes as she'd walked downstairs into the kitchen. Quinn had not been in the hall or the kitchen.

"How about your meeting with the therapist this morning? That went okay?" Garrett asked.

Quinn grabbed a hunk of banana and flung it in the air. It landed on the blue bandana tying back Garrett's hair. He reached for his head, feeling cautiously with his fingers, and grinned when he found the gooey blob. "Bandana saves the day again."

"Again, huh? I don't remember the first time the bandana saved the day." Rowan held out her hand and Garret dropped the mushed fruit into her palm. She tossed it in the sink. "The session went really well. She thinks I might be ready to start weaning off of the antidepressants."

"Yeah!" Garrett yelled more enthusiastically than the moment called for and waved Quinn's arms in the air. "Say, 'go Mommy!'"

"Guh-mmmy," Quinn shouted, giggling and throwing double handfuls of banana into the air.

Rowan screamed and jumped out of the way while Garret ducked, laughing.

"Polliwog," he said, "you're officially done with this banana." He pushed the plate away, shifting his attention back to Rowan. "Look what came in the mail today." Garrett tapped a large white envelope on the table.

She looked at the name of the sender. *Child and Family Services of Northern Michigan.*

"The adoption papers," Rowan whispered. She sank into a chair, the banana on the floor forgotten. "On my way to the jail, I got a call from that publisher."

"The one who wants you to write a book about Helme House."

"Yeah. They offered me a pretty big advance."

He reached for her hand and squeezed, transferring some banana goo onto her fingers. "You deserve it, babe. Are you going to accept it?"

Rowan looked at the envelope and thought back to that long ago day in the park when her parents saw her for the first time. 'Love at first sight,' her mother had said.

Garrett followed her gaze. "We don't have to decide anything right now. We can—"

"Yes." Rowan lifted her eyes to his. "Yes to all of it. The book and the baby or maybe not a baby, maybe a little boy or girl."

Garrett studied her. "Really?"

"Yes."

# ALSO BY J.R. ERICKSON

**The Troubled Spirits Series**

Dark River Inn

Helme House

Darkness Stirring

**Or dive into the completed eight-book stand-alone paranormal series:**

**The Northern Michigan Asylum Series.**

*Do you believe in ghosts?*

# ACKNOWLEDGMENTS

Many thanks to the people who made this book possible. Thank you to Team Miblart for the beautiful cover. Thank you to RJ Locksley for copy editing Helme House. Many thanks to Will S. and Donamarie F. for beta reading the original manuscript. Thank you to Travis Poole. Emily Haynes, Saundra Wright and Tina Keifer for finding those final pesky typos that slip in. Thank you to my amazing Advanced Reader Team. Lastly, and most of all, thank you to my family and friends for always supporting and encouraging me on this journey.

# ABOUT THE AUTHOR

J.R. Erickson, also known as Jacki Riegle, is an indie author who writes ghost stories. She is the author of the Troubled Spirits Series, which blends true crime with paranormal murder mysteries. Her Northern Michigan Asylum Series are stand-alone paranormal novels inspired by a real former asylum in Traverse City.

These days, Jacki passes the time in the Traverse City area with her excavator husband, her wild little boy, and her three kitties: Floki, Beast, and Mamoo.

To find out more, visit www.jrericksonauthor.com.